W9-ARY-710

CONTENTS

inappropriate random

Stories on Sex and Love

Edited by
AMY PRIOR

SEAL PRESS

introduction

The course of true love for the single girl has never been rougher. Even the most wayward of girls and wickedest of women can become confused by some complexities of contemporary romance: detached intimacy-at-a-distance chatrooms and message boards; our greater pursuit of all drinks alcoholic; the growing possibility of cross-country relations; ever-mutating domestic arrangements of friends that extend far beyond the time they ever used to; wider integration and representation of numerous sexualities; intrusion by a variety of therapists; separation as a norm; strictly casual—sometimes casually turning strict, but often becoming disposable—affairs.

A collection of stories by established and emerging writers from Britain and the US, *Inappropriate Random* explores the single female and relationships—acknowledging some of these issues, as well as representing more diverse cultures and experiences than most similarly themed post-Bridget Jones fiction.

Inappropriate Random follows many of our heroines through dazed, sometimes obsessive, pursuit. In Bonnie Greer's "A Map of the Tube", we observe a New York Buppy Princess negotiating her way around London's most undesirable rental options, having trailed a one-night stand across the Atlantic. Julia Bell's Soho cycle courier in "Strictly Casual" fantasizes about and tries to enact a perfectly easy relationship with a chance-encountered married woman, while in "Men Like Palm Oil," Kadija Sesay's T-shirt-sloganed "educated black woman" revels in the potency of an oil that helps bridge the cultural divide between her and the relatives' suggested suitor.

Caren Gussoff admits that finding the right partner is hard work: "Love Story" reduces the social rituals of finding love to the calculated formalities of job hunting. In "Between," a complex living arrangement causes difficulties for Elizabeth Graver's heroine, a thirty-something woman caught in the middle of two men: one a lover; the other, a gay housemate who provides domestic harmony.

Having secured a love, things still may not go so smoothly. In Lynne Tillman's "The Substitute," telling stories about an on-going relationship to a therapist changes its nature and in Lucy Corin's "The Way She Loved Cats," the suitability of a long-term partner is criticized—because of the way he treats a pet.

Post-relationship trauma manifests itself in strange, sometimes disturbing, ways. Bridget O'Connor's drunken, heartbroken lover from "Inappropriate Random" takes chancy revenge on a cheating boyfriend, with the help of her pool-playing female drinking partners. In Tina Jackson's "Rats in the Kitchen," a woman escapes from an impending loveless marriage with the unlikeliest of lovers. "Fish Without a Bicycle" presents Pagan Kennedy's stricken environmental worker, a lady who compares the relative success of her immediate community's relationships following the departure of her live-in boyfriend—then comes to a surprising resolution. Brett Ellen Block's jealous heroine in "The High Month" drives away the result of her boyfriend's mid-life crisis—right down the freeway, and in "The Happening," Laura Hird's morning-after casualty becomes increasingly horrified when she begins to piece together memories of the close encounter that followed her alcohol-fueled office party.

Some of our heroines simply have little interest in loving another person. A. M. Homes' escapee schoolgirl in "Raft in Water, Floating" seems to have given up on real love with her non-communicative boyfriend and family, preferring instead to daydream in the intense summer heat. The star of Cris Mazza's "Cookie" likes to show more affection towards her canine charges than to any human, while the teenaged hearse driver in Barbara Gowdy's "We So Seldom Look on Love" prefers to love non-living bodies. In Anne-Marie Payne's "Web Diary of AMP" we examine our new media writer's preference for detached electronic relations as she rides the downfall of the e-commerce boom.

The days of an easy Mills-and-Boon ride are over. For the single girl, it seems relationships are becoming a much trickier business, fraught with complications and confusions previous generations probably never could have predicted.

The outcome: there are now far fewer ground rules in love. The moral: we just have to make them.

—Amy Prior

between

Elizabeth Graver

For Juda

It is hard to tell among so many bodies—and some of them in skirts—but I think I am the only woman in the bar. Dancing there, close up to the go-go boys on their boxes, the men gleaming like seals, eyes only for each other. It used to be I was a stiff, small dancer, one leg forward, one leg back—jerk, jerk, a tight nod of the head, a bird bobbing for seed. How do I know? I could see my limbs lit red with awkwardness. Now I do not see myself, too small among the bodies, and mine the wrong kind.

I dance myself outside myself. No one looks.

Why does Paolo bring me to the bar? I'm not sure. Sometimes I think it is because he loves me. Other times I think it is because I am a fashion accessory, like the dachshunds or Chihuahuas the other men parade down Commercial Street. I do, in some ways, fit the part, small and lean, almost like a boy, now that we have cut my hair. "Time for a new you," said Paolo this morning on the beach, snip snip on each long strand, and then the ceremonial flinging of my locks into the sea. Sheared I was, cropped close. Paolo held my tiny, light skull between his hands and told me where my hair would go: wrapped around the *Titanic*, swallowed by sharks, part of the great blue.

"I'm ugly now," I said, though I could not see myself on the beach. "No one will ever want me."

"You're adorable, you could be the cutest little dyke."

I shook my weightless head.

"OK, then, just enough boy in you to excite the boys."

"You think?"

He snipped at stray hairs on my neck. "Of course. I could almost have a conversion experience over you."

"Right."

"No, I mean it, with angels and the works. A hundred naked cherubs."

I tried not to smile. "By the time you get through with them, I'll be past menopause."

Paolo brushed off my neck with his towel, backed up and surveyed his work. "Exquisite," he said, turning me around. "I get dinner for this. Let's go home."

When we got back, I saw in the mirror how smooth I had become, my neck longer, my eyes somehow darker than before. And in the shower I was a boy, almost, my hands smoothing away the lines of breast, the hip curves. In the soap dish was a nub of lemon soap, a present Tim had given me before he left. What would he think now, I wondered. Would he want me more, like this, or less?

Paolo and I are in many ways the perfect couple. In the winter, when the town is almost empty, we play at being married, at "Honey, you forgot the coupons," or "No more heavy cream, you need to watch your cholesterol." The locals love us, for we are gentle and playful with each other and look a pair, both of us dark and smallish. "A deal for you," they'll say at a garage sale, "since you're just starting out." It has been five years now since we met through a roommate ad in the paper, and still we cook and clean together, to Bonnie Raitt played loud. At eleven-thirty on nights when both of us are home, we watch *Love Connection* and lament the cruelty of dating, and over the long, bitter winters, we read aloud to each other, mostly from children's books. This winter Tim took turns reading too, from *Alice in Wonderland*. One night tucked between them on the couch, the three of us wrapped in a quilt, I realized that for the first time since I was a tiny child, I knew what the term "well-being" meant.

Sometimes I think Paolo brings me dancing for protection; it has been over a year since he has had a lover, though he is pretty as can be, and even at thirty-eight he is taken for a boy. We have our signals all worked out—the head scratch, the biting of the lip, the yawn. And then, on the way home, his regrets—how this one was all over him, how that one asked him for a walk on the beach. "Why not?" I coax. He has a thousand answers: too old, too young, too queeny, not smart enough, too trendy, never leaving, leaving the next day. All around us men are dying. "It's OK," I tell him, "if you're careful." But under my words I am afraid for him, and even further down, someplace fierce and selfish in my gut, I want him just for me.

We live two lives here. Summers we dance till late at night, then stop at Spiritus for an ice-cream shake. The nursery school where I teach closes for two months, and I spend my days sleeping, reading or making jam. Summer is Paolo's time, men everywhere, and I cook dinner for his friends, lie with them on the jetty, take boat rides with them when Paolo waits tables. They are fond of me; "fond" is the right word, not like Paolo, who loves me. These are men from the city—doctors, lawyers, and models who come down for the weekend. When I sun on the end of their sailboats, they spray water on me and heap careless compliments on my breasts.

Winter is my time. There are fewer men around, but they see me as I walk down the street, and I live the life of a fishing village girl, a date here, a date there, and then, when something goes a little bit right, a nice tousled, salty man in my bed, and then— careful, careful, each step could be the last—maybe another night and maybe I find out what he likes to read and who he voted for, and Paolo says, "This one sounds good" or "A man who hates his mother is bad news."

Tim he approved of from the start. "Notice his chest," said Paolo, "when he comes out of the shower and the hair curls in those little blond tendrils. Plus he's totally in love with you; he picked up your fingernail clippings and *played* with them. He probably saved them to light a candle to."

And Tim, like me, a teacher, tall and bulky and a man, but playful when he rolled down hills with his second graders and did the floppy scarecrow dance in their production of *The Wizard of Oz*.

In the beginning it was fine between the three of us—almost, for a while, perfect. Sometimes I would go to Tim's, a few streets away, and eat dinner with him and his two roommates. More often he came to our place, and somehow the three of us fit into the narrow galley kitchen, where we cooked fish stews and chowders, apple and cheese omelettes. When I told my friend Emily how we were together, she said it sounded great, the best way not to scare Tim off.

"Break him in gradually," she said, and I pictured Tim tossing his hair like a mane, stomping his hoof. "You'll be moving in together before he realizes what's happened."

But the thing was, three was a number that pleased me. I loved being in the middle, the frosting inside the cookie, the door hinge, the go-between. I loved feeling *surrounded*, like a kid between her parents: one, two, and—swing—aloft over the curb. I loved the safety of our threesome, but also the shiver: between Tim and Paolo, maybe even between Paolo and me—nothing strong enough to act upon, but enough to put a gentle buzz of static in the air. With each of my two men I discussed the other, late at night in bed with Tim—"He thinks you're beautiful"—or at dinner alone with Paolo—"The longest time he's been with anyone is a year." And for a time, they liked it too, Paolo happy to have a man dripping in his shower, Tim pleased, I think, to be admired by the both of us, titillated, almost, to be safely with me and yet tousle Paolo's hair goodnight before we went to bed.

And in bed—this perhaps the strangest part—the way we played was not a play of two, but three, although Paolo never came inside the room. It began one night when I made my voice gravelly low and told Tim I liked his chest hair. I was joking, but he kept coming back to it: "My long-haired hippie boy," he called me. "My little sailor." Maybe, I told him, you want to sleep with men, with Paolo, but he said no, he was only fooling around, it was me he wanted. Yet I, too, could feel Paolo's presence through the wall, lying there sad, stiff, and alone, trying not to hear our sounds. And if it hadn't been a move into the outrageous (for Paolo and I were, in our way, the most domestic, conventional of people, with our canisters which said Sugar, Flour, Tea, correctly filled), I would have opened the door and asked him in, if he would come. Then Tim could be in the middle, the boy we both desired. It was too terrible, a house buzzing with sex and loneliness at the same time.

It was my mother who began to worry first.

"You'll never get really involved in a romantic relationship," she said, "as long as you live with Paolo."

"What are you talking about?" I said. "I have a boyfriend. Paolo doesn't keep me on a leash."

"I know you have a boyfriend—this boyfriend, that boyfriend. What about marriage? Children? You're already thirty and if I've understood you right, you want children and a full life."

What she meant was, you must work hard to guarantee your-self a better life than your mother's. Already she was unhappy about the fact that I had done so well in college and was now working for low wages in a nursery school. "It's just for now," I had told her—and myself—at first, but the truth was I loved reading aloud to a ring of sleepy four-year-olds, watching them plunge their fists into tubs of finger paint, seeing how they came into my classroom as stunned toddlers and left as resolute children. Whole families had passed through my classroom in the seven years I had been there.

A good job was one way to a better life in my mother's eyes; the other was a man. First, she thought, I had to transform my boyfriend into a husband. Then (this the trickier part), I had to make sure he did not die on me the way her husband, the way my father did—leaving her alone with me, a girl of six who got too many nose bleeds and would not be good company for many years.

I know, I know, I wanted to say to her. Like you, I feel the world as a fragile, teetering place, your fears all tangled through my veins. But don't you think there are other ways around this? My mother raised orchids, coaxed miracles from plants which have no roots and live in pots filled with stones. Last year she drove from Utica, New York, to Oxford, Mississippi, with her friends Miriam and Charlotte and slept under the open sky. What, I wanted to ask her, is a full life?

"I've got plenty of time," I told her instead. I did not tell her how, when I pictured my children, they sometimes had black hair and brown eyes, slender ankles, Paolo's clever hands. Paolo and I had discussed it, even, but always as an "if"—if I wasn't with someone when I reached the eleventh hour on my ticking clock.

Then it was Tim who began to worry.

"Listen," he said after we had been together for eight months and both had a spring vacation coming up. "What do you think about spending a week away somewhere, just us?"

"Sure," I said, "I'd like that." But when we began to plan a trip to northern Vermont, I couldn't bear the thought of Paolo home by himself.

"He'll be fine," said Tim. "He's a grown man. He lived for years without you."

No, I thought, no, you don't know him, how fragile he is under all his joking. But as we drove to a cabin in the mountains, I began to wonder who, really, I was protecting. How would we cook, just the two of us? How would we sit at dinner, across from each other or side by side? And when we went to bed, what would we do without that feeling of closing the door away from someone else, of being alone but not?

In fact I did sleep, did cook and eat and make love and feel my life begin to take a slightly new shape, like a bubble blown from a child's wand that gets caught by a sideways wind. From the cabin you could see a birch grove on one side, a brook out in front, not another house in sight.

"Someday," said Tim one morning as we walked through the woods, "I'm going to build a place like this, out here somewhere. All by hand—you can help if you want."

It was a voice he used to talk about things he planned to do, which usually involved either wandering the earth or building things. Soon after we'd met, he had pulled out a wooden crate filled with brochures and articles on World Teach, mountain gardens, homesteading, and trekking. At the time I had been half-charmed by his enthusiasm and half-worried by the fact that the one constant theme in the box seemed to be *not here, not you*. Lately he had begun to include me a little more, but his plans still made me nervous for their far-flungness. I pictured the two of us in a country where we were the only ones to speak each other's language, or perched on a mountaintop where the only light for miles was our own.

"It can't be too much fun out here in winter," I said.

He shrugged. "You just stock up on wood and get a car with four-wheel drive. It'd be great."

"You wouldn't miss the sea?"

"The Cape is becoming a zoo," he said. "Look at all these mountains. It's like no one even knows they're here."

"I'd go crazy."

"How do you know?"

How did I know? Maybe it would be peaceful; perhaps I would learn to live more comfortably under the vast arch of sky. But I doubted it. "I just know."

Each night I called Paolo. Each night he told me he missed me and filled me in on pieces of our life: the dryer had broken, a mouse had gotten into the pantry, my mother had called and sounded thrilled to learn I was away with Tim. The first few times

I dialed the phone, I don't think I even noticed that Tim left the room, or sat humming tunelessly, picking at the lint on his sweater. On the third day when I hung up, though, he let out a sigh so loud I could not miss it.

"What?" I asked from the couch.

"How's your husband?" Tim was crouched by the fireplace peeling the bark off a log.

"What?"

"Your husband. Is he managing all alone in that great big house? Has he found out about us?"

"Come here," I said, but he only hunched closer to the log. I went over to him, leaned up against him, and kissed the back of his neck.

"Cut it out," he said, shaking me off. "I'm trying to talk to you."

"Jesus." I went back to the couch. "Look, I don't know what you're reacting to so strongly. I never thought you seemed jealous and anyway there's no need to be—"

"I'm not jealous," Tim said.

"Then what?"

"I'm not jealous, I just—you don't worry about me being lonely, you don't call me up to talk about the dryer—"

"We don't share a dryer, do you want to share a dryer?"

"Don't be an idiot."

"I'm sorry," I said. "If I don't worry about you being lonely it's because you have me."

But in my stomach I could feel fear beginning to stretch and unravel. He would leave me, said a voice in there; I had known it all along, from the day I saw his box of travel plans. And then another voice: But who can blame him, he's right, he should be jealous. You don't want to move to a far-off place where nobody breathes on the other side of the wall and the only way to Paolo is through a stretch of telephone wire.

"You do know," said Tim, "that he'd ditch you in a second if he found the right person."

In his voice I heard a hardness I had never heard before.

"You don't even know him," I said.

"Almost a year and I don't even know him? I've done every-thing but fuck the guy."

"In your dreams."

In my own voice I heard that same hardness. This, I wanted to say, this is what I'm afraid of—how easily, with these men I made love with, I came to be a snarling animal, claws flexed, baring all my teeth. This was nothing, compared to where we might end up. I had been there before—had made the long, cruel lists detailing another person's faults; kept secret count of gifts received, money spent; smashed pottery like a character in a TV movie.

With Paolo, too, I fought sometimes, but it wasn't like this, maybe because we couldn't *break up* (in my mind I saw a stick being cracked in two). I didn't know the smell of Paolo's hair, the feel of his spine, the slippery smooth wall of the inside of his mouth. With Tim—with every man I had ever slept with—I came so close to letting myself be turned inside out. Now I could feel an emptiness in my sternum, my pelvis, everywhere bones came together and formed a space.

"Come here, please?" I said again, and this time he did, though he sat turned away from me, and I wrapped myself around his back and spoke close to his ear.

"It's partly," I tried to explain, "it's maybe really screwed up, but it's partly because I *want* us to work out that I need to have Paolo. Otherwise I get too scared, like I'm putting too much weight on a bearing wall or some thing—"

Tim squirmed. "I'm glad you have such faith in us."

"It's not us, it's the whole thing, expecting that much of one person, it doesn't work, it shouldn't have to work. I mean, look around. But also—" I pictured Paolo stirring soup, tying the tomato plants to stakes with strips of his old shirts, curled before the TV. "Also I do love him, not like I love you, but he's my best friend. I thought you really liked him too."

"Of course I like him. Do I want to marry him? I'm not sure."

I pushed the words out of my mouth. "And me?"

He turned around and looked at me. "I'm not sure. Really I have no idea, but it seems pretty hard to figure out anything the way things are. I want—" He trailed off.

"What?"

"I want to travel again, I told you that before, and maybe end up someplace like this, or someplace else, where there's room to think. The Cape is hardly the most amazing place on earth, you know."

"I like to travel," I said, but my words came out weak. The truth was I loved to sit at home and watch how the dunes shifted, the shoreline changed shape, the summer people came and went and still I stayed.

"Maybe the real problem is you want to marry your room-mate," said Tim.

"Stop."

"I don't think you'd leave him."

"It's not him, I'm settled, I have a whole life there."

"What if I decide to go to India?"

"I don't know." I pictured him with a walking stick, trekking somewhere. A place where there's room to think, he had said, as if thinking couldn't happen in a room. "Would you invite me?"

"Maybe. But not Paolo."

"Paolo hates to travel. He always gets sick." I turned away from Tim; outside the birches were shining in the dark. "Do you think we'll be OK?"

"I guess we should just go slowly," he said, "and wait and see."

I nodded, but as we lay in bed that night I could feel how guarded we had both become. It always happened after eight or nine months, the same time it took to make a baby. Suddenly it was almost a year you'd been together; everything tightened, crystallized. Before I started living with Paolo, I was the one who kept dragging my reluctant boyfriends to look at apartments. My mother, who now told me to want more, used to caution me: "Push too hard, Annie, and they'll run away."

I remembered the Pushmi-Pullyu beast from the Dr. Dolittle story Paolo and I had read aloud two winters before. If I was the one pushing, probably Tim would pull away. And if neither of us pushed or pulled? I wanted to see something lovely, cantering across the sand, but instead I saw a waterlogged, dead beast sinking down into the waves.

What happened instead was the world crashed in, Tim's father in Denver diagnosed with liver cancer. Tim got a month's leave from work and I drove him to the airport and gave him a long, tight hug good-bye.

"I don't know how to handle this," he said just before he got onto the plane. "I honestly have no idea."

"I know. But you will, you'll be OK, I know you will. Call me when you get there, do you promise?"

He nodded. "Listen—"

"What?"

"I don't know. If, I mean if I really flip out or something, do you think you might come out there, I'd help you pay for it—"

My mother crouched in the garden sobbing at night because she thought I could not hear her from my bedroom, but I could hear her, could see her bent shape as I knelt on my bed and bit into the chalky paint of the windowsill. The day of the funeral, she told me later, I brought out crackers into the living room where the aunts, the uncles, my mother sat; I passed around oyster crackers and patted backs, said don't worry, it'll be OK.

"Of course, just let me know," I said to Tim, but I was not thinking the right things. At least you'll know who he was, I was thinking. At least you'll have someone to remember.

After he got to Denver we talked on the phone every few days.

"I miss you," I told him, and I did miss him, but I told him so extra, as if the word itself could save a space for us on his return. He did not ask me to come out there, and I did not offer. Sometimes when we were finished, he asked to speak to Paolo. Once, hearing in my silence some kind of hesitation, he said, "What? He's my friend, I can't talk to my friend?"

"Of course," I said and tried not to listen in or ask Paolo for a report after he hung up.

When I got the letter from Tim it was already July, and I thought, seeing my name on the envelope in his tiny, neat print, that it would tell me his father had died. The letter was short: "Annie, I've realized you're not someone I feel like I can depend on in times like this and so I think we should call things off. I'm too wiped out to explain any better. I'm sorry. Love, Tim."

"What does he mean?" I said to Paolo. "Did he want me to come out there? I said I would—he didn't bring it up again. I should have just gone. He's right, he can't depend on me."

I started crying, the slack sobs of a child.

"He's just going through a hellish time," said Paolo. "He'll be back, he just needs time to figure out his own stuff. Shhh—Stop." He sat me down on the porch steps, rubbed my back. "Don't cry, goose, it's OK. Come inside, we'll cook. Don't cry. The neighbors will think we're getting a divorce."

That night I called Tim. His voice sounded far away and blurry, the voice of my mother when I was six and she came back from the hospital at night, paid the baby-sitter, looked down at me from a great distance, and said, "Hi, Annie, how was school?"

"Hey," said Tim. "How's everything going out there?"

"All right. I mean, not so great, really. I got your letter."

"Yeah—"

"I said I'd come out," I blurted. "I want you to be able to depend on me."

"In the airport, you mean, before I left."

"Yes."

There was a long silence.

"Please talk to me," I said.

"You might have offered again, you could—"

"I will come out. I am offering. I'm sorry, I was waiting for you to ask. I'll come there as soon as you want."

"Look," he said. "It's not just this. I think it would have ended sooner or later anyway, I've thought that for a while."

"Since when?"

"I don't know. Our trip, maybe. Before that, even. I should have talked to you more about it, I just—it just seemed like it had to end."

"Why?"

"I don't know," he said. "A lot of things. I'm not even sure when I'll be back there, or for how long. Look, the hospital might call, I can't tie up the phone. Someday we'll talk about this, I just can't right now. I've really got to go."

"I'm sorry," I said. "You have enough to deal with. Will you call me, if you need someone to talk to?"

"OK," said Tim. But we both knew he would not.

August came. Each morning I woke thinking Alone. Thinking it, but not the way I would have before I met Paolo. The thought felt more like a habit now, a reflex I didn't quite believe. I missed Tim, his hands on my back, his voice in my ear, but I did not feel like a stick snapped in two. Maybe my mother was right. Maybe I was cushioning myself too much; perhaps I needed to live on the thin, sharp edge of desperation in order to find and keep a man. I wrote letters to Tim trying to mend things, read them to Paolo, tore them up. I could not write about lovers' spats to a man whose father was dying.

This morning Paolo said it was time to cut my hair.

"Shorter," I told him when the first clump fell. "Keep going, still shorter."

Paolo snipped and looked and snipped. After dinner he came into my room and pulled out a purple silk shirt from my closet.

"This," he said and grabbed some earrings from my dresser. "And these. And your black jeans."

"No." I burrowed down in my bed.

"Get up," he said. "Get dressed."

Now they make a circle around me, the only woman in the place; they form a ring and clap and have me dance there in the middle. They are not watching so much as protecting me—I can feel it—the way the male whales form a ring around the nursing mothers and circle while they feed their calves. I do not know how they can tell I need that just now. These are men who have been forced to grow good at sensing rawness, at dancing around loss, or maybe Paolo told them about Tim. I know I must look beautiful, that I have found some sort of grace, and for a moment I pretend that with my short hair I am a boy, and they all want me, each and every one of them. But when I start to feel desire in that crowd, my limbs grow stiff and unfriendly, and a few seconds later the circle breaks apart.

When I look for Paolo to go home, I cannot find him.

"Have you seen Paolo?" I ask first this one, then that one, leaning up to their ears, close to their sweat. Finally I start home alone, make my way through the crowds on Commercial Street and then turn down our side street where everything, all at once, is from a different world: the rose hips, shingles, crushed shells, the rusty bikes and creaking gates, not even an echo of music, just the sound of sea and wind.

"Paolo, Paolo?" I sing inside my head, trying to pronounce it the way his mother, born in Italy, does, his mother who wants him to marry so badly that she brought a ring for me when she visited last fall.

"No, no," I tried to explain one morning when I got up early and found her sitting on the porch. "It's not like that. We're just good friends."

"He's a good boy," she said. "I don't care what anyone says."

I gave her back the ring and she tried to slip it onto her own finger, above her wedding ring, but it would not fit.

"Just take it," she said. "Maybe he'll change his mind."

I told her I couldn't, I had a boyfriend already.

"But you live with Paolo. Will you marry this other one? Has he given you a ring?"

I shook my head.

"Just take it," she said, "I have no use for it," and out of awkwardness or maybe something worse, I did take it, and never told Paolo. It is a pretty ring, a tiny diamond chip on a band of braided gold, and though I do not wear it and rarely look at it, it lies in a box inside my drawer.

In the morning when I wake up he is still not there, and by the time he comes home in the evening I have rehearsed what I will say so many times that I am not surprised when it comes out right.

"You met someone," I say. "That's great! That's so great, let me guess, the guy in the yellow shirt, the gorgeous one with the beard, I could see him checking you out all night, and then you disappeared. Tell me everything—"

He throws himself down on the sofa. "What am I doing, Annie? I'm too old for this, what am I doing?" He stretches out his legs, looks down at himself fondly, like someone who has just been tumbling in love. "He's just a kid, he's in his early twenties."

"What happened?"

"He—you know, we just kind of hit it off. I don't even know what happened, you know how petrified I am of all this stuff, we just started talking, it took forever for something to happen, I'm like a goddamn virgin starting all over again—"

"And?"

I know he will not tell me, can feel how a space is opening between us. *I told you everything,* I want to say, but I know it is not quite true, remember how when Tim and I used to close the door at night, Paolo was shut outside of a liquid, salty dark that could not fit inside words.

"He's sweet," Paolo says. "He *is* pretty gorgeous, isn't he? He has a terrible name, Harry, I've got to come up with something else to call him. He's even local, he works in Hyannis, and I guess—I think he likes me, the poor man doesn't know what he's getting into. God, I'm beat." He looks up at me. "Are you OK? Your hair looks great."

I nod. He sits up and glances at his watch. "I'm meeting him at ten at the bar. I've got to go rest for a couple minutes and then jump in the shower. You want to lie down?"

We do this sometimes, lie down together in his room with its gauzy white curtains, white sheets, blue speckled floor. It started when we only had one fan, but it was nice to nap together, to hear another person breathing, watch the curtains billow out, and even when we got another fan, we kept doing it. I tried to explain it once to Emily—how it wasn't sexual, how I didn't want to have sex with him but just liked to lie there. How safe it felt. But she kept saying how cute Paolo was, how could I keep my hands off him? He's not into women, I said, and anyhow, once we did it, it wouldn't feel safe anymore.

"That's OK," I tell him now.

Instead I go down into the basement to do my laundry. It is damp there, the place lit by one dim bulb, but after I put in the load, I drag over an old chair and sit beside the machine for a while with my hand on its belly, feeling its pulse. In my laundry are two shirts that used to be Tim's, one that was Paolo's, a camisole my mother gave me when it shrank. I try to picture which clothes have been mine from the beginning, the ones I bought and have been the only one to wear. The underwear, certainly, but I cannot remember what else is in there, now that it is all sloshing together in the tub.

I am startled by Paolo's voice calling, "Annie? Annie?"

I stand and lean up the stairs. "Down here. I'm doing laundry."

"I'm going to the bar," he calls down. "Do you want to come?"

"Do you want me to?"

"Of course. If you want."

"I might, but not right now. Maybe I'll show up later."

"All right, I'll see you."

I run up the stairs. "Paolo?"

He turns, bright and scrubbed in a turquoise shirt, on his way out the door.

"Huh?"

"Have fun. I hope it works out. He sounds nice." I must look dazed, blinking in the light.

"Yeah," he says. "It'll probably fall apart, he's probably fucked up, I'm probably fucked up." He puts out his hands, palms up. "I'm not any good at this."

"Sure you are," I say. "You'll be great."

And I do want him to be great, do want him to have someone to soothe the places I'll never be able to reach, at the same time that I can already imagine how sweetly he will include me for a while, how we will all three do things together until Harry gets too frustrated, how nicely Paolo will ask me to move out. Or maybe Harry will last two days, or two months; it almost doesn't matter, because eventually someone will come along, if not for Paolo, then for me.

I want to sit him down, then, before he leaves for the bar, and ask him if he thinks three is impossible, if it always comes down to two, or one. I want to ask him if he will marry me in a certain way, or just never stop cooking dinners with me or lying down for naps before the fan.

But this is not the sort of question you ask your friends, not the sort of promise you exact without a contract and a ring. I think of my mother, alone at my age with a skinny little girl who was me, of Paolo's mother, whose husband drank himself to death. I think of Tim's father who is dying like my father has died and all fathers will, and of Tim who is across the country and cannot depend on me.

And then I go down to put my laundry in the dryer. As I sat by the washing machine, I sit now by the dryer and feel my clothes tumble, arms tangling with legs, all of it pressed close around the circle of the sides. Later I will go dancing at the bar. First I will wait for my clothes to come out, and they will be warm and clean, and I will fold them, piece by piece, one by one.

inappropriate random

Bridget O'Connor

"I'm just fond of the drink, helps me laugh, helps me cry"
Jimmy MacCarthy

I was laughing with twins Gina and Tina, as we were in The Galleon, which serves triple gins at Happy Hour (and after the first triple anything's funny). It was that time of day pub-drinking when the afternoon light sort of kicks on the smoke. There's a dotty kind of aerial *fight* and you can see all the things you've breathed out and all the spores and flying creature-things you're just about to breathe in. There was, also, loads of blue smoke stacked above the door and some kid was on the fruit machines making that noise that I don't like. That space ship noise, a *whoop whoop* and then like your brain cells are crashing all pain-filled and confused in the corner of some darkened room. I was still laughing as Gina and Tina started snooker fighting; yelling and swearing over the green baize, rinds of beige fat bulging over their too-tight jeans, and, sitting there at our wet little table watching them joust with the snooker cues, with our tall drinks fizzing up in the colored glass beside me and the ashtray still banked and smoking, I got hit. I got hit by one of those really random London moments where you feel like crying, just breaking completely down, for no good reason.

It's difficult to explain.

I was sitting there—not bawling exactly, but leaking these long molten silver tears, like liquid string, tears which didn't obey gravity neither but kind of veered off to hole up in my ears and, after a while, the twins, Gina and Tina, noticed and scratched their suede heads and that's when everything began going a bit cake-holed.

What 'za matter?

I shook my head.

Come on, darling, tell.

I shook my head. This went on. They tried different angles. Bought a new round, a treble-treble gin which, knocked back, sent my voice box in a rapid crashing descent, like a miniature lift, down to my ankle bones where it stalled itself. Refused to crank back up so even if I'd *wanted* to talk I couldn't have. If they'd been afire and I was designated Fire Watcher and had to yell "Oy, behind you, a *fire!*" I couldn't have. We all would have burned.

I got a back rub, which burped up fresh tears.

Are you on?

Said in a nice, kind voice. And felt their drunken intelligence, their load of bleary eye-mail whizzing over my head. A guilt trip.

Don't you trust us, Janey?

A fight.

Oh leave her, Gina. For once, just give her some space.

Piss off.

They went to pot the black and, after they'd argued about it, came back and stood dumbly in front of me splintering the snooker cues with their weight, big-mouthing, pulling helpless expressions. By then the light had intensified around Marie the Barmaid. It was sizzling on her. The whole of her vast frontage, her polyester frilled blouse, seemed to blow alive with flames as she wiped glass after glass with what looked like a bit of her husband's gray underwear— the Y from his y-fronts. She looked so brave what with her crow-black hair dye and the warped ruler lying in it of pure white root, I cried some more. I was choked. Then Gina jacked up the juke box (there's a trick to it: lift the side, then tease it with a slide-edge of 50p, then ram it with the butt of your hand) and *Sad Sweet Dreamer* came on. The bit where the midgets in white tuxedos give it some, standing up in the juke box with their trumpets raised, made me cry some more. My chin went. Tina took the opportunity to empty my purse, it was pay day, and Gina got in another round of triples. Except it was thirty seconds *after* Happy Hour by then and Gina had to row first with Marie the Barmaid, yelling, *It's an emergency situation, cow.* By then, the random grief had me in a full throttle. I was really bawling, my whole face in a kind of helpless liquid spasm. Another few moments and I'd have hurled myself onto the lino, had a kind of epileptic limb smash like I was attempting to swim front crawl to the ladies loo. All this about what though?

Because there really wasn't anything the matter.

But Tina was crying too now and even Gina had gone glassy-eyed, so I obviously had to come up with something. They had their arms round me as I shivered and blew more wet out of my nose. I used all available tissues and loo roll, and made a sodden mess in the still-smoking ashtray, and Marie the Barmaid had to plonk down her own peach luxury-quilted supply and give me, while she was at it, a look like pub-experience told her my tears were nothing serious; just that bit of inappropriate random which easily could have hit Gina, Tina, the kid on the fruit machine, any one of the potential punters passing by in the pink and gray London dusk.

Then Gina said it, point blank: Jane. Have you got it, cancer?
    And Tina went quiet and held her breath and even the kid on the spacey fruit machine paused in his token plopping. I shook my head for no.

How could I say: No, I'm afraid I've only got, well, just a little bit *sad*.

After all they'd done for me.

There was a long pause, punctuated by fag breaks.

Is it anything to do with, Tina said, . . . that last one (they don't usually remember names), whatzisname . . . Davin or somefink. Gavin. Was it Gavin Cook?

And. I nodded. No I didn't really nod. Coincidentally, my forehead happened to slump forward.

And before I knew it, we were in a taxi on our way to his house. I mean I knew it, I just couldn't believe it! I tried to protest near Newington Green but Gina, puffed up in her black bubble jacket, like a bouncer, was barking into her mobile phone and she wasn't having any of it. She was punching out numbers, gathering more support for my "cause," looking well—scary, feral, the way she does when she overdoes her red lipstick so it looks shiny like a wound. Like she's just had her face in some deer's belly. And Tina had that fixed look on her face too. The kind I've seen her get when her ex-boyfriend talks to some other girl in the pub. Like she's going to have to go over now and glass him, then her, then smash the furniture. Then kill everyone else standing outside at the bus stop.

Drink is a terrible thing.

Because Marie the Barmaid had given us carry-outs. Gin in an

Evian bottle. I was getting nervous so I had a quick swill. Which meant my voice box was still stalling down below in the rusty anchorage of my ankles. I drank and comforted myself with the knowledge that really I hadn't said anything. I'd just nodded at Gavin's name.

The bastard, Tina kept saying.

Did he hurt you?

Nod.

The bastard.

Did you catch him at it?

Nod. Though, again, I didn't *actually* nod. The taxi, cresting speed bumps, made me make a series of unfortunate assents.

Bastard.

And Gina agreed I was most seriously aggrieved. And, by the time we reached the Roman Road, I did feel as though, actually, I did have a bit of a case.

Though I wasn't quite prepared for the large crowd of disaffected women loitering with intent behind Gavin's overgrown privet hedge. Nor for the baseball bat the taxi-driver, a woman, gave Gina as we stumbled out from her cab.

Give him one for me, Gina, the taxi-driver said.

Cheers, said Gina.

And I wasn't prepared for the lift in my gut I got from just seeing Gavin again who is, as it happens, quite a nice bloke. Bit boring. Or the equally pleased look on Gavin's face at first sight of me as he turned the corner with his Friday night Chicken Tikka and Three Popadom Take-away and free Coke.

Hello little stranger, he said. Nice surprise. Great to see you.

But I don't suppose it was really, as it turned out.

we so seldom look on love

Barbara Gowdy

When you die, and your earthly self begins turning into your disintegrated self, you radiate an intense current of energy. There is
always energy given off when a thing turns into its opposite, when
love, for instance, turns into hate. There are always sparks at those
extreme points. But life turning into death is the most extreme of
extreme points. So just after you die, the sparks are really stupen-
dous. Really magical and explosive.

I've seen cadavers shining like stars. I'm the only person I've
ever heard of who has. Almost everyone senses something,
though, some vitality. That's why you get resistance to the idea of
cremation or organ donation. "I want to be in one piece," people
say. Even Matt, who claimed there was no soul and no afterlife,
wrote a PS in his suicide note that he be buried intact.

As if it would have made any difference to his energy emission.
No matter what you do—slice open the flesh, dissect everything,
burn everything—you're in the path of a power way beyond your
little interferences.

• • •

I grew up in a nice, normal, happy family outside a small town in New Jersey. My parents and my brother are still living there. My dad owned a flower store. Now my brother owns it. My brother is three years older than I am, a serious, remote man. But loyal. When I made the headlines he phoned to say that if I needed money for a lawyer, he would give it to me. I was really touched. Especially as he was standing up to Carol, his wife. She got on the extension and screamed, "You're sick! You should be put away!"

She'd been wanting to tell me that since we were thirteen years old.

I had an animal cemetery back then. Our house was beside a woods and we had three outdoor cats, great hunters who tended to leave their kills in one piece. Whenever I found a body, usually a mouse or a bird, I took it into my bedroom and hid it until midnight. I didn't know anything about the ritual significance of the midnight hour. My burials took place then because that's when I woke up. It no longer happens, but I was such a sensitive child that I think I must have been aroused by the energy given off as day clicked over into the dead of night and, simultaneously, as the dead of night clicked over into the next day.

In any case, I'd be wide awake. I'd get up and go to the bathroom to wrap the body in toilet paper. I felt compelled to be so careful, so respectful. I whispered a chant. At each step of the burial I chanted. "I shroud the body, shroud the body, shroud little sparrow with broken wing." Or "I lower the body, lower the body . . ." And so on.

Climbing out the bathroom window was accompanied by: "I

enter the night, enter the night . . ." At my cemetery I set the body down on a special flat rock and took my pajamas off. I was behaving out of pure inclination. I dug up four or five graves and unwrapped the animals from their shrouds. The rotting smell was crucial. So was the cool air. Normally I'd be so keyed up at this point that I'd burst into a dance.

I used to dance for dead men, too. Before I climbed on top of them, I'd dance all around the prep room. When I told Matt about this he said that I was shaking my personality out of my body so that the sensation of participating in the cadaver's energy eruption would be intensified. "You're trying to imitate the disintegration process," he said.

Maybe—on an unconscious level. But what I was aware of was the heat, the heat of my danced-out body, which I cooled by lying on top of the cadaver. As a child I'd gently wipe my skin with two of the animals I'd just unwrapped. When I was covered all over with their scent, I put them aside, unwrapped the new corpse and did the same with it. I called this the Anointment. I can't describe how it felt. The high, high rapture. The electricity that shot through me.

The rest, wrapping the bodies back up and burying them, was pretty much what you'd expect.

It astonishes me now to think how naive I was. I thought I had discovered something that certain other people, if they weren't afraid to give it a try, would find just as fantastic as I did. It was a dark and forbidden thing, yes, but so was sex. I really had no idea that I was jumping across a vast behavioral gulf. In fact, I couldn't see that I was doing anything wrong. I still can't, and I'm including what happened with Matt. Carol said I should have been put away, but I'm not bad looking, so if offering my body to dead men is a crime, I'd like to know who the victim is.

Carol has always been jealous of me. She's fat and has a wandering eye. Her eye gives her a dreamy, distracted quality that I fell for (as I suppose my brother would eventually do) one day at a friend's thirteenth birthday party. It was the beginning of the summer holidays, and I was yearning for a kindred spirit, someone to share my secret life with. I saw Carol standing alone, looking everywhere at once, and I chose her.

I knew to take it easy, though. I knew not to push anything. We'd search for dead animals and birds, we'd chant and swaddle the bodies, dig graves, make popsicle-stick crosses. All by daylight. At midnight I'd go out and dig up the grave and conduct a proper burial.

There must have been some chipmunk sickness that summer. Carol and I found an incredible number of chipmunks, and a lot of them had no blood on them, no sign of cat. One day we found a chipmunk that evacuated a string of fetuses when I picked it up. The fetuses were still alive, but there was no saving them, so I took them into the house and flushed them down the toilet.

A mighty force was coming from the mother chipmunk. It was as if, along with her own energy, she was discharging all the energy of her dead brood. When Carol and I began to dance for her, we both went a little crazy. We stripped down to our underwear, screamed, spun in circles, threw dirt up into the air. Carol has always denied it, but she took off her bra and began whipping trees with it. I'm sure the sight of her doing this is what inspired me to take off my undershirt and underpants and to perform the Anointment.

Carol stopped dancing. I looked at her, and the expression on her face stopped me dancing, too. I looked down at the chipmunk in my hand. It was bloody. There were streaks of blood all over my body. I was horrified. I thought I'd squeezed the chipmunk too hard.

But what had happened was, I'd begun my period. I figured this out a few minutes after Carol ran off. I wrapped the chipmunk in its shroud and buried it. Then I got dressed and lay down on the grass. A little while later my mother appeared over me.

"Carol's mother phoned," she said. "Carol is very upset. She says you made her perform some disgusting witchcraft dance. You made her take her clothes off, and you attacked her with a bloody chipmunk."

"That's a lie," I said. "I'm menstruating."

After my mother had fixed me up with a sanitary napkin, she told me she didn't think I should play with Carol anymore. "There's a screw loose in there somewhere," she said.

I had no intention of playing with Carol anymore, but I cried at what seemed like a cruel loss. I think I knew that it was all loneliness from that moment on. Even though I was only thirteen, I was cutting any lines that still drifted out toward normal eroticism. Bosom friends, crushes, party-party intimacy, I was cutting all those lines off.

A month or so after becoming a woman I developed a craving to perform autopsies. I resisted doing it for almost a year, though. I was frightened. Violating the intactness of the animal seemed sacrilegious and dangerous. Also unimaginable—I couldn't imagine what would happen.

Nothing. Nothing would happen, as I found out. I've read that necrophiles are frightened of getting hurt by normal sexual relationships, and maybe there's some truth in that (although my heart's been broken plenty of times by cadavers, and not once by a live man), but I think that my attraction to cadavers isn't driven by fear, it's driven by excitement, and that one of the most exciting things about a cadaver is how dedicated it is to dying. Its will is all directed to a single intention, like a huge wave heading for shore, and you can ride along on the wave if you want to, because no matter what you do, because with you or without you, that wave is going to hit the beach.

I felt this impetus the first time I worked up enough nerve to cut open a mouse. Like anyone else, I balked a little at slicing into the flesh, and I was repelled for a few seconds when I saw the insides. But something drove me to go through these compunctions. It was as if I were acting solely on instinct and curiosity, and anything I did was all right, provided it didn't kill me.

After the first few times, I started sticking my tongue into the incision. I don't know why. I thought about it, I did it, and I kept on doing it. One day I removed the organs and cleaned them with water, then put them back in, and I kept on doing that, too. Again, I couldn't tell you why except to say that any provocative thought, if you act upon it, seems to set you on a trajectory.

• • •

By the time I was sixteen I wanted human corpses. Men. (That way I'm straight.) I got my chauffeur's license, but I had to wait until I had finished high school before Mr. Wallis would hire me as a hearse driver at the funeral home.

Mr. Wallis knew me because he bought bereavement flowers at my father's store. Now *there* was a weird man. He would take a trocar, which is the big needle you use to draw out a cadaver's fluids, and he would push it up the penises of dead men to make them look semi-erect, and then he'd sodomize them. I caught him at it once, and he tried to tell me that he'd been urinating in the hopper. I pretended to believe him. I was upset though, because I knew that dead men were just dead flesh to him. One minute he'd be locked up with a young male corpse, having his way with him, and the next minute he'd be embalming him as if nothing had happened, and making sick jokes about him, pretending to find evidence of rampant homosexuality—colons stalagmited with dried semen, and so on.

None of this joking ever happened in front of me. I heard about it from the crazy old man who did the mopping up. He was also a necrophile, I'm almost certain, but no longer active. He called dead women Madonnas. He rhapsodized about the beautiful Madonnas he'd had the privilege of seeing in the 1940s, about how much more womanly and feminine the Madonnas were twenty years before.

I just listened. I never let on what I was feeling, and I don't think anyone suspected. Necrophiles aren't supposed to be blond and pretty, let alone female. When I'd been working at the funeral home for about a year, a committee from the town council tried to get me to enter the Milk Marketers' Beauty Pageant. They knew about my job, and they knew I was studying embalming at night, but I had told people I was preparing myself for medical school, and I guess the council believed me.

For fifteen years, ever since Matt died, people have been asking me how a woman makes love to a corpse.

Matt was the only person who figured it out. He was a medical student, so he knew that if you apply pressure to the chest of certain fresh corpses, they purge blood out of their mouths.

Matt was smart. I wish I could have loved him with more than sisterly love. He was tall and thin. My type. We met at the doughnut shop across from the medical library, got to talking, and liked each other immediately, an unusual experience for both of us. After about an hour I knew that he loved me and that his love was unconditional. When I told him where I worked and what I was studying, he asked why.

"Because I'm a necrophile," I said.

He lifted his head and stared at me. He had eyes like high-resolution monitors. Almost too vivid. Normally I don't like looking people in the eye, but I found myself staring back. I could see that he believed me.

"I've never told anyone else," I said.

"With men or women?" he asked.

"Men. Young men."

"How?"

"Cunnilingus."

"Fresh corpses?"

"If I can get them."

"What do you do, climb on top of them?"

"Yes."

"You're turned on by blood."

"It's a lubricant," I said. "It's colorful. Stimulating. It's the ultimate bodily fluid."

"Yes," he said, nodding. "When you think about it. Sperm propagates life. But blood sustains it. Blood is primary."

He kept asking questions, and I answered them as truthfully as I could. Having confessed what I was, I felt myself driven to testing his intellectual rigor and the strength of his love at first sight. Throwing rocks at him without any expectation that he'd stay standing. He did, though. He caught the whole arsenal and asked for more. It began to excite me.

We went back to his place. He had a basement apartment in an old rundown building. There were books in orange-crate shelves, in piles on the floor, all over the bed. On the wall above his desk was a poster of Doris Day in the movie *Tea for Two*. Matt said she looked like me.

"Do you want to dance first?" he asked, heading for his record player. I'd told him about how I danced before climbing on corpses.

"No."

He swept the books off the bed. Then he undressed me. He had an erection until I told him I was a virgin. "Don't worry," he said, sliding his head down my stomach. "Lie still."

The next morning he phoned me at work. I was hung over and blue from the night before. After leaving his place I'd gone straight to the funeral home and made love to an autopsy case. Then I'd got drunk in a seedy country-and-western bar and debated going back to the funeral home and suctioning out my own blood until I lost consciousness.

It had finally hit me that I was incapable of falling in love with a man who wasn't dead. I kept thinking, "I'm not normal." I'd never faced this before. Obviously, making love to corpses isn't normal, but while I was still a virgin I must have been assuming that I could give it up any time I liked. Get married, have babies. I must have been banking on a future that I didn't even want let alone have access to.

Matt was phoning to get me to come around again after work.

"I don't know," I said.

"You had a good time. Didn't you?"

"Sure, I guess."

"I think you're fascinating," he said.

I sighed.

"Please," he said. "Please."

A few nights later I went to his apartment. From then on we started to meet every Tuesday and Thursday evening after my embalming class, and as soon as I left his place, if I knew there was a corpse at the mortuary—any male corpse, young or old—I went straight there and climbed in a basement window.

Entering the prep room, especially at night when there was nobody else around, was like diving into a lake. Sudden cold and silence, and the sensation of penetrating a new element where the rules of other elements don't apply. Being with Matt was like lying on the beach of the lake. Matt had warm, dry skin. His apartment was overheated and noisy. I lay on Matt's bed and soaked him up, but only to make the moment when I entered the prep room even more overpowering.

If the cadaver was freshly embalmed, I could usually smell him from the basement. The smell is like a hospital and old cheese. For me, it's the smell of danger and permission, it used to key me up like amphetamine, so that by the time I reached the prep room, tremors were running up and down my legs. I locked the door behind me and broke into a wild dance, tearing my clothes off, spinning around, pulling at my hair. I'm not sure what this was all about, whether or not I was trying to take part in the chaos of the corpse's disintegration, as Matt suggested. Maybe I was prostrating myself, I don't know.

Once the dancing was over I was always very calm, almost entranced. I drew back the sheet. This was the most exquisite moment. I felt as if I were being blasted by white light. Almost blinded, I climbed onto the table and straddled the corpse. I ran my hands over his skin. My hands and the insides of my thighs burned as if I were touching dry ice. After a few minutes I lay down and pulled the sheet up over my head. I began to kiss his mouth. By now he might be drooling blood. A corpse's blood is thick, cool and sweet. My head roared.

I was no longer depressed. Far from it, I felt better, more confident, than I had ever felt in my life. I had discovered myself to be
irredeemably abnormal. I could either slit my throat or surrender—
wholeheartedly now—to my obsession. I surrendered. And what
happened was that obsession began to storm through me, as if I
were a tunnel. I became the medium of obsession as well as both
ends of it. With Matt, when we made love, I was the receiving end,
I was the cadaver. When I left him and went to the funeral home,
I was the lover. Through me Matt's love poured into the cadavers
at the funeral home, and through me the cadavers filled Matt with
explosive energy.

He quickly got addicted to this energy. The minute I arrived at his
apartment, he had to hear every detail about the last corpse I'd been
with. For a month or so I had him pegged as a latent homosexual
necrophile voyeur, but then I began to see that it wasn't the corpses
themselves that excited him, it was my passion for them. It was the
power that went into that passion and that came back, doubled, for his
pleasure. He kept asking, "How did you feel? Why do you think you
felt that way?" And then, because the source of all this power disturbed
him, he'd try to prove that my feelings were delusory.

"A corpse shows simultaneous extremes of character," I told
him. "Wisdom and innocence, happiness and grief, and so on."

"Therefore all corpses are alike," he said. "Once you've had one
you've had them all."

"No, no. They're all different. Each corpse contains his own
extremes. Each corpse is only as wise and as innocent as the living
person could have been."

He said, "You're drafting personalities onto corpses in order to have power over them."

"In that case," I said, "I'm pretty imaginative, since I've never met two corpses who were alike."

"You *could* be that imaginative," he argued. "Schizophrenics are capable of manufacturing dozens of complex personalities."

I didn't mind these attacks. There was no malice in them, and there was no way they could touch me, either. It was as if I were luxuriously pouring my heart out to a very clever, very concerned, very tormented analyst. I felt sorry for him. I understood his twisted desire to turn me into somebody else (somebody who might love him). I used to fall madly in love with cadavers and then cry because they were dead. The difference between Matt and me was that I had become philosophical. I was all right.

I thought that he was, too. He was in pain, yes, but he seemed confident that what he was going through was temporary and not unnatural. "I am excessively curious," he said. "My fascination is any curious man's fascination with the unusual." He said that by feeding his lust through mine, he would eventually saturate it, then turn it to disgust.

I told him to go ahead, give it a try. So he began to scour the newspapers for my cadavers' obituaries and to go to their funerals and memorial services. He made charts of my preferences and the frequency of my morgue encounters. He followed me to the morgue at night and waited outside so that he could get a replay while I was still in an erotic haze. He sniffed my skin. He pulled me over to streetlights and examined the blood on my face and hands.

I suppose I shouldn't have encouraged him. I can't really say why I did, except that in the beginning I saw his obsession as the outer edge of my own obsession, a place I didn't have to visit as long as he was there. And then later, and despite his increasingly erratic behavior, I started to have doubts about an obsession that could come on so suddenly and that could come through me.

One night he announced that he might as well face it, he was going to have to make love to corpses, male corpses. The idea nauseated him, he said, but he said that secretly, deep down, unknown even to himself, making love to male corpses was clearly the target of his desire. I blew up. I told him that necrophilia wasn't something you forced yourself to do. You longed to do it, you needed to do it. You were born to do it.

He wasn't listening. He was glued to the dresser mirror. In the last weeks of his life he stared at himself in the mirror without the least self-consciousness. He focused on his face, even though what was going on from the neck down was the arresting part. He had begun to wear incredibly weird outfits. Velvet capes, pantaloons, high-heeled red boots. When we made love, he kept these outfits on. He stared into my eyes, riveted (it later occurred to me) by his own reflection.

Matt committed suicide, there was never any doubt about that. As for the necrophilia, it wasn't a crime, not fifteen years ago. So even though I was caught in the act, naked and straddling an unmistakably dead body, even though the newspapers found out about it and made it front-page news, there was nothing the police could charge me with.

In spite of which I made a full confession. It was crucial to me that the official report contain more than the detective's bleak observations. I wanted two things on record: one, that Matt was ravished by a reverential expert; two, that his cadaver blasted the energy of a star.

"Did this energy blast happen before or after he died?" the detective asked.

"After," I said, adding quickly that I couldn't have foreseen such a blast. The one tricky area was why I hadn't stopped the suicide. Why I hadn't talked, or cut, Matt down.

I lied. I said that as soon as I entered Matt's room, he kicked away the ladder. Nobody could prove otherwise. But I've often wondered how much time actually passed between when I opened the door and when his neck broke. In crises, a minute isn't a minute. There's the same chaos you get at the instant of death, with time and form breaking free, and everything magnifying and coming apart.

Matt must have been in a state of crisis for days, maybe weeks before he died. All that staring in mirrors, thinking, "Is this my face?" Watching as his face separated into its infinitesimal particles and reassembled into a strange new face. The night before he died, he had a mask on. A Dracula mask, but he wasn't joking. He wanted to wear the mask while I made love to him as if he were a cadaver. No way, I said. The whole point, I reminded him, was that *I* played the cadaver. He begged me, and I laughed because of the mask and with relief. If he wanted to turn the game around, then it was over between us, and I was suddenly aware of how much I liked that idea.

The next night he phoned me at my parents and said, "I love you," then hung up.

I don't know how I knew, but I did. A gun, I thought. Men always use guns. And then I thought, no, poison, cyanide. He was a medical student and had access to drugs. When I arrived at his apartment, the door was open. Across from the door, taped to the wall, was a note: "DEAD PERSON IN BEDROOM."

But he wasn't dead. He was standing on a stepladder. He was naked. An impressively knotted noose, attached to a pipe that ran across the ceiling, was looped around his neck.

He smiled tenderly. "I knew you'd come," he said.

"So why the note?" I demanded.

"Pull away the ladder," he crooned. "My beloved."

"Come on. This is stupid. Get down." I went up to him and punched his leg.

"All you have to do," he said, "is pull away the ladder."

His eyes were even darker and more expressive than usual. His cheekbones appeared to be highlighted. (I discovered minutes later he had make-up on.) I glanced around the room for a chair or a table that I could bring over and stand on. I was going to take the noose off him myself.

"If you leave," he said, "if you take a step back, if you do anything other than pull away the ladder, I'll kick it away."

"I love you," I said. "OK?"

"No, you don't," he said.

"I do!" To sound like I meant it I stared at his legs and imagined them lifeless. "I do!"

"No, you don't," he said softly. "But," he said, "you will."

I was gripping the ladder. I remember thinking that if I held tight to the ladder, he wouldn't be able to kick it away. I was gripping the ladder, and then it was by the wall, tipped over. I have no memory of transition between these two events. There was a loud crack, and gushing water. Matt dropped gracefully, like a girl fainting. Water poured on him from the broken pipe. There was a smell of excrement. I dragged him by the noose.

In the living room I pulled him onto the green shag carpet. I took my clothes off. I knelt over him. I kissed the blood at the corner of his mouth.

True obsession depends on the object's absolute unresponsiveness. When I used to fall for a particular cadaver, I would feel as if I were a hollow instrument, a bell or a flute. I'd empty out. *I* would clear out (it was involuntary) until I was an instrument for the cadaver to swell into and be amplified. As the object of Matt's obsession how could I be other than impassive, while he was alive?

He was playing with fire, playing with me. Not just because I couldn't love him, but because I was irradiated. The whole time that I was involved with Matt, I was making love to corpses, absorbing their energy, blazing it back out. Since that energy came from the act of life alchemizing into death, there's a possibility that it was alchemical itself. Even if it wasn't, I'm sure it gave Matt the impression that I had the power to change him in some huge and dangerous way.

I now believe that his addiction to my energy was really a craving for such a transformation. In fact, I think that all desire is desire for transformation, and that all transformation—all movement, all process—happens because life turns into death.

I am still a necrophile, occasionally, and recklessly. I have found no replacement for the torrid serenity of a cadaver.

raft in water, floating

A. M. Homes

She is lying on a raft in water. Floating. Every day when she comes home from school, she puts on her bikini and lies in the pool—it stops her from snacking.

"Appearances are everything," she tells him when he comes crashing through the foliage, arriving at the edge of the yard in his combat pants, thorns stuck to his shirt.

"Next time they change the code to the service gate, remember to tell me," he says. "I had to come in through the Eisenstadts and under the wire."

He blots his face with the sleeve of his shirt. "There's some sort of warning—I can't remember if it's heat or air."

"I might evaporate," she says, then pauses. "I might spontaneously combust. Do you ever worry about things like that?"

"You can't explode in water," he says.

Her raft drifts to the edge.

He sits by the side of the pool, leaning over, his nose pressed into her belly, sniffing. "You smell like swimming. You smell clean, you smell white, like bleach. When I smell you, my nostrils dilate, my eyes open."

"Take off your shirt," she says.

"I'm not wearing any sun block," he says.

"Take off your shirt."

He does, pulling it over his head, flashing twin woolly birds' nests under his arms.

He rocks her raft. His combat pants tent. He puts one hand inside her bathing suit and the other down his pants.

She stares at him.

He closes his eyes, his lashes flicker. When he's done, he dips his hand in the pool, splashing it back and forth as though checking the water, taking the temperature. He wipes it on his pants.

"Do you like me for who I am?" she asks.

"Do you want something to eat?" he replies.

"Help yourself."

He gets cookies for himself and a bowl of baby carrots from the fridge for her. The bowl is cold, clear glass, filled with orange stumps. "Butt plugs," he calls them.

The raft is a silver tray, a reflective surface—it holds the heat.

"Do you have any idea what's eating me?"

"You're eating yourself," he says.

A chunk of a Chips Ahoy! falls into the water. It sinks.

She pulls on her snorkel and mask and stares at the sky. The sound of her breath through the tube is amplified, a raspy, watery gurgle. "Mallory, my malady, you are my Mallomar, my favorite cookie," he intones. "Chocolate-dipped, squishy . . . You were made for me."

She flips off the raft and into the water. She swims.

"I'm going," she hears him say. "Going, going, gone."

At twilight an odd electrical surge causes the doorbells all up and down the block to ring. An intercom chorus of faceless voices sings a round of "Hi, hello. Can I help you? Is anybody out there?"

She climbs out of the pool, wet feet padding across the flagstone. Behind her is a Japanese rock garden, a retaining wall holding the earth in place like a restraining order. She sits on the warm stones. Dripping. Watering the rocks. In school, when she was little, she was given a can of water and a paintbrush—she remembers painting the playground fence, watching it turn dark and then light again as the water evaporated.

She watches her footprints disappear.

The dog comes out of the house. He puts his nose in her crotch. "Exactly who do you think you are?" she asks, pushing him away.

There is the outline of hills in the distance; they are perched on a cliff, always in danger of falling, breaking away, sliding.

Inside, there is a noise, a flash of light.

"Shit!" her mother yells.

She gets up. She opens the sliding glass door. "What happened?"

"I flicked the switch and the bulb blew."

She steps inside—cool white, goose bumps.

"I dropped the plant," her mother says. She has dropped an African violet on its head. "I couldn't see where I was going." She has a blue gel pack strapped to her face. "Headache."

There is dark soil on the carpet. She goes to get the Dustbuster. The television in the kitchen is on, even though no one is watching: "People often have the feeling there is something wrong, that they are not where they should be ... "

The dirt is in a small heap, a tiny hill on the powder-blue carpet. In her white crocheted bathing suit, she gets down on her hands and knees and sucks it up. Her mother watches. And then her mother gets down and brushes the carpet back and forth. "Did you get it?" she asks. "Did you get it all?"

"All gone," she says.

"I dropped it on its head," her mother says. "I can't bear it. I need to be reminded of beauty," she says. "Beauty is a comfort, a reminder that good things are possible. And I killed it."

"It's not dead," she says. "It's just upside down." Her mother is tall, like a long thin line, like a root going down.

In the front yard they hear men speaking Spanish, the sound of hedge trimmers and weed whackers, frantic scratching, a thousand long fingernails clawing to get in.

There is the feeling of a great divide: us and them. They rely on the cleaning lady and her son to bring them things—her mother claims to have forgotten how to grocery-shop. All they can do is open the refrigerator door and hope there is something inside. They live on the surface in some strange state of siege.

They are standing in the hallway outside her sister's bedroom door.

"You don't own me," her sister says.

"Believe me, I wouldn't want to," a male voice says.

"And why not, aren't I good enough?" her sister says.

"Is she fighting with him again?"

"On speakerphone," her mother says. "I can't tell which one is which, they all sound the same." She knocks on the door. "Did you take your medication, Susie?"

"You are in my way," her sister says, talking louder now.

"What do you want to do about dinner?" her mother asks. "Your father is late—can you wait?"

"I had carrots."

She goes into her parents' room and checks herself in the bathroom mirror—still there. Her eyes are green, her lips are chapped pink. Her skin is dry from the chlorine, a little irritated. She turns around and looks over her shoulder—she is pruney in the back, from lying on the wet raft.

She opens the cabinet—jars, tubes, throat cream and thigh cream, lotion, potion, bronze-stick, cover-up, pancake, base. She piles it on.

"Make sure you get enough water—it's hot today," her mother says. Her parents have one of those beds where each half does a different thing; right now her father's side is up, bent in two places. They both want what they want, they need what they need. Her mother is lying flat on her face.

She goes back out to the pool. She dives in with a splash. Her mother's potions run off, forming an oil slick around her.

Her father comes home. Through the glass she sees the front door open. She sees him moving from room to room. "Is the air filter on?" His voice is muffled. "Is the air on?" he repeats. "I'm having it again—the not breathing."

He turns on the bedroom light. It throws her parents into relief;

the sliding glass doors are lit like a movie screen. IMAX Mom and Dad. She watches him unbutton his shirt. "I'm sweating," she hears him say. Even from where she is, she can see that he is wet. Her father calls his sweat "proof of his suffering." Under his shirt, a silk T-shirt is plastered to his body, the dark mat of the hair on his back showing through. There is something obscene about it—like an ape trying to look human. There is something embarrassing about it as well—it looks like lingerie, it makes him look more than naked. She feels as if she were seeing something she shouldn't, something too personal.

Her mother rolls over and sits up.

"Something is not right," he says.

"It's the season," she says.

"Unseasonable," he says. "Ben got a call in the middle of the afternoon. They said his house was going downhill fast. He had to leave early."

"It's an unpredictable place," her mother says.

"It's not the same as it was, that's the thing," her father says, putting on a dry shirt. "Now it's a place where everybody thinks he's somebody and nobody wants to be left out."

She gets out of the pool and goes to the door, pressing her face against the glass. They don't notice her. Finally, she knocks. Her father opens the sliding glass door. "I didn't see you out there," he says.

"I'm invisible," she says. "Welcome home."

She is back in the pool. Floating. The night is moist. Vaporous. It's hard to know if it's been raining or if the sprinkler system is acting up. The sky is charcoal, powdery black. Everything is a little fuzzy around the edges but sharp and clear in the center.

There is a coyote at the edge of the grass. She feels it staring at her. "What?" she says.

It lowers its head and pushes its neck forward, red eyes like red lights.

"What do you want?"

The coyote's legs grow long, its fur turns into an overcoat, it stands, its muzzle melts into a face—an old woman, smiling.

"Who are you?" the girl asks. "Are you friends with my sister?"

"Watch me," the old woman says. She throws off the coyote coat—she is taller, she is younger, she is naked, and then she is a man.

She hears her mother and father in the house. Shouting.

"What am I to you?" her mother says.

"It's the same thing, always the same thing, blah, blah, blah," her father says.

"Have you got anything to eat?" the coyote asks.

"Would you like a carrot?"

"I was thinking of something more like a sandwich or a slice of cheese pizza."

"There are probably some waffles in the freezer. No one ever eats the waffles. Would you like me to make you one?"

"With butter and syrup?" he asks.

The girl nods.

He licks his lips, he turns his head and licks his shoulder and then his coyote paws. He begins grooming himself.

"Be right back," she says. She goes into the kitchen, opens the freezer, and pulls out the box of waffles.

"I thought you were on a diet," her mother says.

"I am," the girl says, putting the waffles in the toaster, getting the butter, slicing a few strawberries.

"What's this called, breakfast for dinner?"

"Never mind," the girl says, pouring syrup.

"That's all you ever say."

She goes back outside. A naked young woman sits by the edge of the pool.

"Is it still you?" the girl asks.

"Yes," the coyote says.

She hands the coyote the plate. "Usually we have better choices, but the housekeeper is on vacation."

"Yum, Eggos. Want a bite?"

The girl shakes her head. "I'm on a diet," she says, getting back onto her raft.

The coyote eats. When she's finished she licks the plate. Her tongue is incredibly long, it stretches out and out and out, lizardly licking.

"Delish," she says.

The girl watches, eyes bulging at the sight of the tongue—hot pink. The coyote starts to change again, to shift. Her skin goes dark, it goes tan, deep like honey and then crisper brown, as if it is burning, and then darker still, toward black. Downy feathers start to appear, and then longer feathers, like quills. Her feet turn orange, fold in, and web. A duck, a big black duck, like a dog, but a duck. The duck jumps into the pool, and paddles toward the girl, splashing noisily.

"These feet," she says. "They're the opposite of high heels and still they're so hard to control."

They float in silence.

She sees her sister come out of her room. She watches the three of them, her mother, father, and sister, through the glass.

She floats on the raft.

Relaxed, the duck extends her neck, her feathers bleach white, and she turns into a swan, circling gracefully.

Suddenly, she lifts her head, as if alerted. She pumps her wings. She is heavy, too heavy to be a swan. Her body is changing again, she is trading her feathers for fur, a black mask appears around her eyes, her bill becomes a snout. She is out of the water, standing on the flagstone, a raccoon with orange webbed feet. She waddles off into the night.

Below ground there is a shift, a fissure, a crack that ricochets. A tremor. The house lights flicker. The alarm goes off. In the pool the water rolls, a small domestic tidal wave sweeps from one end to the other, splashing onto the stones.

The sliding glass door opens, her father steps out, flashlight circling the water. He finds her holding onto the ladder.

"You all right?" he asks.

"Fine," she says.

"Come on out now," he says. "It's enough for one day. You're a growing girl—you need your beauty sleep."

She climbs out of the pool.

Her father hands her a towel. "It's a wonder you don't just shrivel up and disappear."

the high month

Brett Ellen Block

Adrienne broke into Richard's car with a wire hanger, then she drove until the car was out of gas.

The tank ran dry near a highway on-ramp, about a hundred yards from a bar appropriately named the End of the Road Watering Hole. On the bar's roof stood a wooden cutout of a cowboy on a rearing horse that was silhouetted against the white December sky. Crested by the cowboy's lasso, the listing building was so glum and tacky it was almost comic. Of all places, Adrienne found it fitting she would end up there.

Richard had given her a key to his apartment—a gesture he said proved how serious he was about their relationship—and Adrienne knew where he kept a spare for the ignition, so jimmying the door to his vintage Mustang was the only part of her plan that had involved any real risk or effort. After she had gotten the button lock up, she let her guard down and took off. When the car coasted to a stop, Adrienne realized that the lesson she had been trying to teach Richard about priorities—namely obsessing over his car— would not be nearly as apparent to him as the one she had just learned about keeping her eye on the gas gauge. The irony wasn't lost on her.

Adrienne folded the hanger into her purse and locked the doors, then left the car in the ditch where it had stalled and headed for the End of the Road.

Upon entering the bar, a voice called out to her, "Is it raining?"

Adrienne could make out a few dark forms in cowboy hats sitting on stools, and there was a couple in a booth by the door, but because she was looking into the shadowy room with daylight behind her, Adrienne wasn't sure exactly where the question had come from.

"No," she said tentatively.

"As long as it's not raining, I'll be happy," the voice announced. "It shouldn't rain on Christmas. That'd be just plain wrong."

Once inside, Adrienne could tell that it was the bartender who had spoken. He was a hefty, solid man and he wore a bandanna around his forehead. He was leaning into the bar like he was the only thing holding it up.

"Is there a service station around here?" Adrienne asked. "I ran out of gas up the road."

"Afraid not," the bartender said, shaking his head sympathetically. "Next one's up the highway a good five miles."

There was no way she could walk that distance. And none of the other men at the bar were jumping up to offer her a ride. Though all were squarely in their sixties and seemingly benign, Adrienne doubted whether she would have gone even if they had offered.

"Maybe you could call somebody to come and get you," the bartender suggested.

Adrienne wished it were that easy. She had called in sick that morning to the insurance company where she worked, so she couldn't phone anybody there for help. And if she called a friend, then she'd have to tell them just what she had been up to. Adrienne's only other option was to call Richard. He was an accountant, a serious yet thoughtful man who, like any of his spread sheets, looked good on paper. He was loving, had a steady job, his own home, and most of his hair. To Adrienne, who at thirty was already once divorced, Richard was a real catch. However, this stunt she'd pulled with the car would likely scare him straight off the line.

"Nobody to call," Adrienne said, answering the bartender. An empty tank had not been part of her scheme. She slumped down on a stool to think.

The syrupy twang of a country ballad filled the bar, which, Adrienne judged, had probably been a barn in a previous incarnation. The place still had the drafty feel of a building not meant to be lived in. All of the wall studs were exposed, and the light fixtures hung from sagging rafters alongside alternating rows of spurs and branding irons, the only visible nod to a cowboy theme besides the cutout on the roof. Strands of colored Christmas lights strung around support beams did little to brighten the decor or the room itself, which was so dimly lit that Adrienne found she could no longer see the couple by the door from where she sat. When she squinted, all she could discern was a poster at the end of the bar bearing a photograph of a wrecked pickup truck surrounded by cartoon sprigs of holly. The poster read: "Don't take the *Merry* out of Merry Christmas."

"We have drink specials," the bartender offered. "Half-price shots for ladies. That's not supposed to start until seven, but I'd make an exception."

Adrienne attempted a smile. "It's a little too early for me."

"Suit yourself," he said. "But the offer stands."

He went back to watching the television that was mounted on the wall. A weatherman was tracing a path of storm clouds that was moving up the southern coast. The satellite showed a staticky haze whirling its way toward the ocean, hiding brown stretches of land all over the state. Adrienne tried to focus on what to do about the car but, like the land on-screen, any ideas were quickly swept over by indecision.

Adrienne had been with Richard when he purchased the midnight blue, '69 Mustang a month earlier. It was a present to himself. "I know midlife crises are really '80s," Richard said, "but this car makes me feel good." Adrienne had to admit that it was a handsome automobile, practically a work of art. It sat low to the ground and looked razor sharp. But there was one problem. Richard's answer to his midlife crisis had quickly turned into Adrienne's current predicament.

In the beginning, she could overlook it when he would scold her for shutting the car door too roughly or pulling the seat belt too hard. She had been willing to put up with it because when they weren't actually in the car, Richard turned all of his attention over to her, acting as if she were a delicate flower he'd been given to hold. No other man had ever treated her that well. They saw each other every day, and Richard wouldn't take no for an answer when it came to wining and dining her. For Adrienne, it was as though she had her own spotlight, like a jewel in a museum case, and she had gotten accustomed to it. Richard was a sweet, gentle man, quick to give his heart, but Adrienne soon discovered that it was possible to go beyond love. And that was what he had done. Only not with her.

"Hey, it's OK," the bartender said to Adrienne. She knew she must have looked upset. He probably thought she was going to cry. "It's only an empty gas tank," he declared. "It's not like your car blew up."

Adrienne had to laugh. The bartender was right. The car wasn't gone. It just wasn't where it was supposed to be.

She had planned to move the Mustang while Richard was at work, to park it around the block from his apartment and wait for him to return. When he came home, he would immediately notice that the car was missing, but before he could get too worked up, Adrienne would step in and explain everything in the hope that he might realize just how ridiculous he was behaving about his car.

Once Adrienne was on the road, however, she found it difficult to turn back. She had never been behind the Mustang's wheel and hitting the gas felt like an overdue snub. Each night before Richard would get into bed with her, he would check on the car from the window. He washed it every week by hand. He still doted on her, but Adrienne didn't like sharing the spotlight. She had daydreams of taking a sledgehammer to the car's hood, a chainsaw, a container of lighter fluid, wild visions. In the end, that was why she thought her trick would work. If Richard wasn't so preoccupied with the Mustang, then she wouldn't have to be either. It hadn't dawned on Adrienne that *anybody* would be upset to find their car missing, not until it was too late.

As she sat at the bar tracing the nicks in the shellac, Adrienne tried to predict what Richard would do when he found out what she had done. Realistically, he would break up with her. She didn't want to think about it.

Adrienne forced herself up. "Ladies room?" she asked. The bartender poked his thumb toward the rear of the building. She pushed in her stool and headed towards the back, then something moved at the edge of her vision, and Adrienne stopped short.

There was a man sitting at a table in the far corner of the room. She hadn't noticed him before. He was watching her.

"Excuse me, miss," he said in a mellow drawl. "Mind if I ask you something?"

The man was dressed in a Santa suit. His beard and cap lay on the table beside several empty bottles of beer. Two of the buttons on his red jacket were open, exposing the pillow that was stuffed inside. Adrienne couldn't understand how she had missed him, but the dim, old barn did offer plenty of room to hide in. That may have been the very reason he was there.

"I know you don't know me," the man intoned. "But I'd like to ask you for a favor." He cheerfully motioned for Adrienne to join him.

His scalp was gleaming and he needed a shave, but he had a wide, ingratiating smile. He was, she guessed, no younger than fifty. He was probably also drunk, but Adrienne's instincts told her that he was harmless. Anyway, if he tried anything, she felt sure she could get to one of the empty beer bottles before he could get to her.

"Come on," the man said. "I didn't ask you to sit on my lap. That's not the favor. What I want is of a purely innocent nature."

"I have Mace," Adrienne lied.

"And I value my eyesight."

"So what's the favor?"

He pushed a chair toward her with his foot. Adrienne took a seat cautiously, keeping her distance. The man shoved up the furry cuffs of his coat and put out his hand, which Adrienne shook quickly. He said his name was Bruce.

"My job," Bruce began, gesturing to his suit, "is complicated. To say the least."

Bruce spoke with such intensity that Adrienne had to reconsider exactly what was involved in playing Santa. Bouncing children on your knee and listening to their Christmas lists didn't sound all that complex. Bruce must have read the doubt on her face. "What? You don't believe me?"

"No. Really I do," she told him. No need to get the man riled up, Adrienne thought.

"Well, I guess I should say my job *was* complicated. I was fired," Bruce said, taking a swig from his beer. "Thank Christ."

Then came a strained silence. Adrienne examined the floor.

"It wasn't a good job. It was worse than I expected. But what isn't?" he added. "I had children asking for Ferraris and a million dollars, which is typical. I also had two kids ask if they could have their schools burned down before the end of the holiday break. And one who wanted to know if he could have his stepfather killed. Literally killed." Bruce rubbed the corners of his mouth. He looked as though he was having trouble forming his next sentence. Adrienne was beginning to regret her decision to sit down.

"After that," he went on, "I started telling kids they could wish for whatever they wanted, but that it didn't mean they were going to get it. In fact, I said, the odds weren't good. The mothers did not appreciate this, of course. Neither did my boss." The cuffs of Bruce's coat slid back down his arms. "I know I'm not the first Santa to feel like this, to have this reaction. I know this isn't an original complaint. But let me ask you something," he said, locking Adrienne in a soulful stare. "How can I be Santa *and* be a moral guy?"

He let the question hang between them, acting as though he hadn't asked it and rolling the bottom of a beer bottle over the wet ring it had left on the table. Then, to Adrienne's astonishment, he began to unbutton the top of his pants.

"Wait," she cried, reaching for one of the bottles.

In a single swift motion, Bruce ripped the pillow from under his pants and shirt and threw it to the floor. Relieved, Adrienne fell back into her chair.

"What a terrible job," Bruce stated flatly.

Outside, drops of rain began to hit the windows. From what Adrienne had heard on the television a few minutes ago, it was going to rain on Christmas. The weatherman had put up his hands defeatedly and wagged his finger at the swirling clouds. The forecast made no difference to Adrienne. Whatever the weather, she rarely looked forward to the holidays. Like trying to decorate a palm tree instead of a pine, Christmas was always especially difficult and unsatisfying and, in the end, it only reminded her of what she didn't have to celebrate. This year, it seemed things would be no different.

Bruce eyed the television. The volume had been turned up, and the bartender was flipping channels. It seemed as though Christmas music was playing on every station. Adrienne decided to give Bruce another minute to ask his favor, then she was determined to excuse herself. She thought about calling Richard, but still hadn't come up with a way to explain herself. Each minute that passed was more time that he had to agonize over his missing Mustang. She was making the situation worse simply by sitting there.

"Just look at him," Bruce said.

Adrienne thought he meant someone on television.

"Who does he think he is? It's not like this is the Ritz. It's only some dirty, old honky-tonk bar." Bruce wore a wounded expression but sounded angry.

Adrienne followed his line of sight straight to the bartender's back, and finally she understood. She was surprised that she hadn't figured it out sooner. The bartender must have cut Bruce off, and the favor he was going to ask was that she buy a round of beer for him. It was as if he was trying to work off a stubborn soberness, but because Bruce wasn't acting totally bombed, Adrienne wondered why he didn't just go to another bar. Then she remembered shifting the Mustang into drive, what little effort it took to lose herself in the lull of the motor. Getting caught up in something was the easy part.

"That man doesn't have the giving spirit," Bruce hinted.

"Another one of these?" She pointed to the label on one of the bottles.

"You read my mind," he said, grinning.

Adrienne went up to the bar and ordered. The bartender glanced in Bruce's direction. "This for you?" he asked.

She wasn't expecting the question, so she hemmed and hawed and took too long to answer.

"Sorry," the bartender said. "I already told that guy enough is enough."

When Adrienne returned to the table empty-handed, Bruce was grave. She thought he might leap up and sweep all of the bottles onto the floor. It was possible, though unlikely. When Bruce wasn't smiling, the deep creases in his face gave him a harsh, ravaged look, something the fake beard must have covered, but his body didn't appear as if it would cooperate for such a feat of exuberance.

"It's all right. It's not your fault," Bruce said, beckoning for her to sit back down.

"Look, I should be going," Adrienne said, a little louder than she'd intended.

"Where are you going to go? You don't have any gas." Bruce nodded toward the bar, indicating that he had heard her talking before. He wasn't threatening her, merely pointing out what she'd let herself temporarily forget. Once reminded, Adrienne could picture the empty tank turning into a vast cavern. She imagined an eerie wind whistling through its darkness, her mind manifesting stress in cartoonish horror.

"So where could you go?" Bruce asked.

"Nowhere, I guess."

Now Adrienne sounded as bitter as Bruce did. She didn't like her choices—calling Richard over for a confrontation she wasn't prepared for or walking out in the rain in search of a gas station. Neither was appealing, and both would speed up the inevitable.

The rain had picked up. Adrienne found herself listening to its rhythm on the roof as though it was a favorite piece of music. She waited, anticipating a break like the end of a song that would signal her to move, to do something about the gas. The interruption came instead from Bruce saying, "How far away is your car?"

"Why does it matter?"

"How far?"

"Just down the road. Why?"

Bruce grabbed the pillow off the floor and stood up. "Let's go."

"Where?"

"Parking lot," he said. Hesitant, Adrienne remained. "Come on," Bruce said, waving her along. He was halfway across the room. After a few seconds, Adrienne acquiesced.

They stepped outside and stood under the overhang for a minute. The sky, heavy and gray as iron, seemed to be only a few feet overhead. Rain was streaming down, filling the potholes in the bar's lot.

"Now what?" Adrienne asked. She was willing to follow Bruce out of the bar, but not much farther.

"Wait here a minute," he said.

Bruce ambled across the lot to a beat-up sedan and opened the trunk with a key. After tossing the pillow inside, he pulled out a gas can and a piece of tubing, then held them up for her to see. "You need gas, right?"

He went over to the car parked in the space marked Reserved for Staff that was next to the building and removed the gas cap. "Come and hold this can," Bruce said. Adrienne did as he asked.

"Are you really that pissed off at the bartender that you would steal the gas right out of his tank?" She huddled her shoulders and cupped one hand over her eyes. The rain made her feel like she had to shout to be heard.

"One good turn deserves another, don't you think?" Bruce picked up the tube and stretched it out so it would reach his mouth. "How badly do you want this gas anyway, huh?"

Adrienne thought about all the time she had already wasted and moved the can into place by the end of the tube.

"Have you ever done this before?" she asked.

"No, but I know how to do it. And I've tasted gasoline before, so I think I'm prepared."

"Somebody else cut you off and you got desperate?"

"Funny," Bruce said, glowering. "I used to be a fireman. But I lost that job too. Guess red really isn't my color."

Bruce took a few deep breaths, put the tube to his lips, then inhaled one long drag. The gasoline came coursing out of the tank and he dropped the tube into the can, spitting and choking on the mouthful of gasoline he'd gotten. Adrienne searched for a spigot somewhere on the building. Unable to locate one, she gave Bruce a napkin from her purse. He wiped his tongue with it, gagging.

"So they make you drink gasoline before you fight fires?" Adrienne asked as the can began to fill. She felt like talking, an anxious response to her impending meeting with Richard.

"No," Bruce said with a cough. "That was an accident, a mistake during a demonstration. One of many."

The gasoline was pulsing through the rain-spattered tube, causing the can to rock in the mud. Bruce brushed down the sleeves of the Santa suit and patted out the rainwater.

"This is a pretty good coat. Doubt if I could wear it that often, but at least I didn't have to pay for it."

"Do you still have your fireman's outfit?"

"I had to turn it in."

"That's too bad."

"The whole thing was too bad," he said, checking the can. "I'd just washed it."

Bruce wiped the rain from his face. "Jeez, that was ten years ago," he said, remembering. "It was August, and I'd been hanging my uniform up to dry when I heard a call come in over the police band radio. A man had jumped off a bridge. The police were trying to find his body in the river."

Adrienne was taken aback. She wasn't sure what to say or if she should say anything at all. Bruce looked around and over his shoulder like the memory was coming up on him from behind.

"My house was right on the bank of that river," Bruce said. "I knew where the cops were looking. And I knew they were up too high. I could tell that the current would've swept the body much farther downstream. I had a little motor boat back then, and I took a sheet and a net and went out on the water." Bruce bent down and shook the tube to encourage the gasoline to flow. "I didn't really think about what I was doing. I was already on probation for not showing up and for screwing around, and I was trying to make right. Redeem myself, I suppose. Show everybody that I wasn't the guy they thought I was."

Bruce held the tube as the last bit of gasoline filled the can, then pulled it from the tank. After a moment, he said, "I found the body and brought it to shore. It was like it was right there waiting for me. But when I called in, they told me I'd broken procedure in a big way. A day later, I was out. I had to bring all of the gear back to the station or else they'd fine me. The uniform was still wet from when I'd washed it."

"But you found the body," Adrienne said.

"That's right." Bruce took the tube back to his trunk. "And they were dragging bodies out of that river for weeks after that. August is what cops call a 'high month.' There are others but, really, it's any month where people start acting crazy or, more to the point, when a lot of people die. December's one because of the holidays and all. In August, though, it's the heat. It changes people. They either lose their minds wanting to be cool, wanting it so badly, or they drown trying to get cool." Bruce slammed his trunk. He walked back over to Adrienne and looked at her squarely, thick drops of rain pelting his face. "Maybe after all those bodies went missing, they were sorry they fired me."

"Maybe," Adrienne replied.

Rainwater was getting into the gas can. Bruce put the lid on it. "We don't want any rain getting in our perfectly good gas," he said.

The humming sound of traffic on the nearby highway made it seem as though the air was quivering, being split by the rain. Adrienne thought she could feel the motion on her skin.

"You did me a favor, well tried to, so now I did you one," Bruce said, hoisting the can up onto his knee. "Go on," he told her. "You can go home now."

"What about the gas can? It's yours."

"Keep it," he said, staring out at the puddles that had collected on the lot.

Bruce passed Adrienne the hefty container, which she had to hold with both hands, then he went over to the side of the building to stand under the overhang. Adrienne trailed him.

"But isn't there something else I can do for you? Give you a ride or something?" She was biding time. She wasn't ready to face Richard.

"Nah. You've done your good deed for the day."

The rain was coming down hard now. The grass at the edge of the lot shuddered under the torrent.

"You're going to have to make a run for it," Bruce said. "Do you think you can make it?"

Adrienne felt herself nod yes, though she wasn't sure just how she would make it, not in any sense. She lifted the can into her arms and let it press its weight into her wet shirt. As it fell, the rain sounded like clapping hands, an audience after the curtain had closed. Adrienne thought about the pale leather seats in Richard's car, how the water would stain them and how her body would leave a shadow of itself there, maybe permanently. That was the image she clenched in her mind as she stepped out from under the overhang into the downpour.

a map of the tube

Bonnie Greer

SLOANE SQUARE: THE DISTRICT AND CIRCLE LINE

I'm here and I'm scared.

Some people may think what I am doing is impulsive. Just take off. Just go running transatlantic after a guy I met only once, I slept with only once or the fact that I was wearing my red vintage Yves St Laurent shirt with the red heart. Lucky I didn't wear my China-town cheongsam, which would have been too Kate-Moss-six-years-ago, but, well, I admire her and there's nobody better to have as your icon than Kate. I can say that now. When I first saw her, everyone else in school couldn't understand, but I did. We don't look alike, of course, but I transferred her to me. I mean, she's too cool to even do the catwalk, not like Naomi who just won't give it up.

No, it wasn't the full moon over Martha's Vineyard that did it to me. It wasn't the fact that he asked me to "prepare" a "proper" American hot dog and that he said "proper" and not "real." Leave it to Daddy to make a big thing about taking the ferry out to the Vineyard, *in August,* the time when I like to just lie around in my air-conditioning, and come to see him.

Glad I did. Glad I did. Glad I decided to renew my gym membership, too (Why do people who go to gyms look like they don't have to?), and schlep all the way down to the Battery and do the treadmill and the rowing machine and the sauna—duh-duh-duh—and then came the call to meet my destiny.

Just the day before, I was sitting at an outdoor cafe in Bleecker Street, trying to get through Zadie Smith (again) and I saw this bunch of sixteen-year-olds in teeny tops and shorts up their cracks yelling at the top of lungs on their cell-phones. I don't care what anybody says, no way was I that gross at sixteen. And, OF COURSE, I looked at their skin in the sun, the way the light just slid over it and there were no shadows. Madame Mui who's got this facial salon in Chinatown where all the models go—(My theory is this: models are composed by the camera. They do not exist anywhere else. Because you would not give these under-nourished giants another glance on the street.)—Madame Mui told me that girls of sixteen are doing Botox—oh my God!, what will they have to look forward to?—so everything is not what it appears. I didn't start until I was twenty even though, like they say, "Black Don't Crack," who wants to take chances what with all the environmental factors, the ton ozone, etc. Besides, all my ancestors had to do was pick cotton, not deal with New York City, right?

Before Scott, the long, dull summer stretched ahead. Before Scott, maybe graduate school in the fall. BS—what was the point? I've learned to face the reality of life, thanks to Hortensia Poole. What would I do without her? Her latest book *Want It: A Sister's Guide To Having It All—And More* says simply: "Make a wish."

Well, I made a wish and The It-Man appeared. Half African and half English. He should wear a shirt that says "Lick Me." A babe and he's mine. Yes, Lord, I'm so glad I wore my La Perla that day! Almost couldn't find any in my size. Not made for colored women's behinds, but I got lucky. The salesgirl said that I wouldn't have found this size in Paris because they don't have behinds like mine in Paris (That supposed to faze me?), so I said, "But I'm not in Paris, I'm on Fifth Avenue and I've got a platinum Am-Ex." She tried to get an attitude. I didn't want her to nut up and pull those panties, so I smiled, thanked her and SCOTT SAW THEM, TOO!

After Daddy realized that he couldn't stop me, he insisted that I do first-class to London. Knowing him, he thought that I would turn around at JFK and come back. He insisted on coming to the airport with me. I asked him not to. I just didn't want anyone to recognize him. I didn't want a "fan" to ask for his autograph. Why don't these people get a life?

But I was glad that he drove me himself to JFK. I'm still enough of a Daddy's girl to relate. Yes, and I like the Lexus, so shoot me. Whenever he drives it, the playas salute him with this little jump thing they do with the front of their car. They recognize a fellow playa, a fellow hustler, even if it is a respectable hustle like having worked for Dr. Martin Luther King in the Stone Age.

Daddy kept yakking all the time, asking me why, why, why follow some guy you don't even know 3,000 miles to London? Is it the length of time, the place, is that it, Daddy? We were yelling all the way to the airport, real high-school prom stuff, like I'm trying to borrow the car keys or something—hello, Pop! I-am-following-my-heart, doing a truly American thing, lighten up.

He's all "Let me take you, take more money." For once, I've got enough. I'm only going to be there a week (I thought). A few pieces of plastic will do. Sadly, Daddy tried the race thing. He kept saying that Scott was a white boy. He's bi-racial, Daddy, let it go. His last trump card.

As he begged and begged me to stay—"What if he's a serial killer?"—I looked out of the window and gazed at NYC, trying to burn it into my memory. I am not coming back unless I come back with Scott.

Thanks again to Kate, I packed my essentials: four miniskirts (black, khaki, denim, vintage Levi); pants—three pairs (Earl and Levi jeans); two sweaters (black and white); four '50s prom dresses, black chiffon, lemon chiffon, gingham (very Terry Moore in *Peyton Place*), a Prada (don't leave home without it); two black jackets (Chloé and Galliano); the red vintage YSL (for luck), shoes (yes!) Manolo, Dior, Marc Jacobs, Vivienne Westwood, my Jimmy Choo fuck-me-shoes for Scott; two belts, and three bags: vintage '20s beaded, Chanel power bag, and a simple black nothing from Canal Street, plus my Hermès "Birkin" bag which I was so lucky to find! (Mix the Birkin with *cheap* jeans, etc. so I don't look like the daughter of some African dictator who stole all the aid money and lives in a villa above Cannes.)

The flight was great, first class is wonderful. Seats where you can sit back and put your feet up. They give you your own shoes. I will never enter a plane and turn right again! There was some stupid

Helena Bonham Carter movie on in-flight. I looked at the flight pattern. The complimentary bag was filled with goodies. Nice chocolatey François Nars make-up, YSL perfume, essentials. Make-up from make-up people.

I learned long ago from Daddy's third wife, Frances, to never buy cosmetics from a fashion house or shoes from a guy who makes dresses. These things have to be kept separated.

I like Frances a lot. We'd go to the East Village when she was married to Daddy and shop vintage dresses, big, frothy prom dresses that I used to wear to school until Daddy sent me to that hole on Fifth Avenue. No, it wasn't because of Daddy that I grew my dreads, it was because of "Miss Walker's." All those Long Island and Connecticut dorks with their chauffeur-driven limos and their skinny little bodies. I was the only black kid there and didn't I know it. I had to slap down many of them because they wanted to touch my hair, they were used to doing that shit to their nannies and mammies. Not to me. Those girls were put on diets at eight, gym at twelve ... I had to be "street" 24/7. Carried around anything by Angela Davis (she still looks great!), real loud and proud. I mean, I am my Daddy's girl. I was. Before Scott.

"Stay in the moment," Hortensia says. Right.

My room here at the hotel in Sloane Square is white on white complete with scented candles from Harrods. The concierge said that Lily Langtry and the Prince of Wales slept here. OK. The taps are gold-like. I've spread out my shoes, including my custom-made Jimmy Choos, in neat little rows like soldiers. That's what Frances taught me. To keep my shoes lined up and labeled. And to polish the soles every night, like Diana Vreeland did. I will go to Jimmy Choos while I am here to have another pair made. It takes about two weeks, but the wait is worth it. First they measure every inch of your foot. Weird to find out that one of my feet was smaller than the other. Then you come back for a fitting with the dummy shoe and then the real thing. My first pair were a college graduation present from Daddy. Compensation for my lost childhood, I always tease him. Ha-ha-ha. I like the sound of English car engines, I like that putt-putt-putt thing. "Masterpiece Theatre."

Poor Daddy has left several messages and as soon as I'm ready, I'll call him. Or should I say, I "shall" call him (I'm in England now).

Room service here is OK. I mean, can you screw up a BLT with potato chips? After that I painted my nails with the new YSL color that makes my nails look like a vampire's.

And that feeling came back again. Like I'm in a fog, lost, choking. I'm caught, caught, caught. Shit. I'm twenty-five, a quarter of a century old and what do I have to show for it? All those years on earth? I ask this question because just before I left I had dinner with my best friend, Charlie. He told me that he's dyeing his hair gray. Crazy, but he said that with the recession, the old and the tried and true is best. Kids are out. Lot of his friends crashed and burned with the dot com thing and took a few people with them. So the kids is out. Will learn to cook. Food is always important.

My life! Is it my fault that Daddy is famous? Is it my fault that I have to weigh every ounce, every fucking crumb in order to maintain my weight? They say, at least in *Vogue*, that love makes you lose weight, but not me. After the BLT, a store was open and

I got all my favorite fashion magazines: Anna Wintour is God, let's face it. She's so cool and mature. Even when those animal rights activists threw that dead animal on her plate while she was EATING, she was still cool. What does Oprah say: "Those minks were born to die for me" or something like that. What's a mink? It's a rodent, look at it!

In the morning, I've got to get my food together. My new diet—this one will work—is eat for your blood type. I am Blood Type A—we came after the hunter-gatherers and built civilization and don't need so much meat.

However, with the BLT I had a bunch of stuff that I shouldn't: bread, bacon, tomato, mayonnaise, potato chips . . . only the lettuce is acceptable. Oh shit, I have to call room service for a cup of hot water and lemon. This will help my digestion, according to the diet. Plus, I've got to do my Pilates before I go to sleep. "Zip and hook." Tried it on the plane. I think the guy next to me thought I was choking. Scott, Scott, Scott, Scott, Scott, Scott . . .

RUSSELL SQUARE: THE PICCADILLY LINE

What do I have back in New York? Managing my little brother's rap group? Guess he has a point. Taye's idea is this: that rap, especially gangsta, is listened to by white suburban kids anyway, and besides, how would they know he went to a prep school? They can't understand the lyrics.

Taye estimates that it will cost $245,000 to produce the video. Something like twenty people at MTV sit around and decide what's going to get airplay and Taye figures that they would be so impressed with Daddy's rep . . . you got to use everything these days. If not, a quarter of a million down the drain.

He showed me a lyric before I left. Drove his Range Rover Discovery over to my apartment and almost blocked the entire street. He goes: "Some folks think God is gone. Too bad for them, I pray to Capone." This little kid who gets straight A's in Latin calls himself "Big Pimpin" and now wants to pack a Glock. Well, if Puff Daddy can come from the 'burbs so can "Big Pimpin." Daddy's really stressed. He screams stuff like: "Is that why I did all those sit-ins, so my son can sing about 'ho's and bitches'!!"

What does he want him to do? Join Farrakan? Not with those tiny red clip bow ties. Taye would die.

The tube . . . an experience. Don't sit down on the seats. You could get lice, they're cloth! Unfortunately, I wore my white Prada pedal pushers—dumb. I tried to look back at myself as I stood up . . . thank God, Daddy told me that the word "fanny" in England means the vagina, so I was careful not to ask anybody if I had any dirt on my fanny.

Another thing: people drop stuff on the street all the time. I think it must be their medieval heritage. Oh, and they eat candy bars and smoke cigarettes at the same time. I'll have to find a place to get a facial soon and I've only been here a day.

Most of all: NO EYE CONTACT. You buy your ticket, NO EYE CONTACT. This old guy was tumbling down the stairs on the other side, and nobody budged. The tube workers rushed down to help him, but everybody just kept going and NO EYE

CONTACT! Scott is half-English, he'll explain it to me. The black folks don't look either. Maybe it's all the colonialism. Scott's father's people are from Jamaica. He told me some wild stuff his father found out when he first came here: outdoor toilets! That had to be the worst. I would have turned around and gone right back, fuck that! I've brought my own toilet liners. I'm not sitting on a toilet seat I don't know.

On the way to Scott's university, I tried to make eye contact with this one woman. I smiled at her. She turned her head away from me, which was real strange because she had dreadlocks, too. Speaking of which, where in the hell will I get my hair done? I left my custom-blended moisture spray at home. I will have to find the "community" soon.

I got precise directions to SOAS off the Web and a detailed map. Turn right out of Russell Square. Pretty drab area, everybody looks pretty harassed. I noticed that all of the women had their purses strung across their chest. I think I know what's up. Mine is a $1500 Chanel bag, as in Rome. Present from Shelley, Daddy's fourth and current bride. Shelley is five years older than me. She's already had a full face lift, nose job, lipo, The Six Million Dollar Bitch. She met Daddy at a lecture called "Why the '60s Will Never Die" at the 92nd Street YMCA, and Daddy, very susceptible to young blonde JAPs in his old age, fell for her. The first time I met Shelley was at the Tribeca Bar And Grill because she's a friend of a friend of Robert DeNiro's and like, who cares, but for Daddy's sake I showed up. Decided to do neo-Nirvana, low-slung jeans ("Earl"), uncombed hair, a hooded jacket ("Tommy Hilfiger"),

OK, not quite Nirvana. What really got her was that I hadn't shaved under my arms.

I took the occasion (Hortensia always says to make sure that every day you do something FOR YOU) to announce my decision: I was going to London, England. Of course they were freaked. "London is some place you VISIT, are you crazy!" the fourth wife yelled.

I endured it. Neither of them understands what it's like to be a quarter of a century old right now. It's not a matter of being like Taye's generation, totally corporate, totally after the bling-bling. That kid's talking about platinum watches after he cut his record deal. I just want to hide inside Scott, just get lost in his love, be like . . . a Mariah Carey lyric.

I can see the writing on the wall. I need Scott. At Russell Square, I walked the path over to SOAS just the way he described it: past the movie house where he goes to see his favorite French films, and then to the university. That big, gray building where I'll be waiting for him. After hanging around, I saw a Japanese restaurant and had a lot of sushi, good for my diet. Ate too much of it. So had to top it off with a Diet Coke and McDonald's French fries—a small one. I sat in Mickey D's and watched the people in there. One of the things that I've always found interesting is comparing the different *Vogues*. French *Vogue* is very tight. To be a French woman you have to be skinny and very pulled in. Not a hair out of place. Italian *Vogue* is the best, very raunchy and artistic. They also used the black models first. That's where I first saw Naomi Campbell. American *Vogue* is about (How'd that rap song go?) "dollah bill, y'all, dollah, dollah dollah bill y'all." Now British *Vogue*—this is different. Can't make it work yet. But Scott will help me. Have got to find a gym because otherwise all of these crunches that I'm doing will be buried under fat. What was that article I read in *Mademoiselle*, that you have to be genetically disposed toward a six-pack . . . something to do with fat distribution. Scott has a six-pack. He has everything.

Back at the hotel, I went over Hortensia Poole's *Three Steps Toward a New You*: 1. Kick That Sucker to the Curb—get rid of negativity. 2. Don't Sweat the Small Stuff—brush little things aside. 3. God Don't Like Ugly—people who do you wrong will get what they deserve, don't you worry. 4. Keep Your Eye on the Sparrow—don't lose sight of your goal. It's about creating this place inside yourself, the way Madonna did, just really believing in yourself and eventually the rest of the world will. That's why she's my idol. If you look at her, there's nothing really special going on. Except when I was eight and saw her *Like A Virgin* video where she's in Venice with this lion—the guy in it looked like Scott. It's destiny, I know it. Got to stay focused like Madonna. How can you beat it? You're whipped by the will power!

That is why, dear map of the tube with your squiggly lines, I embrace you. Soon I'll be with him. Wish it and it will come true.

But sometimes, I ask myself in my darkest moments what it must have been like to have been young in a time when it meant something, like in Daddy's time. Taye and I just roll our eyes and look at the ceiling when he starts with his '60s thing. Being black is just one of the components, part of the mix, not the end all and be all. Anyway, it must have been nice to have been young in the old days when your lifestyle wasn't instantly appropriated and sold back to you in Gap ads. I buy Gap, OK, but what can I do about the kid in Pakistan who doesn't have pee breaks because he's making a pair of combat pants.

It's just too big, too fucking big. You're a cog in a gigantic machine, so deal with it.

I said this to Scott and he understood perfectly. Englishmen are extremely well educated, such gentlemen. No wonder Madonna married one.

They eat with a knife and fork. Just watching Scott eat with a knife, then cut with it just like Princess Diana's butler said in his book, almost made me come! Can't wait to be an English wife!!!!

HOLLAND PARK: THE CENTRAL LINE

Very nice of the Filipina maid at the hotel to tell me about this park. Did Westminster Abbey and all that. Bought another pair of Manolo's at his shop in Chelsea, $600!! Maybe Scott won't be impressed with this. He's really preppy, sweaters and slacks.

Great park. Since I'm a native New Yorker didn't know I need the fresh air, have never had that sensation. And it's another place to chill out, plan my strategy. Guess she knows that I've been in the hotel for a week and am not doing any touristy things. Also walked to that park in *Notting Hill* where Julia Roberts and Hugh Grant hung out. Couldn't get over the fence, have more body fat than Julia. Must work on that.

Running out of money because I have been eating in Nobu every night like *Vogue* suggested. How do people eat here? The proportions are miniscule and $100 for two courses.

Also got into Ivy. Sat next to Jerry Hall. Realized old guy sitting next to her was Mick Jagger! Couldn't eat my crab cakes! Learned how to get a cab if I need one. Slip through the main entrance of The Ivy, then come out. Doorman thinks you ate there. Like Nobu better. Also Anton Mossiman's next to Harvey Nicks. Bought a pair of Donna Karan black pants that cost a fortune, just to cheer myself up, plus had a facial in the salon, another fortune. Had my first Havana cigar in Mossiman's, so strong I got stoned. And then did something really stupid. Thought I saw Scott on the street. Ran outside like a crazy woman and turned the guy around. It wasn't him. Losing it. Must practice my power mantra. Envision my dream.

Feel really good in my hotel. Don't have the feeling that I'll get mugged for my hand-made Jimmy Choos in Sloane Square. If ever run over in street because I looked the wrong way have a note in my purse asking to remove the Choos before I go into ER. Can't stay in the hotel much longer.

Seriously running out of money.

And no Scott.

Stood at entrance to SOAS for eight hours yesterday.

Nothing.

HAMPSTEAD: THE NORTHERN LINE

After two weeks here, have had to leave the hotel or will be out on the street big time. Frances' idea to always carry Louis Vuitton luggage has paid off. It got me a room in a big house in Hampstead. Furniture like *Brideshead Revisited* plus dust, but I must be really in London now. I'm staying in one of the son's rooms. It's really the den, with a small couch and a window that looks out at a garden. People must really trust each other here because there are no bars on the window. Hair is seriously dry and needs help. Weather getting cold and clothes will no longer work. But I did have the foresight to get one of those shrinking devices I saw on television, so a couple of big sweaters (New Jersey warehouse sale) are shrunk down to the level of three handkerchiefs in my suitcase. Pays to watch those early morning infomercials between exercise classes.

Had to talk to Daddy for AN HOUR long distance in order to explain to him that I was trying to save money, that was why I was moving out of the hotel. Told him that I've made friends, OK, it's the guy who sells papers near SOAS, but so what?

Anyway, how can I stay here and be with Scott if I'm spending money on hotels and Nobu and stuff? Daddy just doesn't get it. He just doesn't get it. I'm IN LOVE, I'm IN LOVE!! That's all that counts.

Hampstead. Everybody I ask directions is American. Am I in *The Twilight Zone?*

My landlady is divorced and writes soaps for the BBC. She's a chain smoker, too. A soap star who also rents a room with her just got busted for bringing a joint back from Spain. That's the good news. The bad news is that she was with her girlfriend.

Last night couldn't sleep because landlady was on the phone all night, plus reporters hanging outside waiting for the soap star to show up. Need sleep because of the days I am spending hanging out waiting for Scott and am very tired when I return. Skin getting very gray because there isn't much sun here. Hair needs help. Locks starting to fall out.

Tonight had dinner with landlady. Had lots of salad. Landlady understood. She's on a diet, too. Used to eat lots of Marks and Spencer's TV meals, but I told her about all the e's and stuff, so she will stop.

Told her about Scott and me, about how we met at a function for Daddy and how . . . I don't want to say that we had sex. We made love. It was once, only once, but I know. It's so cool that he's studying Arabic. He doesn't have to do that. This alone makes him so fantastic. He's going to do something in this world.

Jenny, that's my landlady, told me about a shop where I can sell some of my clothes, if it comes to that. A red Lolita Lempicka dress that Frances bought me in Paris should get something. I have a vintage dress from Granny Takes A Trip which cost a fortune but is an investment piece. That will all go anyway because even if I have to live in some cramped place with Scott, it'll be worth it.

Found a bar—I mean pub—not far from Jenny's house. A guy tried to pick me up. Very cute but didn't like the tattoos. Showed him my engagement ring. Bought it myself the other day at Harrods, maxed out my VISA but, Scott's a student, we're—and I can say that now, I'm empowered by my mantra—not into that guys-buy-the-ring stuff.

It looks great. Well, not a great diamond, tiny. But it's pinkish, which looks great on my complexion, even if it is getting gray.

RUSSELL SQUARE: THE PICCADILLY LINE

Been coming here for weeks and weeks and weeks now.

No Scott.

Asked at the Arabic Department at SOAS if a Scott Fairburn was registered there but they couldn't find his name. Daddy's threatening to come and get me. Jenny looks at me funny. Getting cold outside.

Took some clothes to a store in Chelsea and got some money. Can't stand to even list what is gone.

Have streamlined everything. Can't survive on salads, don't want to get foot and mouth. Jenny told me foot and mouth is what we call mouth and hoof, but what difference does it make?

Going to that pub a little too often. Can't do too many more Bacardi Breezers, coming home a little out of it. Teeth are getting dingy and the hair and the skin! Can't afford a gym. I know this is my call. I take full responsibility for my life.

Hope that I have my grandmother in me. She walked with Daddy from a burning building that the Klan tried to destroy. She walked with her baby, Daddy, in her arms. I can see her sometimes, sitting in her big chair, telling me never to give up, never to let go.

I didn't, and finally . . . Hortensia's affirmations kicked in!!!

I saw HIM!!! Scott!

He didn't go inside SOAS, but was walking past. I ran up to

him. Well, maybe I was too forward. But it was like he had a light around him, a big halo. He is half English. I just wasn't cool. But I've been waiting so long. He was happy to see me. He's still sooo beautiful. But he looks different here, can't pinpoint it. He had on a funky pair of Diesel jeans and a Gap T-shirt. Wish I couldn't tell a label just like that. Wish I could be simple . . . just not give a damn. Labels, money, possessions, Scott doesn't care, he's not into it. He's British. My American shallowness will be burned away in the fire of his love. Just like Madonna who, too, has found her British love.

We ate at a Chinese around the tube station. It was a little bit greasy spoon, but Scott's a student. I wanted to take him to Nobu to celebrate. He had a better idea. Much, much better.

VICTORIA STATION: THE VICTORIA LINE

I'm going to say it straight up: I was a little shocked to find out that Scott was bridge and tunnel. Croydon. Cool to do the tram, though, better than the tube. Saw a postcard comparing Manhattan skyscraper to Croydon. They call it a mini-Manhattan. Ugh . . . but night I can kind of see it. Better than a pitch-black postcard they sell in New York called "New Jersey by Night."

Problem. Scott told me in New York that his parents had a place in the country and that he came from money. His parents live by the sea in Margate. He looked apologetic. Why? Margate. That sounds great. Bottom line, this is his world. I love it. He lives in a studio with no elevator and no shower. The floor is creaky. I saw a roach! Oh, and he has a White Pearl, my favorite vacuum cleaner. White Pearl is the Rolls Royce.

Been here in walk-up studio for four days, wrapped in love. Actually and truly can see myself here. Weird. Me, Buppy Princess with the big dreads, living near Wimpey's hamburgers, and drinking Tia Marias with the ladies of Croydon.

But this is suburbia, I'm not fooling myself. Is this where Kate Moss started?

Seven days later.

Things are eating at me. No books. Weird. Maybe he works at the library. Cut off my cell phone. Don't want to hear from Daddy. He's even got Taye on my case, and even Frances who doesn't even speak to Daddy anymore, they're all calling me. Taye wants to know if he can use my apartment. The Land Rover got shot at in The Bronx after a gig.

I've been living in the *same clothes* for four days, the hair, the nails, the skin, the teeth, who cares! I'm with Scott.

I White Pearled his place to death. Scott doesn't talk much and he's gone a lot of the time, but we're together.

Used Daddy's platinum VISA at Harrods. Le Creuset pots and pans, burnt orange, a beautiful Iranian rug just like the one I saw in a *People* magazine story about Mariah Carey (Why does she *always* know the score?), plus lots of Moulinex appliances and an espresso machine. Also did the Harrods spa thing because I had read about it in *Vogue*: CACI facial, etc. and a Gucci jacket for Scott. He looks a little like Tom Ford, but thankfully Scott is straight.

Worried about the jacket. Don't know how much it would be

appreciated in clubs where they only drink Malibu and Coke, and something called Babycham. Took him and jacket to Nobu. Can't do that anymore.

Oh, and he smoked through his meal!!

ST PAUL'S: THE CENTRAL LINE

Seven days later. Near Scott's office.

Scott does not go to SOAS. It was a scam. A way to hook up with women while on vacation. Feel like some seventy-year-old scammed by some condo Casanova who ends up giving you HIV and the nurse at the clinic says "I'm so sorry that you contracted this through bad blood" and you say "Actually I had sex without a condom" and everybody in the place goes "Sex at seventy—how disgusting!" And the sex is the worst part!

Using Hortensia's books as my guide. She says "Sisters—no matter what: DON'T LOSE THE LESSON!!"

I won't. Called Jenny up in Hampstead to give her two weeks' notice so that she can rent her room out.

Scott is my future (Say ten times before I sleep as according to Hortensia).

VICTORIA STATION: THE VICTORIA LINE

Three weeks. Did some drug. What I remember is that we went to a club not far from studio. Things are breaking up. Feel sick. Can't give up.

Wore my denim mini skirt, shiny shirt from Anna Sui, and stuck my extra Master Card in my "Victoria's Secret" maxi-thong to club. People drink a lot. $18 to get in but all drinks are free. Scott wore what looked like stay-pressed slacks and pretty cheap shirt hanging out of his waistband. But, like Hortensia says, look below the surface. Did lots of Bailey's, not much else there. Tons of Lionel Ritchie.

Cash advances on the card will soon cease. Think Scott wants me out. Staring at Scott's sleeping back. Don't want him to use condoms . . . want to get pregnant . . . have to check cycles, can't do it in front of him . . .

He thinks am here on a visit.

Have to make things clear to him immediately.

BRIXTON: THE VICTORIA LINE

Found place to get hair done. Got to look good for Scott.

Had appointment for two o'clock, but didn't get into chair until four. Real laid-back place. Need this chilled-out vibe. Get in touch with blackness. Need to be more laid back. Scott half West-Indian, but maybe English part is what is weird . . . he is very cruel now.

I am ignorant. Reggae, don't get it, but must learn. Scott's half Jamaican. Learn to cook peas and rice, or is it rice and peas? Where to buy?

In beauty shop only person who smiled at me was the Rasta who swept the floor.

Wash, hot oil treatment, head rub, re-twist. Caught my face in a store window. Have lost weight, but not in a good way. Sat in

Mickey D's, had a coffee, staring at the street. Watching all the black people. Want to connect with them, but how?

Rang Daddy to talk, make him remember what love is about.

Must get a job, anything.

ST PAUL'S: THE CENTRAL LINE

I am praying at cathedral . . . can you believe it?

Reason: Got back to Scott's three days ago. Note asking me to move out. Sat there for two days, eating nothing, waiting for him to return. Have to make it very clear that we are meant to be together.

Elle said that this was the month that I would meet my destiny. *Elle* has been right before. Got that vintage Betsy Johnson at the sale, didn't I?

Window-shopping in Notting Hill. Found a mini-trampoline. Intend to jump on it one hundred times a day to reinforce bones and stimulate calcium. Have given up dairy, puts on the pounds. He'll love me skinnier.

Last night he came back with another girl. I didn't want to leave, couldn't. What if locked out?

TOTTENHAM COURT ROAD: THE NORTHERN LINE

Can't tell Daddy that working illegally. Get money in hand at the end of the week. Answer the phones. Television production company makes reality TV. Reality? What's that?

Doing a show based around a refrigerator. It's like this: get four fatties in a house and give a million to the first one who loses four-teen pounds. Stuff the refrigerator with food. Interviewing people all week now, all kinds of losers. Lots of loser dust in this place, too. Have to get out soon. They all want to be in front of camera. Guess you don't really exist unless you're on TV.

Asked about Margate, everybody looked at me like I was crazy.

Got a room in a boarding house owned by a church near Charlotte Street. Think it's about a hundred years old or something. Room is the size of my shoe closet back in New York. The bed sags in the middle and whole place smells like cabbage. Have to share the bathroom, which has this air freshener beside the toilet that makes me sick. Afraid to bring my Harrods scented candles in here because I might burn the place down. At least we're all women here, but the girl next to me has a boyfriend and at night it's gross.

Scott changed his phone number.

Sold more stuff, one of the Vuitton pieces. Did really well in Chelsea with that, though I bet they'll unload it for more. Have to bang on these paper-thin walls so that I can get some sleep.

Can't they understand that must get up early? Must try to talk to Scott before I have to go to work?

TOTTENHAM COURT ROAD: THE NORTHERN LINE

Scott said get out of his life or he'll call the police. Told him to go and accuse me of stalking. After cops hear who my father is nothing will happen anyway. Told some of the dorks here about Daddy but they never heard of him. Funny how history just washes over people, how people and their deeds just vanish in the mists of time.

In Daddy's day, I would have been doing something meaningful. I would have been marching for freedom or fighting the police or burning my bra.

Too young to know my mother, but she was the love of my father's life. "A little blond girl from a good family who had a heart of gold," he always says, "the love of my life."

Feel so sorry for Daddy. To live to be fifty-two, all those years and not find it. I have.

TOWER HILL: THE DISTRICT AND CIRCLE LINE

Daddy is somewhere over the Atlantic. But he won't find me. Daddy used to FIGHT the CIA but I truly believe now that he WORKS for them. Hired a detective to keep an eye on me.

I tried to tell this to Scott, but he doesn't want to know. He even came out of his office to beg me to leave him alone. I would, I swear, if I thought that we weren't meant to be together.

Am going tomorrow to start the process of getting a visa. An Australian who works with me says that Lunar House, where you have to go, is the pits. But at least it's in Croydon. Something I know. Got to look over my shoulder to make sure no one's following me.

At a quarter of a century old I actually don't have much energy, all the energy necessary to deal with all the people who want to keep on living: the old who won't die, the middle-aged who won't slow down, all the ones younger than me, plus the trees, the insects, so much life. So much.

Daddy used to laugh at me—the only black girl into Nirvana, his child, into a grunge white boy band from Washington. Daddy, I'm not like you.

Figured out why I like *Blair Witch* so much. See, the thing they were looking for in the wood was not a witch, but Kurt Cobain's body. Kurt blew his head off in the woods, didn't he? His death belongs to me. I get it.

I said this to Scott, in New York, after we'd made love, and he got it. This is one of our many bonds and you don't throw that away.

Men are from Mars, and Women are from Venus. I can deal with that. To my right is the Tower of London and some great postcards of Princess Di. I'm here to stay. I know that my friends envy me back home.

An Englishman! I have followed my love and my dream. We will marry right here on this bridge. Right on the spot I am standing. In a white Vera Wang dress, shoes by Manolo Blahnik, real diamonds, La Perla undies.

I am strong, just like my grandmother who defeated the evil around her and with her child in her arms, walked through the flames.

cookie

Cris Mazza

She first encountered the neighbors on the steep adjoined drive-ways they shared. With an armload of letters, ad circulars and mag-azines from the mailboxes on the street, Nan's neighbor was making her way back down toward the houses on her white con-crete half of the driveway, just as Nan was headed up her own black asphalt side to collect her daily barrage of junk. The neighbor was in her fifties, wearing a long cotton skirt, her hair in a babushka, and was accompanied by a child of around seven years dressed in purple shorts and a green sleeveless top. The family, Nan knew, were Eastern-European, but they hadn't fled poverty. The man was a contractor, had built several houses in the area, then he'd moved his wife and children into the one that hadn't sold, a monstrosity with a Sleeping Beauty tower on the flag lot next door to Nan.

Below the houses, a resort golf course meandered through bot-tomland, as though the native chaparral floor of a Southern Cali-fornia watershed had instead been flooded with a thick coat of green paint. Nan's lot, a carved-out level spot, was halfway up the canyon wall, overlooking one of the sea-level fairways. From there, her driveway was another steep climb to the road above. Called a "flag lot" because the perimeter shape of the parcel plus driveway was the outline of a flag and pole—with the flag completely unfurled in a stiff breeze. Near perfect privacy, except the flag lot next door whose driveway ran adjacent to Nan's, their flag extended the opposite direction, as if blowing in a different wind.

Nan had bought the lot overlooking the golf course with her inheritance, then built a modest house and dog facility. Six runs, a grassy exercise yard, small outbuilding with two rooms: one for crating, the other equipped for bathing and grooming. She bred, trained and showed Shetland sheepdogs, and was paid to train and show other people's dogs, often dogs owned by wealthy people who rarely had their animals at home.

Nan wasn't sure the neighbors spoke English, wasn't sure what to do that day, passing so close on the driveway. The woman gazed away, seeming to have eyes only for the tomato vines and squash her husband had planted on the strip of dirt bordering their driveway. But the child spoke up. "Hi!"

The child was chubby with a full moon face. Nan answered, "Hello."

"Hi," the child said.

Nan replied, "Hi, how're you?"

The child said, "Hi!"

"Hellllo there," Nan exclaimed softly.

"Hi!"

By this time Nan had passed the woman and child, but she

turned quickly and looked closer, just for a second. Something definitely wrong there. The child clasped her hands together in front of her stomach, twisting her wrists back and forth like unscrewing a jar, fingers entwined. "Hi!"

It had been months before, when the European family first moved in, that Luke, the man who delivered drinking water, had told her there was a husband and wife and several children, he couldn't be sure how many children, maybe a baby too. In fact, Luke thought another one could've been born since the family moved in, but he hadn't heard a baby in a while, those babies may have died. He said he heard, from someone on his route who'd bought one of the man's other houses, that there was one of those problems between the man and wife, both negative or both positive, one of those mismatches that caused some of the children to sicken and die or have other defects. He meant, of course, the Rh factor. These things didn't happen with dogs. Or if they did, perhaps it was one of the conditions that caused a bitch to absorb her litter while gestating, or caused her to eat the newborn whelps, or ignore them and let them die of exposure.

"Hi," the child uttered, and before Nan turned to continue her ascent to the mailboxes, she thought she saw the woman smiling, even laughing behind a dour face.

The rest of the way up her driveway, her own face burning, Nan couldn't help but remember a news fluff piece she'd seen the other day, a story about one of those child geniuses who'd graduated from college at fourteen and passed the bar at seventeen, ran his own law firm for ten years then decided on a career change and went back to college for a Ph.D. in neuro-physiology. His mother reminisced that while she was pregnant with him, her doctor warned her the fetus could be born retarded. Was it a case of a medical opinion being wickedly wrong, or were there two equivalent possibilities at either end of a spectrum? Despite study and care in dealing with heredity, it still seemed such a grab bag.

Around this same time Nan's foundation bitch, Daphne, was pregnant with the litter that would contain her Best-in-Show Champion *O'Nan Call The Wind Mariah*, a future Register-of-Merit dam of champions. Of course that day she didn't know how successful the breeding would be, and even though she endeavored to continually expand her understanding of genetics, her knowledge of the traits, good and bad, supposedly carried by both sides of the pedigree, it still seemed that all the possibilities, even probabilities supplied by the sire and dam just swirled somewhere in chaos, like bingo balls in a big glass box, until the moment of conception, or the bingo lever is pulled, and random numbers—or haphazard traits of appearance and personality, proficiency and malady, strength and incapacity—are whisked up, called out and displayed—or manifested in whoever, whatever is finally born. You get what you get, that's all you have to work with, that's all there is to it.

Well, except the rhynoplasty her parents bought for her sixteenth birthday because, despite the blizzard of freckles and cloudy green eyes, despite the name O'Flannary, her original nose took a long bumpy trip down her face. Of course she also taped and braced her puppies' ears, the whole first year of their lives, to ensure a high, tight earset and perfectly tipped ear leather.

It wasn't long before Nan noticed, in fact heard persistently all day, the child next door repeating "Hi", sometimes in the slow redundant rhythm she'd used on the driveway, sometimes a louder call as though to a friend across a restaurant, although still the same clipped monotone inflection. The rest of the time Nan could hear the girl bellowing, not words, just open-throated wailing or guttural cries. And she heard the other children, a few older girls, admonish her, "Maria, be *quiet*." Sometimes the utterances or shouts were muted, other times the child was obviously outside the house, and Nan easily discovered—because the only barrier between her nearly-private back lawn and the neighbor's yard was a small trellis of string beans on a corner of their property—that the neighbors had put the child out on their raised patio deck where a redwood fence railing kept her penned five feet off the ground, and the glass slider to the house must've been locked. The girl stood leaning on the banister, almost as though enjoying an afternoon or morning interlude overlooking the golf course, and called "Hi" to each group of golfers who passed. Most answered her, then when she repeated her short greeting, they answered her again. After her third "Hi" they might wave, or glance up sharply. By that time they were usually on their way again, heading down the fairway after hitting their balls a second or third time. They got into their golf carts and took a long last look over their shoulders, up the hillside toward the girl on the patio deck, still saying "Hi."

Nan planted a fast-growing eugenia hedge on the property line between her place and the neighbors', from the end of the driveway, alongside the house, ending where a steep landscaped embankment plunged down to the golf course. When Mariah was born, the individual eugenia bushes were only as tall as Nan, and the spaces in between each were as wide as the plants themselves.

Mariah was everything a dog should be. In fact, she was exceptional in every way and demonstrated her comprehensive quality from the getgo. From the flashy full white collar, white up to her foreleg elbows, on the plume of her tail and a perfect triangle snip of white on her muzzle, to the deep sable red of the rest of her coat. From the sweet, merry expression of her dark, almond-shaped eyes, to the elegant length and arch of her neck. She was, in fact, difficult to fault: her muzzle full, her backskull lean and flat, the angle of her shoulders laid back, her hocks parallel, her feet catlike and round, her tail long enough to brush the ground, her topside level, her body shape cobby, her coat long and profuse, her teeth perfectly scissored, her movement at a trot swift and fluid with astonishing extension and flawless single-tracking. Add to all this a high-energy, confident, seize-the-day attitude that radiated not only health but spirit and vivacity. When Mariah was a year old and already a Best-in-Show Champion, Nan had to recognize that the limitations and faults in her first three dogs—including her foundation bitch, Mariah's mother—were sufficient to thwart their show careers, so she placed them in pet homes to make room for Mariah's more successful descendants.

Including other people's dogs who were being kept for showing or breeding, but not counting litters of puppies, Nan usually had at least six dogs requiring daily attention—cleaning and hosing down kennels, dispensing food (at least four different preparations due to special dietary requirements) and changing water, then basic grooming of all dogs, bathing as necessary (sometimes five or six before a show weekend), not to mention nail clipping, cleaning of ears, trimming hair on feet and ears, and dental cleaning. The dogs took turns out on the exercise lawn—certain pairs could be together, but many combinations were not possible—while Nan road-worked those being actively campaigned for championship points. She had a special bicycle with a fixture to which the dog was secured on a buckle collar, and she rode at a steady pace, keeping the dog at a trot for twenty minutes.

Nan's house had picture windows and glass sliders overlooking the resort. Outside the sliders, she had a few flowerbeds and one strip of lawn between her house and the steep downhill embankment. Separated from the dog facilities by her house, and finally separated from the neighbors by the eugenia hedge, it was a secluded part of her property where clients never came. But Nan sometimes went out there with Mariah in the evening, after the last of the golfers was gone, listening to ravens squabble with the hawks they chased from fir trees growing along the fairway whose tops were just about level with Nan's lawn where she sat throwing a ball for Mariah or just resting quietly while Mariah viewed her territory. If a late jogger came by, especially one with a dog, Mariah would growl low in her throat and stand at the lip of the embankment, neck arched, ears quiveringly alert, hackles raised. Her only breed-standard imperfection was that when guarding territory, when asserting her alpha position, she carried her tail straight up, a flag over her back. The profuse fur on her tail bristled out, and, combined with the abundant puffed-up hackles around her neck, clearly functioned to make her appear bigger to whoever she was warning away, so Nan hardly considered the gay tail a fault, it was natural and necessary.

After a few years the girl next door developed a second word, *cookie*. This could have been funny because all of Nan's dogs understood that word, although they didn't seem to respond to it when the girl bellowed it incessantly, inside the house and out on the patio deck, following her babushkaed mother up the driveway and back down. Nan herself used the word in the show ring, to bring the dogs' ears up and give them the necessary posture and presence. Sometimes, with a difficult dog who wouldn't show, she wondered if she shouldn't have named the dog *cookie*. But then, of course, the word's special meaning would be lost.

During the week, two or three people might have appointments to come by, to deliver or pick up dogs for showing and training, to have their show dog groomed (ostensibly to learn to do it themselves), to drop off a bitch to be bred or to look at a litter of puppies. They always wanted to see Mariah, or came into the enclosed kennel area and immediately spotted her, "That must be Mariah!" Mariah would be standing upright with front paws on the edge of her exercise pen, back feet hopping up and down, eyes laughing, her plume tail waving like a banner, as usual drawing every eye to see her first, capturing attention and not relinquishing it easily.

And yet, the consultation did often stray.

She was affixing a patch of adhesive moleskin to the inside of each ear on a four-month-old, then using yarn glued to the moleskin to draw the ears together, higher on the puppy's head, tying the yarn in a bow between the ears, and the puppy's owner, helping to hold the pup still, said, "What's with your neighbor? I said good morning and she looked away."

She showed a new owner how to line-brush: lie the dog on one side and start just behind the dog's ears, make a part down to the skin, a "line," brush the long thick guard hairs and undercoat against the growth grain, then, by bringing more and more hair forward, brushing it smooth against the grain, the line will move further and further down the dog's body. This kept the wavy undercoat from matting flat, gave the whole coat its profuse, full bushy appearance. The owner said, "Hmmm, yes, I see." Then, "I think someone next door wants a cookie."

She tried to avoid answering her clients' extraneous observations, but when she did reply, she made every effort to keep her responses nonchalant and indifferent.

While Nan snipped off each whisker at its base on the muzzle of a young show prospect, the dog's owner, hovering too close and blocking part of her light, remarked, "Your neighbor's gardener gave me a long, hard look when I came down the driveway."

Nan said airily, "That's not a gardener, that's him."

When Nan took one dog onto the grass exercise area to train, the dogs remaining in kennels and crates in the outbuilding yelped a jealous, joyous chorus. Those who belonged to Nan could wear

electronic bark collars, delivering a minor jolt of electricity if they
made any noise while wearing the apparatus, but the collars
couldn't be used on boarding dogs, and she no longer put one on
Mariah, who was often free to roam the outbuilding and patio and
walkway around the exercise yard. But almost every visitor asked
about the other noise that Nan barely noticed anymore.

"Who's being killed next door?"

"What's with all the yelling?"

"Someone please give that child a cookie!"

"Is there something wrong with that kid I saw in the
driveway?"

"What's going on over there, is that a TV?"

"There's a kid screaming next door, shouldn't you call
someone?"

"I don't think that would help anyone," Nan said mildly. The
consequences of neighborhood animosity could be, for a kennel
owner, catastrophic. Antifreeze, for one, was something everyone
had, was sweet and attracted dogs, and was lethal. Around this time,
Mariah had her first litter. Despite several serious inquiries from
reputable breeders, Nan kept three of Mariah's first puppies and
sold the two lesser-quality pups to novice clients who were interested in starting a dog-showing hobby.

Nan needed eight 5-gallon jugs delivered every week because she
only let the dogs drink purified water, but she'd been looking for
a reason to switch water companies, since Luke had asked her to

dinner or a movie. She'd tried the kind of answer meant to say *no* without having to say it directly. "I'm so busy, and I go to shows every weekend." But, if he found her around the kennels or in the outbuilding, if she didn't disappear into the house quickly enough when she heard his truck come down the driveway, he'd ask again if she had a show that Saturday.

"Every weekend," she smiled. "There's always a show somewhere. Even if it means I go five hundred miles."

"Even Thanksgiving week, even Easter week?"

"There's no holiday big enough to deter dog-show people from our pursuit of points, it's crazy, I know, we have no lives of our own." She was standing with her back to the door, at the stainless steel sink in her outbuilding, washing all the aluminum water and food bowls in a basin of hot soapy water with bleach, then rinsing and setting them in a rack to dry. Viruses and bacteria were so easy to pick up at a show, no matter how hard you tried to keep the dogs' noses off the ground by carrying them from pen to ringside and wheeling them from the parking areas into the grounds still in their crates stacked on carts. Not to mention the dogs her clients brought, despite her requirement of a health certificate and certain extra tests, for giardia, for brucellosis, for coccidia, and other parasites, protozoa or bacteria that cause chaos in the animals' intestines or reproductive systems. Now was a good time for extra caution, with Mariah's promising offspring being grown out, and it looked like none of the three was going-off and losing quality.

"What are the points for?" Luke asked, pushing his dolly with the last two jugs through the door. "You win money?"

The room was more crowded than usual, with a pen for Mariah's six-month-old pups set up in the center. Nan dried her hands. "When you win, you earn points. Toward a championship."

"So how do you win? The biggest? The fastest? Or just the prettiest? Like Miss America?"

"No, not like that, they're judged against a standard," Nan said, unable to stop herself, even though it meant he was putting his clipboard down, leaning over to lay a ham-fisted rap on the back of a young bitch's head—the way you'd lovingly cuff a Lab or Golden Retriever. But the Shelties always ducked away and barked, they had no use for rough affection. "Besides," Nan added, "the Miss America judges would never admit they're using a standard, even if they are."

"How's that?" He squatted outside the exercise pen. The dogs came forward slowly, their cautious bodies low and slinky, then they stopped, braced, stretched their necks so just the tips of their noses almost reached the side of the pen where Luke was poking his thick fingers through the wire.

"A standard describes the perfect breed specimen," she said, counting while she poured daily heartworm pills from a bottle into her palm. "Shape of the skull and muzzle, angulation of the shoulders and hips, length of neck, earset, tailset, shape of eye and foot, balance of length to height, texture of coat, everything about the dog structurally, overall appearance and minute details." The dogs in the pen stood up against the edge and licked their lips, muzzles straining toward Nan when she turned toward them with the heartworm pills. "Then there's the proper temperament—

behavior and attitude—for each breed. The dogs are judged against that written standard."

Luke half-sat on a large crate with his thick thighs spread, his hands folded between his knees. His coarse black hair was slightly greasy and had only a few strands of gray. "So they have to win or they don't deserve to live?"

She knew he was kidding, but couldn't refrain from answering earnestly, "If they don't win, they just don't deserve to reproduce." Then Nan smiled when the young male yapped—as though in answer, but really was just aroused by the animation in her voice.

"Whew," he chuckled, "good thing *we* don't have a standard!"

She smiled again, but not at him. Mariah, trotting breezily with her tail up, had come into the building from the run area and dropped a tennis ball at Nan's feet. Didn't spook when she saw Luke. Didn't even give him a sideward glance. No need for his attention. Nan picked up the ball, watching Mariah's eyes glint and body brace in anticipation. "How do you know we don't have one?"

A lot of things had not measured up to the standard. Hadn't books and movies made sex seem glowingly, even cloyingly beautiful, all that burning and yearning, the slow tenderness and ardent pleasure of being the beloved. What it came down to had been a boy who took her home from high school and stopped somewhere, every day, to play a game that must've been called *See if You Can Get Out of This One* because that's what he'd said as he pinned her arms with one hand and half his body, used a knee to pry her legs apart, so he could dig his free hand under her skirt.

From next door the invocation began: "Cookie!"

"Back," Nan said quietly, and Mariah took two steps backwards. "Tail," Nan murmured, and Mariah lowered her bush tail to her breed's correct carriage. "Stand." Like a tap dance, Mariah lifted and repositioned each of her four feet, almost too quickly to see, so she was standing foursquare, stacked and poised as she would be in the show ring to show off her angulation and body-balance, her springy and durable musculature. She was rewarded with a toss of the tennis ball—Nan gave the release word, "OK," as the ball arched high over Mariah's head, and Mariah jumped straight up, all four feet off the ground, to catch the ball in her mouth.

"Cookie!"

"There she is," Luke said, still in no hurry to resume his route, "The Cookie Monster. My daughter used to watch that on TV."

Nan paused from cleaning fur from a slicker brush, but didn't look at him. "You have a daughter?"

"Eleven years old. I'm divorced."

Was he waiting for her to say *that's good* or *how long?* Should she just ignore it or change the subject, or would that keep him there longer and seem like interest?

"Cookie!"

Mariah carried her tennis ball cocked in her mouth at a jaunty angle and trotted out the door with her tail back up. Behind her, Nan also walked toward the door—ordinarily an effective hint that a lingering visitor should do likewise. She paused in the doorway.

"Cookie! *Coooookieeeee!*"

"A human being who only says two words and knows the meaning of neither, would she know to go sit on a toilet when she has to go? I wonder." She'd spoken without planning to. Ordinarily the only direct comments Nan made about the child next door were offhand remarks to the dogs, like, "Do *you* want a cookie too?"

"Did you see, they got a visit from child welfare over there?"

"No. Why?" She took a step back inside.

"Shit—pardon my French—that kid's yelling all the time, who knows what's going on over there, they parade her up and down the driveway like nothing to be ashamed of, then I think they lock her up. Is she getting any help, any training, she's about the same age as my kid, I don't know what I'd do if she were mine, but . . . maybe some home for people like that, I know everyone thinks that's cruel, but what about the rest of the kids? Someone had to call the authorities . . . I'm glad someone did."

"But who *did*?"

"Well . . . whoever did, it was the right thing to do, they shouldn't worry about sticking their nose in. Like you said, who knows the whole story over there? If nothing was wrong, no-harm-no-foul, everyone just goes on with their lives as usual."

"I didn't say that. Now they probably think *I* called."

"So? What're they gonna do?"

"I think they. . . ." Nan turned sideways at the doorway, how much more obvious could an usher-out be? "Uh, I'm expecting a client soon, so maybe you'd better move your truck. . . ."

"Yeah, I'd better get to my next stop. Maybe next week you'll find a night when you'll want some dinner?" He winked when she moved aside to allow his dolly room to get out of the door.

After Nan switched to a new bottled water company, Luke had come back once and rang the doorbell. All the dogs in the runs and in pens in the building sounded off with rapid-fire barks, including Mariah, who now lived in the house with Nan. Nan didn't answer the door. Each time he pressed the doorbell, a new eruption of barking broke out. Finally he waited long enough for the noise to die down, then called out, "Miss O'Flannary, our customer service would really like to know how we could've kept your patronage." It seemed like a long time with no barking while Nan waited, standing frozen and listening, watching as Mariah snuffled at the crack where the door met the jamb then stood tensed in anticipation, neck cocked and ears alert, for whatever excitement might ensue when the door opened. Nan tried to barely part the blinds and peek to see if Luke was finally gone, but he wasn't, he hadn't even turned away yet, and the blind snapped like an electric shock when Nan flinched back and released it. Luke leaned on the bell so it rang over and over like a car alarm and the dogs burst forth into a new frenzy. Next door, someone banged something metal, a spoon against a frypan or a metal pipe against a flagpole. By the time all the noise died down, Luke's truck had already screeched backwards up the driveway.

Maybe it was the new water company delivery truck that

dented her mailbox. Her driveway was always difficult to maneuver, and the new driver was inexperienced. She changed services again, this time to a built-in water purification system which only needed to be serviced once a year.

Twice a day Nan walked up her driveway, in the morning for the newspaper and in the afternoon for the mail. The newspaper, always rolled inside a plastic bag, was supposed to be thrown to the black side of the double driveway, but often it had skidded to the neighbor's concrete. But she started finding the newspaper, almost every morning, just off the street in the gutter. She called the delivery service complaint number a couple of times, but the gutter delivery continued and too often she found the plastic bag filled with water, the newspaper soaked and ruined. She finally canceled the paper.

In the afternoons, the neighbors were often out tending their garden. The strip of dirt running uphill beside their driveway, still thick with squash and tomatoes, green peppers and eggplant, now also had mature dwarf fruit trees. In the summer apricots and nectarines ripened, fell and rolled down the driveway, most of the time veering right—because at the bottom where the driveways split, Nan's was steeper—so rich-smelling fruit collected and drew flies and bees in front of Nan's garage and outbuilding. Nan picked up the bruised, sometimes split apricots and tossed them up beyond the fruit trees to the empty lot on the other side of her neighbor's driveway where ground squirrels and birds could eat them. One morning the fruit must've had an interesting trip down the driveway—instead of collecting against her curbing or in front of her garage door, four or five apricots were smashed against the front windshield of her van.

Going up for her mail, Nan started to hear the neighbor woman muttering. At first Nan thought she was grumbling to her husband in another language—the dialogue was curt and one-sided, just the woman spitting one or two words at a time. Then Nan thought she made out some of the words: "nosy" and "dirty" and "ugly." Nan contemplated answering, but a returned insult was too easy to volley. Instead Nan considered looking the woman in the eye and saying "Cookie." Of course, she never did.

Because all three offspring Nan had kept from Mariah's first litter finished their championships—the male and one bitch finished simultaneously at under two years old, taking the points from the dog and bitch classes at the same shows—Mariah's entire second litter had been sold before it was whelped. People were calling to be put on the waiting list before Mariah was even bred. Then the con-tracted new owners had visited weekly, sometimes more than that, as the whelps grew into pups. Their reports about her neighbors were no longer throwaway comments, jokes or offhand questions. One woman said, "Do your neighbors know you have a kennel here? I think that guy next door said 'more big stink' as I walked by." Another reported that the long-skirted wife came up the driveway shouting for her to move her car, even though she was parked on Nan's black asphalt side as Nan had instructed. A man had a flat tire just blocks after leaving Nan's driveway. Someone else's car was scratched, a single unbroken line from the headlights to the rear fender on the side that was closest to the neighbor's side of the driveway. Only once or twice Luke's truck, parked in the neighbor's driveway, blocked her clients, and they had to honk to ask him to move.

But her clients had seemed to stop noticing the girl, and Nan realized the middle of the day was punctuated with a long span of relative quiet, other than whatever hammering or whirring of machinery the man was involved with in his garage or garden, and the cackle of chickens from a coop hidden on the far side of their house. On weekday mornings Nan still regularly heard the girl on the next-door patio firing off strings of *Hi* very early when joggers would be using the golf course before it opened; then for an hour or so the girl would yell inside the house, long unbroken cries or shouts, the way a baby wails, but in a near adult voice, and completely sobless. After that, at around eight when Nan would be loading Mariah and her champion son and one or two clients' dogs into the van to take them to a track where she would road-work them on her bicycle, the neighbor girl—now as tall as her mother and built thick and square, still always dressed in cotton shorts and top or sweat pants and sweatshirt—would be following a parent or one of her sisters up the driveway, twisting her hands in front of her stomach and reciting, or shouting *cookie*. As Nan slowed at the top of her driveway before pulling out into the street, she often saw them standing beside their mailbox. Then one day Nan had to wait because a school bus was stopped in the road blocking the driveways, and the girl was being helped from behind to climb aboard, yelling *cookie* to the driver, and *cookie* as she lurched down the aisle toward a seat. In the afternoon, Nan started waiting until after five to get her mail, because between 3:30 and 4:30, without seeing the bus arrive, she would once again hear the cries of the girl as she came back down the driveway with her mother or a sister, bellowing *cookie*, which, it seemed, had mutated into a less recognizable word, something like *soo-tay*.

Animal control wouldn't tell her who filed the complaint, but the officer's unannounced inspection and list of possible violations— too many animals on the property, unlicensed animals, unsanitary conditions and noise infractions—were easily dispensed with. First of all, Nan's kennel license had been grandfathered when the area was zoned as a residential neighborhood. There had been no neighbors, nothing but the golf course, when she first bought the lot and built here. Secondly, there were obviously no unsanitary conditions, the dogs that didn't belong to Nan often came from other counties and were either licensed there or had health cer-tificates, Nan's dogs were all properly registered, and the kennel license allowed her more dogs than the current laws specified.

But right around the time animal control came, indicating a "series of complaints," Nan noticed her eugenia hedge, now eight or nine feet tall and too dense to see through, was burned and dying on the side facing the neighbors. A landscaping contractor postulated the bushes had been sprayed with herbicide on that side, so Nan hired his company to replace the hedge with an 8-foot cedar fence.

As he measured the side of the lot where the fence would go, and made an estimate that included calling a surveyor to re-establish where the property boundary between Nan's lot and the neighbors actually lay, the girl was out on the patio deck chanting *Hi!* The word sounded like *aye* with just a wisp of *h* at the beginning. "I see why you need the fence," the contractor said. "I can enclose your whole lot."

Nan just said "No, thanks," and didn't try to explain that she didn't fear trespassing any more than she feared her dogs getting loose and leaving her property, and the girl next door was either penned on the patio, inside the house, or supervised in the driveway. So the fence was just erected where the hedge had been, starting from the end of Nan's driveway and extending back along the side of her house to where the embankment suddenly sloped down to the golf course fairway.

The sweet cedar scent still wafted through the windows Nan kept open throughout the house—the fence was less than a month old—when Nan heard hammering and sawing coming from that part of the property line. In fact something was knocking against the fence itself. The contractor had warned her new zoning laws might stipulate that a fence could only be six feet, but since she had a kennel, he'd noted, maybe her neighbors would overlook the breach. But she had a year-old bitch from Mariah's second litter in the sink in the grooming room, almost thoroughly soaped, so Nan couldn't run to see if her fence was being razed. She not only had to work the soap through the undercoat and down to the dog's skin, she had to add the bluing shampoo to the dog's white collar and chest, then let the soap sit for five minutes for conditioning, before thoroughly rinsing, then toweling the dog with three dry towels and doing an initial blow-dry, finally put the wet dog in a pen flanked by heat lamps before she would be able to run to the fence line and see what was happening. An adjoining pen of ten-week-old puppies, Mariah's grandchildren, yapped and clamored when Nan, in one motion, turned off the dryer, put the wet dog in the heated pen, and sprinted for the doorway.

The fence was still standing. The hammering and sawing had stopped. But she could hear someone just on the other side of the fence, breathing hard and moving something, a soft scrape of wood-against-wood, something brushed a few times against the fence, then an almost imperceptible thud. But since there obviously wasn't any disaster occurring, Nan hurried back to the wet dog who needed to have her undercoat line-brushed. Later, before dusk, after giving Mariah her game of ball, while Mariah lay like a lioness on the Serengeti surveying the territory she controlled, Nan went to the fence, and peeked around the end. A low bench had been con-structed and pushed up against Nan's fence, and atop the bench sat three white beehives. No bees were visible, but it was almost dark. By the next day, Nan could see the bees' comings and goings over the top of the fence, like an almost imperceptible trail of smoke, and she noticed a few more bees always in evidence in her flowerbeds around the lawn. When she and Mariah sat quietly on the grass, she could hear a thin, low buzzing.

One day as Mariah stood poised on the edge of the embank-ment, using three keen senses to study something down on the golf course, slowly lifting her tail like a banner over her back, Nan got up from where she'd been reclining on her elbows and crept on her knees to the edge of the grass to see what Mariah saw. There was an unusually large group of golfers, well over the usual four. This group had four carts, probably four men actually playing golf and at least two others in sport jackets standing around without golf clubs, another had a large video camera—much bigger than the personal kind almost every dog handler used to tape and review how their dogs look in the ring—plus there were two women seated in golf carts who hadn't gotten out to swing at a ball. The man with the camera was keeping his lens trained on one of the golfers, a tall Black man wearing a chauffeur's cap backwards on his shaved head, a white shirt, baggy shorts to his knees, and two-tone golf shoes without socks. Even though she followed no sport, Nan recognized the man as a famous, recently retired athlete, known all over the world—of course he would play here eventually, this was a world renowned resort golf course. It was not one of the usual times the girl next door would be outside calling "Hi" but Nan suddenly wished she were so the athlete would be prompted to look up, and would then see Mariah—after all the things he'd done that had struck awe in the eyes of the whole world, he'd be struck by the dog's elegant, sublime beauty. Mariah had five all-breed Best-in-Show trophies, numerous group placements, at least twenty-five Best-of-Breed awards from all-breed shows and over a dozen Best-of-Breeds at specialty shows, including once at the national specialty. Nan was considering retiring her from showing. Now nearing seven years old, she was close to achieving five champion offspring and could have one more litter.

• • •

It was a rare Sunday when Nan didn't have a dog-event, but Mariah had been bred for the last time and was due to whelp in two weeks. Besides, Nan hadn't liked Sunday's judging panel and had already exhibited Friday and Saturday, so she had an extra day to catch up with bills and paperwork, with weeding flowerbeds and mowing the lawn, washing dog bedding, bleaching the concrete floor of the outbuilding, and spraying around the perimeter of the property for ticks. In the late afternoon, Nan was in the kitchen making liver biscuit. She'd long since stopped using the pure boiled-then-baked liver at dog shows and now bought freeze-dried liver, ground it and added it to a biscuit recipe. She pressed the dough in a pan and baked it like brownies, but long enough to make it dry and hard so when cut into cubes it didn't crumble, and it didn't stink nearly as much as pure cooked liver. It smelled enough, though, that she always baked a pan of real brownies right after the liver biscuits, to chase the odor of liver from the house.

While the brownies cooled on the shelf and the liver biscuits cooled in the washroom, Nan roused Mariah from a nap on the sofa, and they slipped through the slider to the fresher air of the lawn that overlooked the golf course. It should have been ethereal and tranquil. Sunday afternoons, when Nan returned from a show, were usually—and thankfully—refreshing times for a nap because the neighbors spent all day somewhere else, possibly at church, until past nine at night, so there was no pounding or chopping, no sweeping or digging or sawing or motorized leaf mulcher, no sound like the scraping of shingles from the roof and hammering on of new ones that had gone on most of last week. And no yelling. When the family came home from whatever they did all of Sunday, Nan was usually getting ready for bed—the car would pull in, doors open, and immediately it began: *soo-tay, soo-tay, sooooo-tay!* and "Come on, Maria, be quiet," footsteps in hard-heeled shoes on the concrete, until they were inside, maybe just the man remaining out in the garage, some small sound of tinkering, as though inventing something to do to keep himself from having to go inside too.

But that Sunday afternoon was not quiet. Nan didn't know why she hadn't noticed while inside baking, but the girl was outside on the patio, and her shouts were markedly different that usual. Usually she only said "Hi" while on the patio, but it was the other word Nan was hearing. It had mutated again: *toot-say, toot-say, toot-say.* The girl repeated it faster than her normal rhythm, with an edge of panic in her voice, then ceased the word for a series of continuous wordless cries, like howling except there was no *oooo*, it was more *aaahhhhhhh, aaahhhhhh.* Then back to *toot-say, toot-say, toot-say*, and there was a low thudding sound. Even Mariah noticed the difference in what had essentially been white noise for around eight years. She barked, growled, then approached the fence cautiously, neck stretched low, stalking catlike, so unlike her customary bold demeanor. Nan followed slowly, staying behind Mariah to watch her. *Aaahhhhhhh, aaahhhhhhh, toot-say, toot-saaaaaay!* The voice more feral and raw, but still without the wet sound of tears, the thumping faster but no louder. Mariah advanced along the fence line toward the end then stood with tail up and bristled but head very low, trying to use her nose instead of her eyes to explain the disturbance she heard. Holding onto the end of the fence, Nan also crouched low and leaned around, her body hovering above Mariah's.

The girl was in pajamas. The thumping was the glass slider rattling because she was violently pulling on the handle, as though trying to open it like a regular door. Then she left the glass, turned and walked to the railing, hands waving about her face, calling rapid-fire, *toot-say, toot-say, toot-say, toot-say!* The current of bees leaving and returning to the three hives seemed a little more visible, and perhaps less orderly as though some bees were circling, unsure whether to come back or venture out. But, under the girl's commotion, Nan didn't know if the bees were buzzing any louder. From what she could see, the girl seemed huge, her head enormous, her hair tangled and awry, her eyes thin slits in a very round high-cheeked face, but whether this was from bee stings or her genetic appearance, Nan couldn't tell. It had been too long since she'd taken a long, direct look at the girl. She must be fifteen or sixteen years old by now.

A bee buzzed close, zooming past Nan's ears. She backed up, took Mariah by the collar and pulled her back too. "Come on, girl, let's not get your babies in an uproar." She brought Mariah inside the house. *Toot-say, toot-say, toot-say.* The cries were more muffled. The thudding, if the girl returned to rattle the glass slider, couldn't be heard at all. Mariah stood outside the washroom, bright eyes back and forth between the door and Nan's face, shifting her bulky weight from left to right on her back feet—ultrasound had predicted she was carrying five or six whelps—then she whined a perky sound and stamped one of her front feet. Finally she barked: not an alarm, a requisition. Nan laughed and went to cut a liver biscuit for her from the pan in the washroom.

Toot-say, toot-say, aaahhhhhhh, aaahhhhhhh!

Nan looked up and paused, cleaning the knife blade between her thumb and index finger. Mariah was vacuuming the last crumbs from her biscuit from the floor at her feet.

Soo-tay, soo-tay, hi, hi, hi, soo-tay, aaahhhhhhh!

Nan made two or three swift cuts across the brownies both ways, then left the knife in the sink and took the whole pan of brownies. Mariah tried to follow, but Nan told her to stay and shut the slider as Mariah's nose tried to slip into the shrinking opening. Mariah hit the glass with her front feet and barked in mock anger.

As soon as she spotted Nan come around the fence, the girl's voice modulated. "Hi." She paused. "Hi." Once on the neighbor's side, Nan had to make her away past the beehives then through some straggly geraniums growing amid loose rocks, then bare ground and plenty of foxtails. Around the base of the neighbor's raised redwood patio was a curved row of cauliflower and purple cabbage and tall rubbery stalks that appeared to be the tops of onions. Nan stepped between the plants, her head level with the floor of the deck.

The girl said, "Hi."

"Hi," Nan answered, standing below her, then lifted the pan of brownies and the girl reached down to take it.

· · ·

At first Nan didn't see the policeman come around the corner of the neighbor's property. The girl's mouth was too full to speak, crumbs caking her lips and cheeks, a big ragged piece of brownie in each hand. Nan waited below for the empty pan.

Nan started when the officer said, "Hello? Everything all right here?"

The girl didn't respond. The policeman was beside the corner of the house, more on the same level as the deck. Nan raised her hand. "Down here."

"You live here?"

"No. Next door."

"We received a call from the resort about a problem here, someone screaming." Then he looked up at the girl. "Retarded?"

"Yes."

"Where're her folks? They leave her alone here?"

Nan hesitated before answering. Then the girl said "Hi". Crumbs flew from her mouth. Nan reached up and pushed the pan back and forth on the floor of the deck to draw the girl's attention back to the brownies. "Just this once," Nan said softly. "Maybe there was some emergency. They must've forgotten she was out here."

"Looks like she's wet herself. She's still in pajamas."

"Very unusual," Nan murmured.

"She pregnant?"

Nan looked up sharply. Looming above her, the girl was large and thickset. Her big thighs and arms were fleshy, and she had ample, mature breasts. Her midsection was as bulky as any of the rest of her. Nan could smell chocolate and the urine on the girl's pajamas. "I don't think so." Nan's voice was still feathery, although her heart thudded.

"I'll have to have someone check her out," the policeman said, but Nan had already turned, leaving the brownie pan, and was making her way through the geraniums and the flow of bees toward the fence.

Almost two months later the neighbor woman knocked on Nan's door.

For the first several weeks, Nan had felt herself awaiting the next shoe to drop, tiptoeing around the house and compound, alert to any clang or rustle from next door, shushing the dogs more often, keeping them inside in the crates more of the day, and often caught herself listening for the cry of a newborn. Whenever she heard a vehicle on the driveway, she had put down whatever she was doing and had gone to the nearest door or window to check, watchful for any sign of subsequent official action—child-protective services, additional police involvement, public health or social workers—and for any clue that might denote increased rancor. She especially checked the lawn overlooking the golf course each time before allowing Mariah out there. Despite the fence, it was the only spot, besides the adjoined driveways, where the neighbors had easy access to her property. She looked for pieces of bread or crackers, dog biscuits, even pieces of meat or soup bones on her lawn. But Mariah wanted to go out less and less as her whelping time drew near. It still took some time after the pups arrived for Nan's vigilant preoccupation to snap.

Mariah's last litter of five pups were four weeks old and beginning to wean when Nan noticed Mariah leaving food in her bowl, even though, while nursing, the high-protein kibble was mixed with yogurt. Nan realized she'd been preparing the meals as usual, but without Mariah at her feet, urging her to hurry. She opened a special canned diet for lactating bitches and filled Mariah's bowl. The pups clamoring at her nipples, Mariah walked away, humped over, retching, but the vomit was not the sort produced by a dam for weaning pups to eat. It was bile, and not even the usual bright yellow. This was a foul brown.

Yes, it could be a slow poisoning, the vet said, but on his initial palpation of Mariah's abdomen, he felt something right away, an enlarged liver he said at first, but it was probably standard procedure to not say cancer until the x-ray and ultrasound were performed and the diagnosis confirmed: Lymphoma that had already metastasized. No recommendation of surgery, the liver was already overwhelmed, and the pancreas, stomach and gall bladder were affected.

Facing the vet, Nan stood at the stainless steel examination table where Mariah reclined with her head up, relaxed and panting gently, in a leisured posture as though stretched out serenely at a spa for her weekly massage, seemingly drowsy and content. "But . . ." Words had to be squeezed slowly through Nan's constricted throat, one at a time. ". . . She never . . ." and the vet waited, his hand slowly stroking Mariah from her neck to her ribs, "I mean . . . so sick . . . and didn't even . . . kill her puppies."

"Yes, remarkable. But she has no knowledge of what cancer is. She doesn't know she's terminal."

"But . . . all this time . . . it must've been . . . growing in her . . . for so long. . . ." Nan's eyes stayed on the vet's hand moving over what was left of Mariah's burnt-red coat after being shaved for the ultrasound, ". . . and she . . . never . . . showed . . . any sign . . . unless . . . my fault . . . I didn't . . . notice. . . ."

"Some dogs have huge pain thresholds," he said. "Their drive to continue being the dog they always were is much stronger than any debilitation-driven impulse to let down and admit they can't. Until they really can't."

And a week later—her body shaved in more ragged patches to allow IV attachment, still eating nothing, vomiting viscous sputum and peeing blood—this time completely devoid of any remaining poise or vigor, lying with head down in her own foam bed on the examination table, while Nan cupped Mariah's face and pressed her nose to Mariah's perfect muzzle, the vet injected an overdose of an anesthetic agent, and Mariah quietly surrendered her final breath.

When the doorbell rang, every dog, de-barked or not, went ballistic. In both hands the neighbor woman held Nan's brownie pan, washed clean. In the middle of the pan were two peanut butter jars with wax paper inserted between the lip of the jar and the screw top. The jars were filled with a dark amber, almost brown substance resembling transparent sap that has dried while dripping down a tree trunk.

"For thanks," the woman said, smiling. There were gaps between every one of her small teeth. Her babushka was brown and white and matched a homemade-looking shawl across her shoulders. "Fence good. Protect bee from wind. Finally make honey."

Nan had one hand on her forehead, holding dirty hair from her eyes, then waved vaguely in the direction of the still-barking dogs in the runs. "Sorry about the noise."

"We like," the woman said, "good protect." She held the pan further out and Nan felt herself reach to accept it. Then the weight was balanced in her own hands.

"Have in tea. Feel better," the neighbor said, turning to go. "Have with more chocolate cookie you make."

Nan took the honey to the kitchen where most of the linoleum floor was taken up with a pen holding Mariah's six-week-old puppies. She lit the burner under the kettle and stood staring at the glowing electric coils until the kettle whistled, causing a chorus of aggressive yaps from the brash whelps. After dunking a teabag, Nan unscrewed one of the jars and dipped a spoon into the dark gluey honey, let it drizzle into her tea, then caught the stream with two fingers, reached down and let the eager pups lick and bite the sticky sweetness from her skin. Their blissful tails wagged straight up over their backs.

the way she loved cats

Lucy Corin

One of the things he liked best about her was the way she loved his cats. She'd never lived with cats before, but when Beth moved in, she commented about how cats made everything look picturesque, just by being there. She said the cats brought out part of the pattern on her dress, and how that was a funny, good sign about her moving in. Walker told her that in the eighties, Bloomingdale's bred a bunch of cats to go with the upholstery of the couches they sold. When you got a couch, you got the cat to go with it, if you wanted. Some of their best times were watching TV, whatever was on, really, it didn't even matter, each with a cat on the lap. He sat stroking a cat on his lap, and she sat stroking a cat on her lap. Seeing the same thing, doing the same thing, it was almost like accidentally *being* the same for a while, unlike that awful feeling you can get on a family vacation that's not working.

Sometimes if you're at a stoplight and you and the car in front of you both have your turn signals on, it's interesting to watch the car's blinker and listen to your own, and notice how they ease in and out of synch. It's mind boggling and soothing at once. In fact, both of them, when they were sitting with separate cats, equated it somehow with what it was like to lie in bed next to each other, each masturbating, which they did routinely as well, although neither of them mentioned this equation.

About a year later, Beth got transferred, so they had to move several states over. Walker was supposed to make sure the movers got everything right, and meet her there, in the new place she'd picked out. After the move was complete, they were watching TV and Beth said, "When will the cats get here?"

Walker said, "Good idea. I'll get some tomorrow. I miss sitting here with the cats."

It turned out Walker didn't believe in moving cats. He said it wasn't fair, to uproot them. He said it was also unfair to just leave them, not fair to the cats, who were domestic and couldn't be counted on to reassimilate into the natural order if abandoned, and could also cause a traffic collision. He'd shot them and buried them in the old back yard.

This was shocking; shocking enough that it shocked Beth, who generally wrinkled her nose at gore on television, or furrowed her eyebrows at the evening news, but made little more of it. Walker, certainly, didn't do it to be shocking, but he did it. Beth's face had both wrinkled and furrowed when he told her, and he said, "What? What? Are you mad?" but she didn't say anything. She thought about saying something, and she thought enough to have the conversation out in her mind. It was one she didn't like, and she didn't want to have it.

She thought about it enough to make herself able to see how this aspect of him could have been there all along. It was a wide and latent layer that had surfaced, states away. She could see him states away, in their old back yard, and could imagine the moment when this aspect emerged, in the same way a memory he hadn't remembered might have lifted itself and started walking around, instantly familiar. She could see him in the backyard, watching the cats walk around when she hadn't been looking.

When she sat in her chair watching television in their new living room and glanced at him as he sat on the couch watching television, she did it quickly: glanced in a flash to make sure that indeed, their eyes were facing the same direction, and that he sat as he sat. And then she thought about the image of him sitting there as she watched the television. She kept her arms on the arms of her armchair, and thought about how he was sitting with both hands on his Pepsi, which was in its cozy, between his thighs.

She started thinking there was a problem with the way they watched television, but of course it was more than that. I mean suppose Beth and Walker had a thoroughly admirable relationship, whatever kind it is that everyone wants, instead of whatever kind of relationship it was they had. Like more books and less television, suppose, or hikes in the forest with picnics, or soul-dumping conversations into the night. I don't see it saving them from the cats. They're there or they're not, and you know it or don't. You can't be too careful, and you can't be careful enough.

And also, I'm not saying she was a cat, specifically, but about a year later, Beth got transferred again. "I don't want to move," she told her boss. "We're really settled here, and we'd really like to stay," she said. "I don't want to uproot."

strictly casual

Julia Bell

"Our little chats," that's what she calls them.

"I do so love our little chats," she says, covering your hand with hers, squeezing meaningfully so the points of her nails dig into your skin.

You meet her every Wednesday in Espresso Espresso. At one. She's always early, you know because you watch from the telephone box across the road as she picks a window seat, arranges her cigarettes, mobile phone, on the table in front of her. You wait until she orders something, then give her another five minutes on top. You always make a point of being five to ten minutes late, you don't want her to think you're keen or anything. After all, like she says, it's strictly casual.

You saunter in, checking to see if she looks at all ruffled by the fact that she's been sitting on her own for ten minutes. You left her for half an hour once, walked in just as she was packing her cigarettes into her handbag. You thought she was going to go into one about keeping her waiting but she didn't. She fussed around you, stroking the air: "Are you all right? I thought something terrible had happened."

She's a busy woman, she runs a magazine or something. You're not really sure, your conversations never seem to go into detail about these kinds of topics, like what you do, where you live. All you know of each other is what you have learned from this cafe, from your little chats.

You've brought her flowers, like you always do, a bunch of purple irises, her favorite. "You're gorgeous," you say, meeting her eye, forcing her to look away.

You know that she is only shy like this with you. You know that in her real world, outside this cafe, she is used to telling other people what to do, how to be.

You order a latte and a salad. She frowns. "Don't you want anything else?"

Your friends think you're mad. They push the lonely hearts pages in front of you, tell you to get out more, to get a life.

"You can't survive on an hour a week," they say, "it's not enough for anyone."

"You're getting obsessed with her."

"And what do you do? I mean, no sex or anything, I got to say it to you, that's twisted, I mean, what kind of game are you playing here anyway?"

She wears a wedding ring, and you know that her husband runs a company, because every now and then, there is a break in your little chats when she follows him on business trips. She brings you presents, jewelry from Amsterdam, clothes from New York, expensive, duty-free perfumes. You wonder about him, you know he doesn't know about your little meetings, that she won't mention you to him as she glides around her immaculate house, pressing play on her Bang and Olufsen, wiping specks of dust from the glass and chrome. Of course you don't even know if this is true but you imagine that her house must be like her: pristine, perfect.

"Had a good week?" She covers your hand, strokes it. Her touch, even after all this time, is full of static. In your real life, no one asks you questions like this about yourself.

"Kind of," you say. When you think of your life outside of this cafe, it's a strange, solitary blur of people and cars, of zipping through traffic at high speed.

"You should take care out there."

"I do," you say, pushing her hand away.

She sighs. "Cyclists in London think they're invincible."

Invincible. Maybe you do think that when you're biking from Soho to the South Bank in the rush hour. Weaving between cars and taxis, through pedestrians, up pavements, over curbs, through red lights. You know it's easy to get so caught up in your own commotion that the rest of the world just becomes one big obstacle, something to be outmaneuvered, overcome.

"Least it keeps me fit," you say, clenching your forearms slightly to show off your muscles. She notices, the color spreading across cheeks.

"Mmmm." She strokes your arm with the back of her fingers, the rocks in her wedding ring gently grazing your skin. "It's quite romantic really."

"What is?"

"Doing what you do. Throwing your body against the city like that. A whole, huge, city." She lifts her hand to brush her fingers across your cheek. "Day ninety-nine," she says. "You made it this far. Who'd have thought it?"

You met at a party. A loud, drunken, semi-celebrity affair at some semi-celebrity's show home. Polished oak wood floors, a baby grand piano in the bay window, sophisticated, urban jazz in the background. You recognized a few people from magazines or TV, a couple of writers, an indie film actress. It wasn't really your scene, but you'd gone with your flatmate, Kerry, as a show of support. She'd just landed herself a job on a TV game show and thought it was the most glamorous job in the world, to be locked in a claustrophobic studio being bossed by all the crew, coddling the celebrities, and making endless cups of tea.

"You can't let me go on my own," she said. "What if no one talks to me? Please, it's for my career," and she widened her eyes in her I-know-I'm-irresistible-when-I'm-pleading-with-you kind of way and, being a sucker, you had to say yes.

"It's important to network," Kerry advised, as she squeezed herself into her best red dress. "It's the only way to get ahead." She was always saying things like this to you.

Of course she abandoned you along with her coat as soon as you walked through the door. You wedged yourself between the marble fireplace and a leather Chesterfield and listened politely to two very young and very stupid writers arguing about a colleague and trying to smile and look interested and hope that they wouldn't ask you anything about yourself. That, more than anything else was why you hated those kinds of parties. You could see people's eyes glazing over when you told them. Especially at semi-celebrity parties where what you did was your key to social success. Being a cycle courier wasn't really going to help anyone on their ladder to the stars.

You sighed and leaned against the fireplace, the stupid writers moved on to books. Listing everything that had been published in the last ten years and finding ever more convoluted and clever ways to declare them all crap. No one else in the room had stood still for more than a few minutes at a time, and the circulating was at one point so frenzied it seemed as if the party was in danger of creating a vortex, a whirlpool of people spinning round and round each other in a desperate, mad rush of air. And that's when she walked through the door.

You always thought people were lying when they told you their eyes met across a crowded room. You were unmoved by all that Disney bullshit, sex was what mattered. Good, old-fashioned, oblivious, fucking. But then you saw her.

• • •

It was as if the rest of the room stopped, although, thinking back, it was probably only you who came to a standstill. She looked you dead straight in the eye and held you in her gaze. You couldn't look away, you couldn't breathe, you couldn't.

"I want you," you blurted, before you could stop yourself.

She cupped your cheek in her hand, her wide palms cradling your face.

"Meet me," she said. "Meet me every Wednesday, at one, in Espresso Espresso. The little cafe just near the station, you know the one?"

You nodded.

"One hundred times. We'll meet one hundred times. You'll come to me every week at one." She paused, and brought her face close to yours. "Strictly casual."

"Of course," you said, but she had already gone, the heat of her attention already cooling in the air around you.

The first time was an experiment really, to prove to yourself that it wasn't just a dream. You took the bike and a book and figured if she didn't show you wouldn't look foolish to anyone but yourself. Espresso Espresso is a little Italian place, in Soho. Proper Italian, fizzing with family business and strong coffee.

At a quarter to one you nearly bottled it. What were you doing? You hardly knew the woman, you could barely remember what she looked like. It had been nearly a week since the party and in that time she had become a shape, a color, a smell, a pair of dazzling eyes, dark, glossy hair.

When she touched you on the shoulder you nearly jumped out of your skin. But you held it in, tensing your muscles instead of letting them reflex. This is a trick you learned from cycling, it's how you avoid accidents. When all your instincts are telling you to cover your head and close your eyes, you keep them open, stamp on the pedals and look for the narrowest of margins to squeeze yourself through.

"I didn't think you'd come," she said, sitting opposite you. She crossed her legs, skirt riding up her thighs. You tried not to look.

"Well here I am," you said.

"Like your cycling gear."

Immediately you wished you'd made more of an effort. Here she was, polished, immaculate. You hadn't bothered getting changed: still in your lycra top, scruffy shorts, cycling shoes.

"So I can make a quick getaway," you said, daring yourself to look her in the eye. "And it's my job."

"Ah." She looked you up and down, approvingly. "Of course, those muscles."

Ninety-nine dates. Nearly three years of your life. You've both been counting the time, even though sometimes, you both pretended to have forgotten. "What is it this week? Fifty-two or fifty-four, I forget."

Every week you bring her flowers and compliments, you think about her, about what will happen to you when this is all over. You imagine how it will be when you finally make love.

You also get on with your job. You learn every shortcut in central London, smash up three bikes and move companies twice. You're now with City Quick, a net-based firm that text jobs to your yellow mobile phone. It makes you queasy, all this future, like you're a character in a dense, uneasy, Manga film.

"What are you thinking?" She nudges your leg with the point of her shoe. You are both leaning in so close that were it not for the table, you would fall into each other's laps.

"How we met."

She smiles. "That awful party."

You catch the clock from the corner of your eye, it's nearly two already. Your throat tightens.

"Next week then," she says.

Her hand glides down your arm, pausing on the scars to run a musing finger across the papery skin. You shiver.

"Next week," you mutter at your hands. You can't look her in the eye.

Your phone beeps. Half an hour to get a videotape from a production company in Hoxton to a studio up west and twenty minutes for a zip disk from a design agency in Fulham to a publisher somewhere in Piccadilly. Cycling fast through London traffic is about a series of controlled risks. Of deciding that the blue van at the lights is turning right, even though it's not indicating, and chancing that you can zip across the junction, inches in front of the bumper, before it accelerates on the turn and spreads you across the road. Or more accurately, probably, if the van isn't traveling too quickly, crunches up a wheel, maybe a leg, and puts you in hospital for a couple of months.

Sometimes, when the traffic's heavy, when you're speeding down Victoria Embankment, weaving between the cars that are jostling for lanes, there isn't even time for thinking. You're all instinct: reacting second after second to keep yourself alive, just a heartbeat in between events. From the outside, a blur, a ghostly movement in the wing mirror, never slowing down enough for anyone to see who you are.

You do Hoxton to Shepherd's Bush without using the brakes once. Arrive at reception, sweating, legs trembling and you have to sit outside when you've made the drop to get your breath back.

Next week. Next week. Thinking about her is making you nervous. You haven't really talked about what Next Week means. Does she want you to be lovers? Or girlfriends? Or just a one-off one-night stand? Or will she give you a whole new set of terms and conditions?

Trying to double-guess her is giving you a headache. Whatever she wants, whatever you want, you know that things have shifted since your last little chat. You get back on the bike, settle yourself in the saddle for the ride back into town.

You figure that as you're in love with her, you're already her lover, and being her girlfriend is out of the question—too much baggage with her husband and everything. Perhaps a one-night thing, just to end it, that might be kind of poetic. You can't decide, as you weave down Tottenham Court Road, counting off the traffic lights—red: she loves me; green: she loves me not—what you really want.

The phone box is full of escort cards. Stuck up with blu tack or sellotaped to the glass. You notice that all the women's names all end in "a"—Angelica, Katrina, Tanya, Gabriella, Roberta, Trans-sexual Najhuaa. You wonder if it means anything. Perhaps someone has done a study—on why "a" is a sexier end letter for a name. The pictures on the cards are crude color repros, soft-porn shots of girls in lacey underwear, or dominatrix in cheap PVC. Some offer a meeting within the hour, some a full-body massage, all are discreet with satisfaction guaranteed. One, Lady Lula, advertises herself as passive, fully-functional, a genuine female experience. You remember that you read somewhere that school kids were trading these cards instead of Pokemon, and you wonder how much Lady Lula is worth in the playground. Three Tanyas? One Roberta and two Katrinas? And how are you supposed to know if you've got a full set?

You peel away a couple, Mistress Strycta and Delila the Domina, so you can see across the road. Espresso Espresso is half-empty. It's drizzling, a courier's dream, the work rate goes through the roof in the rain, and the streets are slippery as wet soap, upping the ante another notch higher. You heard that there was another wipeout on Monday. A rider from another company went under a skip truck. When his parents came to ID him, the coroner kept his helmet on, to stop his brains oozing out all over the slab.

You check your watch. Ten to. She's not here yet. You always knew that she might not show. In fact, you think, it would be quite a relief. At least you wouldn't have to make a decision.

At five to, you're disappointed. You thought you meant more to her than that. The last date. She could have made the effort.

At two minutes to you spot her. Your heart beats faster than it ever does on the road. The familiar shape of her moving through the crowd makes you want to run over to her, bury your face in her hair. But you hold it in. As she gets closer, you see that she is pulling something behind her: a white suitcase. Immediately you wonder what it means.

As she approaches the cafe, she has to sidestep to avoid a couple pushing a pram, and the suitcase, swinging on wayward wheels, bounces over a curbstone and off the pavement into the gutter. She loses her grip, and the suitcase topples into the road, splitting open as it does so.

You're across the road in a second. Dodging traffic to get to her. You didn't even think about it. In the split lip of the suitcase you see material, that in the shudder of the accident, seems to be alive. It's high quality lingerie. Slippery satin knickers, delicate lace bras. Some of them get caught in the wind and blow across the road like flags, a thong slithers into a puddle, cream silk floating on the oily water.

"I—I—," she's blushing furiously as you gather her suitcase in your arms, holding it shut across your chest. "Thank you," she says.

You seem to look at each other forever. She looks puzzled. "Don't I know you from somewhere?" You stare at her, willing her to remember it like you do, but she shakes her head, and mumbles, "Maybe, I'm going mad lately, I don't know." She holds out her arms for her suitcase.

Close up she's not quite how she seemed from across the road, the fine lines on her face have accumulated to make her look dehydrated, crumpled, slightly defeated. She's smaller and shorter too. You wrap your arms tighter around the suitcase and give her your best smile.

"Fancy a coffee?" you ask.

the substitute

Lynne Tillman

She watched his heart have a small fit under his black T-shirt. Its unsteady rhythm was a bridge between them. Lost in the possibilities he offered her, she studied his thin face, aquiline nose, tobacco-yellow fingers. In the moment, which swallowed her whole, she admired his need to smoke. She wouldn't always, but not being able to stop meant something, now. Certain damage was sexy, a few sinuous scars. He'd be willing, eager maybe, to exist with her in the margins.

She'd set the terms. Ride, nurse on danger, take acceptable or necessary risks. Maybe there'd be one night at a luscious border, where they'd thrum on thrill, ecstatically unsure, or one long day into one long night, when they'd say everything and nothing and basely have their way with each other. She wasn't primitive but had an idea of it—to live for and in her senses. She'd tell him this. Then they'd vanish, disappear without regret. She was astonished at how adolescence malingered in every cell of her mature body.

Helen met Rex on the train. She taught interior design to art students in a small college in a nearby city. He taught painting. She liked it that he sometimes smelled like a painter, which was old-fashioned, though he wasn't; he told her he erased traces of the hand (she liked hands), used acrylics, didn't leave his mark and yet left it, too. Still, tobacco, chemicals, alcohol, a certain raw body odor, all the storied ingredients, reminded her of lofts and studios and herself in them twenty years before, late at night, time dissolving. Between Rex and her, one look established furtive interest, and with a fleeting, insubstantial communication they betrayed that and themselves. They were intrigued dogs sniffing each others' tempting genitals and asses. Being an animal contented her lately, and she sometimes compared her behavior with wild and domestic ones. Reason, she told an indignant friend with relish, was too great a price to pay daily.

Her imagination was her best feature. It embellished her visible parts, and altogether they concocted longing in Rex. She could see it; she could have him. She couldn't have her analyst. She held Dr. Kaye in her mind, where she frolicked furiously in delayed gratification. But Rex, this man beside her—she could see the hairs on his arms quiver—engaged her fantastic self, an action figure.

Rex's hands fooled with his cigarette pack. Her analyst didn't smoke, at least not with her, and she didn't imagine he smoked at home, with his wife, whose office was next door, she discovered, unwittingly, not ever having considered that the woman in the adjoining office was more than a colleague. Cottage industry, she remarked in her session. Dr Kaye seemed amused. Maybe because she hadn't been curious about the relationship or because it took her so long to catch on. That meant more than what she said, she supposed.

Rex's hands weren't well-shaped, beautiful. If she concentrated on them . . . But she wondered: would they stir me, anyway. She shut her eyes. She liked talking with her eyes shut, though she couldn't see her analyst's face. Dr Kaye wore a long tie today. It hung down over his fly and obscured the trouser pouch for his penis. When she first saw him, she was relieved to find him avuncular, not handsome like her father. Men grew on trees, there were so many of them, they dropped to the ground and rotted, most of them. Dr. Kaye hesitated before speaking. She imagined his face darkening when she said things like that. Whatever, she said and smiled again at the ceiling. I like men. I'm just pulling your leg. She could see the bottoms of his trousers.

When she approached him on the train, Rex had a near-smirk on his lips, just because she was near. She liked his lips, they were lopsided. If he didn't speak, she could imagine his tongue. He might push for something to happen, actually, and that was exciting. Her heart sped up as Rex glanced sideways at her, from under his . . . liquid hazel eyes. She squirmed, happily. Hovering at the edge tantalized her. The heart did race and skip; it fibrillated, her mother had died of that. What do you feel about your mother now? Dr. Kaye asked. But aren't you my mother now?

They flirted, she and Rex, the new, new man with a dog's name. Did it matter what he looked like naked? They hadn't lied to each other. Unless by omission. But then their moments were lived by omission. Looking at him staring out the window, as if he were thinking of other things than her, she started a sentence then let the next word slide back into her mouth like a sucking candy. Rex held his breath. She blushed. This was really too precious to consummate. Dr. Kaye seemed involved in the idea.

He had shaved closely that morning, and his aftershave came to her in tart waves. She inhaled him. She—Ms. Vaughn, to him—weighed whether she would tell him anything about Rex, a little, or everything. With Rex, she wasn't under any agreement. She measured her words for herself and for him, and she told him just enough. He was the libertine lover, Dr. Kaye the demanding one. With him, she drew out her tales, like Sheherazade.

First, Dr. Kaye, she offered, her eyes on the ceiling, it was the way he looked at me, he was gobbling me up, taking me inside him. I liked that. Why did I like that? Because I hate myself, you know that. Then she laughed. Later, she went on, I pretended I didn't see him staring at me. Then I stopped pretending. In her next session, she continued: He wanted to take my hand, because his finger fluttered over my wrist, and his unwillingness, no, inability, I don't know about will, I had a boyfriend named Will, he was impotent, did I tell you? His reluctance made me . . . wet. She sat up once and stared at Dr. Kaye, daring him. But he was well trained, an obedient dog, and he listened neatly.

Rex was sloppy with heat. Their unstable hearts could be a gift to Dr. Kaye. Or a substitute, for a substitute. She trembled, bringing their story—hers—to Dr. Kaye in installments, four times a week. It was better than a good dream, whose heady vapors were similar to her ambiguous, unlived relationships. Not falling was better, she explained to Dr. Kaye; having what they wanted was ordinary and would destroy them or be nothing, not falling, not losing, not dying was better. Why do you think that? he asked. This nothing that was almost everything gave her hope. Illusion was truth in a different guise, true in another dimension. Dr. Kaye wanted to know what she felt about Rex. I don't know—we're borderline characters, she said. Liminal, like you and me.

And, she went on, her hands folded on her stomach, he and I went into the toilet . . . of the train . . . and fooled around. She laughed. I was in a train crash once. . . . But the toilet smelled. . . . Like your aftershave, she thought, but didn't say. Say everything, say everything impossible.

Looking at Rex reading a book, his skin flushed, overheated in tiny red florets, Helen wondered when the romance would become misshapen. Her need could flaunt itself. She wanted that, really, and trusted to her strangeness and his eccentricity for its acceptance. Or, lust could be checked like excess baggage at the door. They'd have a cerebral affair.

But their near-accidental meetings sweetened her days and nights. They were sweeter even than chocolate melting in her mouth. Dark chocolate helped her sleep. She had a strange metabolism. How could she sleep—Rex was the latest hero who had come to save her, to fight for her. If he didn't play on her playground, with her rules, he was less safe than Dr. Kaye. But Rex was as smart, almost, as she was; he knew how to entice her. She might go further than she planned.

Dr. Kaye's couch was a deep red, nearly purple, she noted more than once. Lying on it, Helen told him she liked Rex more than him. She hoped for an unguarded response. Why is that? he asked, somberly. Because he delivers, like the pizza man—remember the one who got murdered, some boys did it. They were bored, they didn't know what to do with themselves, so they ordered a pizza and killed the guy who brought it. The poor guy. Everyone wants to be excited. Don't you? She heard Dr. Kaye's weight shift in his chair. So, she went on, Rex told me I'm beautiful, amazing, and I don't believe him, and it reminded me of when Charles—that lawyer I was doing some work for—said, out of nowhere, I was, and then that his wife and baby were going away, and would I spend the week with him, and it would be over when his wife came back—we were walking in Central Park—and I said no, and I never saw him again.

One night, Rex and she took the train home together. When they arrived at Grand Central, they decided to have a drink, for the first time. The station, its ceiling a starry night sky, had been restored to its former grandeur, and Helen felt that way, too. In a commuter bar, they did MTV humpy dancing, wet-kissed, put their hands on each other, and got thrown out. Lust was messy, gaudy. Neverneverland, never was better, if she could convince Rex. How hot is cool? they repeated to each other, after their bar imbroglio.

Helen liked waiting, wanting, and being wanted more. It's all so typical, she told Dr. Kaye, and he wanted her to go on. She felt him hanging on her words. Tell me more, he said. The bar was dark, of course, crowded, Rex's eyes were smoky, and everything in him was concentrated in them, they were like headlights, he'd been in a car accident once and showed me his scar, at his neck, and then I kissed him there, and I told him about my brother's suicide, and about you, and he was jealous, he doesn't want me to talk about him, us, he thinks it'll destroy the magic, probably . . . stupid . . . it is magic . . . and he wanted me then, and there. . . . But she thought: Never with Rex, never give myself, just give this to you, my doctor. She announced, suddenly: I won't squander anything anymore.

The urge to give herself was weirdly compelling, written into her like the ridiculous, implausible vows in a marriage contract. Dr. Kaye might feel differently about marriage, or other things, but he wouldn't tell her. He contained himself astutely and grew fuller, fatter. He looked larger every week. The mystery was that he was always available for their time-bound encounters, in which thwarted love was still love. It was what you did with your limits that mattered. She imagined she interested him.

Listening to her stories, Dr. Kaye encouraged her, and she felt alive. She could do with her body what she wanted, everyone knew that; the body was just a fleshy vehicle of consequences. Her mind was virtual—free, even, to make false separations. She could lie to herself, to him; she believed in what she said, whatever it was. So did he. To Dr. Kaye, there was truth in fantasy. Her half-lies and contradictions were really inconsequential to anyone but herself. He might admit that.

But the next day, on the train, Rex pressed her silently. His thin face was as sharp as a steak knife. He wouldn't give her what she wanted, he didn't look at her with greedy passion. There was a little death around the corner, waiting for her. She had to give him something, feed his fire or lose it and him.

She would visit his studio, see his work, she might succumb, Helen informed her analyst. She described how she'd enter his place and be overwhelmed by sensations that had nothing to do with the present. In another time, with another man, with other men, this had happened before, so her senses would awaken to colors, smells and sounds that were familiar. Soon she would be naked with him on a rough wool blanket thrown hastily over a cot. Her skin would be irritated by the wool, and she would discover his body and find it wonderful or not. He would devour her. He would say, I've never felt this way before. Or, you make me feel insane. She wouldn't like his work and feel herself moving away from him. Already seen, it was in a way obscene, and ordinary. She calmly explained what shouldn't be seen, and why, and, as she did, found an old cave to enter.

Dr. Kaye didn't seem to appreciate her reluctance. Or if he did, in his subtle way he appeared to want her to have the experience, anyway. She knew she would go, then, to Rex's studio, and announced on the train that she'd be there Saturday night—date night, Rex said. He looked at her again, that way. But if she did, she knew it would hasten the end, like a death sentence for promise. Recently, Helen had awaited Timothy McVeigh's execution with terror, but it had come and gone. No one mentioned him anymore. Others were being killed—just a few injections, put them to sleep, stop their breathing, and it's done, they're gone. Things die so easily, she said. Then she listened to Dr. Kaye breathe.

Saturday night Helen rang the bell on Rex's Williamsburg studio. All around her, singles and couples wandered on a mission to have fun. Soon they'd go home, and the streets would be empty. Rex greeted her with a drink—a Mojito—which he knew she loved. His studio was bare, except for his work and books, even austere, and it was clean. The sweet, thick rum numbed her, and she prepared for the worst and the best. There was no in-between.

His paintings were, in a way, pictures of pictures. Unexpectedly, she responded to them, because they appreciated the distance between things. Then, without much talk, they had sex. She wasn't sure why, but resisting was harder. Rex adored her, her body, he was nimble and smelled like wet sand. He came, finally, but she didn't want to or couldn't. She held something back. Rex was bothered, and her head felt as if it had split apart. But it didn't matter in some way she couldn't explain to Dr. Kaye. She heard him move in his chair. She worried that he wasn't interested. Maybe her stories exhausted him. Rex called her every day. She wondered if she should find another man, one she couldn't have.

rats in the kitchen

Tina Jackson

Masha was a classic case of the Valium housewife in spite of not being married and never having had psychiatric treatment. At twenty-five, her daily routine was get up, take drugs, go to work, come home, take drugs, sit on the sofa, take drugs, fall into bed. Her drugs were off-prescription; she self-medicated. It didn't really matter what they were; she had what you might call a psychological dependency rather than anything physical.

Sometimes she had sex with Joe, her boyfriend, but more often than not she tried to get away without having to do it. Sometimes, instead of going to work, she sat for hours, wired and scared, pinned to her seat on the Circle Line, going round and round without getting off. Sometimes, when she got home before Joe did, she'd sit in the dark in the bedroom, rocking backwards and forwards. Sometimes, he found her there. "What on earth are you doing?" he'd ask, and she wouldn't be able to tell him she'd been trying to will him not to come home.

Joe met Masha when she lived in happy nightlife squalor. He wanted her because he thought she made him look more interesting than he was. He loved the time he walked into his office and proudly informed his colleagues that he'd been at an illegal after-club drinking den with her, where he'd drunk home-made poteen and smoked sensi and then come straight into work without going to sleep at all. The admiring looks on their faces had made him feel cool. When he took her to the pub to meet his workmates, her multi-colored hair and ambivalent smile excited a degree of sexual speculation amongst his colleagues which he felt reflected enormously well upon him.

After a prolonged siege which included roses, presents, weekends away, lots of giggling and continuously enthusiastic sex, he'd convinced her that she wanted to pack up her belongings into a shopping trolley and her cat into a cat-basket and come to live in a happy-ever-after eggbox with him. The timing was good; she hadn't had a proper boyfriend for over a year, she owed masses of back-rent and her flatmate had taken to painting everything in the flat black. But once she'd moved in, Joe didn't want her to be interesting anymore. When she was, he felt he wasn't the center of her world. He liked doing coupley things like the shopping, together, and having friends round (his). He wanted her to spend a lot of time with his mother.

He disapproved of her old ways, which had initially seemed lively and appealing, and every now and then, when she sneaked off with a friend to revisit her old life, he was a bit sniffy about it. He felt there was something about her he'd never quite managed to catch and tame, which made her seem unknowably remote at times, as if she was miles away even when she was lying next to him in the bed.

Joe was the kind of man who always brought flowers and chocolates home on a Friday, on his way home from his well-paid job with good career prospects. He'd never have admitted it even to himself, but he liked it best when she was ill, so he could look after her. Tucked up on the sofa in their rented living room, she seemed frail and vulnerable rather than distanced and other-worldly. "You're so sweet," he'd gush, bringing her flowers and herbal remedies. The flowers stayed in their vases until all the petals dropped off and she put the herbal remedies down the sink when Joe wasn't looking.

She'd also medicine herself when he wasn't looking, and gradually the color began to drain out of her. When the washing machine broke down, sending a torrent of soapy water gushing all over the lino in the bathroom, she phoned him at the office. "The washing machine's broken down," she squawked. "You've got to come home and mend it. I don't know what to do." He did come home, leaving unfinished work on his desk, and he did mend it, and afterwards he felt very pleased with himself. "Poor silly little thing," he thought tenderly. "She'd fall apart if I wasn't there."

Masha seemed to spend a lot of time in the kitchen. Joe liked to be well catered for. If he didn't feel his stomach was pampered, he didn't feel loved. Masha got hooked on the soothing rhythms of cutting up and weighing and watching things not burning. Her brain could detach itself from any emotional engagement with what she was doing whilst nevertheless being assured of a result. She felt like a human kitchen device, a stirrer, chopper, blender. Some kind of human magimix. She'd watch herself as if from down a very long tunnel, a tiny figure moving according to a set of pre-planned steps.

Joe wasn't allowed in the kitchen. She liked it that there was a part of the flat he didn't fill. When he hung around, hovering in the doorway, it made her impatient, and on bad days, panic stricken, as if she was under attack.

"Get out!" she'd squawk, backing herself into a corner. "Let me get on with it! I can't bear it when you hover!" At those times, Joe would console himself with the thought of PMS and make himself behave with extra tolerance.

Sometimes, Joe would go to conferences, which meant he'd be away from home for a few days, or even the odd week. When this happened, Masha would phone in sick and sit on the sofa with the cat, gazing into space, which, free from the invader, was all hers. It was on a morning like this, eyes glazed contentedly over and a mug of coffee in her hand, that she realized they had rats. Just beyond the living room at the far end of the corridor by the open back door, she could see an enormous rodent helping itself out of the cat's bowl. It took her several transfixed moments to work out that it was real.

It was so large, mangy and repulsive it made her flesh crawl. At the sight of its malevolently beady eyes, scrofulous coat and bald, scaly whiplash tail, Masha came back into her box with a jolt. She watched in horror as it bolted the cat's dinner and oozed its way under the inch-high gap under the bathroom door. She watched paralyzed as the cat jumped off the sofa and scurried behind it. Then Masha seized her mobile, jumped onto the nearest table and telephoned the one person she knew could deal with it.

"Mother!" she shrieked. "An enormous rat has just vanished into the lavatory!" Her mother, despite the bad tidings, was delighted to hear Masha sounding with-it. "Go and put on your biggest boots," she said sensibly, "and find a big stick." Masha did what she was told, but before she could attack the rat, it slithered out from its hiding place and, rudely helping itself from the cat's bowl again, scurried out of the back door.

And you're no use, she hissed exasperatedly at the cat, who gazed back at her inscrutably. Masha sat back on the sofa. She hadn't used her brain for so long that it felt odd, but gradually some facts filtered through. London was in the grip of its worst ever rodent infestation. In London, you were never more than two yards away from a rat. Sundry recent patterings and scufflings and bitten bin-bags which Masha had put down to the cat doing her nocturnal thing suddenly took on sinister overtones.

Every time anything in the house creaked, Masha imagined it was caused by the army of rats, on the move. Rats outnumbered the city's human inhabitants by millions. And the rats themselves were mutating, breeding themselves into ever larger, stronger and more poison-resistant species. It was called survival of the fittest, and all the rats were in prime fighting condition.

She remembered hazily how a friend's derelict flat had been infested by rats who'd eaten through the brickwork, developed an immunity to Warfarin, invited all their rat-friends round to share the feast of poison which had been left for them, smacked their lips over the delicacy and come back for more. Masha recalled how urban myth had it that the rats traveled on the underground, the scourge of the Metropolitan line, looking for places where there were good chances of finding a bolt-hole to house their ever-increasing numbers. Her friend had moved out, at first temporarily, and then for good. The rats had won. Now it was Masha's turn.

The cat took off with its tail in the air, at a jaunty angle, which seemed to suggest she washed her paws of the whole thing. She meowed gently but firmly as Masha tried to call her back, as if to say that she was sorry.

Masha was on her own.

That night, preternaturally aware of anything which suggested rodents, she realized she had a full-scale occupation on her hands. Her eyes were out on stalks as a rat watched the television with her, settled into the shade beneath Joe's precious stereo. Gnawed holes in the bin liners she'd left outside convinced her that the rats were helping themselves to leftovers she'd scraped into the rubbish. She caught a glimpse of a rat preening itself in the bathroom mirror. A brave, solitary rat made its way along the corridor to join her in her bedroom. When she heard scrapings and scufflings, her initial thought was that it was a rustling paper bag. When she realized it was alive and doing the rat dance of the boudoir, she hid under the covers and wished desperately that she had something to batter it with. She didn't dare get out of bed to find a weapon, so she stayed where she was and quivered.

She hardly slept. When she got up, the rats, overnight, had made their presence felt. The day before, they'd been inconspicuous, vanishing when they heard the tread of Masha's footstep. But once in occupation, they got cocky. One fronted Masha out in the bathroom, staring insolently at her as if to say, why should I go just because you're here? Masha screamed and shouted and stamped, and eventually the rat disappeared down a hole with an insolent flick of its tail, as if it was doing her a favor. Masha couldn't help feeling it had given her the rodent equivalent of a finger. It set off a reaction she hadn't expected: she felt more alive, more energized, than she had for a year.

It was ages since she'd done anything without consulting Joe, but she felt a new sense of determination. Getting the Yellow Pages, she looked up pest control. They promised to send someone round the same afternoon. Masha dug out the poker and sat on the sofa. She'd forgotten to take any drugs all day. Instead, she poured herself a stiff vodka. As she slugged it back, she silently vowed a toast to revenge.

As promised, the rat-man made his entrance. He was unexpectedly prompt, and not at all what Masha had envisaged. When her friend had had rats, the pest controller sent to deal with them had been rodent-like himself, with hairy, pouchy cheeks, beady eyes, elongated front teeth and furtive, jerky, shuffling movements. It had crossed Masha's mind that he might have been on the side of the rats because none of the rodents had actually died as a result of the poison he'd left. Conspiracy theories had riddled her mind for ages after that; they were one of the things she'd dwelt on obsessively whilst riding round and round on the Circle line.

Fey and fairy-like, Masha's rat-man couldn't have been more different. This was no ordinary little man carrying a bucket of poison. He was slim, lithe and dark. You could have eaten your dinner off his cheekbones. He had a sly foreign accent. He looked like a pixie.

Masha stared at him for a moment before she noticed what he was wearing. Rats' tails and paws dripped from his belt, decorated his shirt and encircled his hat. A necklace of rat's bones was knotted around his neck and a polished, shining rat's skull was pinned to the lapel of his jacket as a brooch. Masha's jaw dropped.

The rat-man looked understanding. "You see I am wearing some rat things," he said in broken English, which revealed a broken tooth at the front of his mouth. "I am born in the Year of the Rat. I live with rats. I understand rats. To fight them I have to know their ways."

Masha's jaw was still on her chest. She shook her head uncomprehendingly. The rat-man smiled. His broken tooth flashed at her disarmingly. Masha felt herself staring, then beckoned him inside.

"To be a person who can make rats go away, I have to be like them. I have to understand what it feels like to be a rat," he explained, leaning comfortably against the kitchen door. Masha put the kettle on. She still hadn't said anything except to ask him if he'd like a drink. "So to make me a little of a rat myself, I wear rat things. I try to think my way into what it feels like in that skin. Looking always for an opportunity, or a place, to find a way in. To be always hated and to have not to care, just to make a place for myself. To be the thing that is disgusting, just for doing what it cannot help. So maybe, by wearing their flesh and their bones, I show them that I do not hate them, even that I respect them. Because everything that lives has some purpose. But also it is my job to make the rats not be where they are not wanted. I have to make them go away. Go to someplace else."

Masha had never expected that anyone could have been mystical about working as a pest controller. Now she had a rat shaman in her kitchen. As she tried to get her head round the sudden strangeness of her life, the rat-man flashed her a smile so dazzling she stopped thinking and just smiled back.

"You try to understand and it is hard," he agreed. "But I like that you make the effort." He drank his tea when she finished making it, hot water on leaves in a pot, not bags, and looked at her strangely. "I think is a while since you did that," he said. Masha had the odd idea that he was talking about making an effort, not about making proper tea, and she blushed.

She showed the rat-man where the rat sightings had been. Then he asked her to leave him to deal with them, so she left him to get on with the problem and sat back on the sofa. She tried staring into space but instead found herself thinking. Some of the conclusions she came to surprised her. When the rat-man knocked on her door to tell her he was going, she noticed the clock. Hours had passed.

"I think they won't come back no more," said the rat-man. "I have deal with them. And I see you try to deal with me. So I leave you this. Goodbye." He tipped the brim of his rat-skull encrusted hat at her, flashed another intoxicating grin and all but disappeared in a puff of smoke, kissing his fingers at her.

Masha looked at the folded paper he'd put into her hand. She was expecting a bill, but instead she saw a recipe in curly script. And a telephone number.

Masha put the recipe in a cookery book she hadn't used since domestic science at school. She didn't want it anywhere Joe might look. Then he came back, and as the rats had miraculously vanished, she didn't tell him anything about her adventure. It felt amazingly exciting to have a secret which had nothing to do with him. But as her daily life returned to normal, she went back to turning herself into a human chemistry set. The rats didn't put in any further appearances and her recent experiences merged into a haze which she wasn't sure might not have been the product of her imagination.

Joe had decided they ought to get married. His mother agreed with him. She liked Masha because she was slimmer than her daughter, less expensive, and apparently devoted to Joe. She thought Joe would do well to marry Masha so he would keep on getting his shirts ironed and such good food cooked.

Between Joe and his mother, the wedding arrangements were stitched up. Masha looked at a lot of magazines with wedding dresses in them. It vaguely crossed her mind that she would look like an alien in the frocks, but it all seemed unreal to her anyway.

With the wedding idea launched, Joe became proprietorial. He wanted to know what she was doing, what she was thinking, what she'd eaten at lunchtime. He phoned her at work every hour. She couldn't think of anything to say, but that didn't seem to bother him. He bought her things all the time. Gadgets for the home. Cute socks. Flowers. Chocolates. The odd ornament. Records he thought she'd like, which she listened to as if they were in a foreign language.

He started making all sorts of reservations and penciling in dates on the calendar like, Liberty's, Wedding List, 2:30 P.M., Possible Caterer, 4:30, and Florist, 12:15. The dates seemed far enough away not to matter at first, but gradually it dawned on Masha that they were becoming more real and more frightening, like the bars on the edge of a nightmare that gradually materialize into a prison. Masha woke one night to realize she'd been so occupied with pushing reality as far away from her as possible that she'd been backed into a corner. She lay quivering next to the inert Joe with her eyes stretched wide and her mouth in a rictus grin to stop her teeth from grinding. When Joe woke up, he found her next to him, wound tighter than a snare drum. "You must be ready to come on," he consoled her.

That night he brought her a handbook on dealing with painful periods. She threw it at him and locked herself in the kitchen. He shouted and battered on the door and pleaded with her to let him in. She curled up on a tea towel in the gap where the bin went. It wasn't until he left for work the next morning that she came out.

When he'd gone, she picked up the phone. She had a scrap of paper in her hand and she realized it was the only thing which could save her life.

Early that afternoon, the rat-man dropped round with a small parcel. He stayed for longer than it takes to drink several cups of coffee and when he left, he was empty handed.

Masha spent what was left of the afternoon in the kitchen. The recipe wasn't one she'd ever used before, the handwriting was curly and hard to read and the ingredients were both unfamiliar, and initially unpleasant to work with. But when she'd finished, she was dead pleased with the result.

Then she carefully checked she had the piece of paper with the address on it which she'd found on the dresser just after the rat-man departed, and left, empty-handed, locking the door carefully behind her. When she got to the end of the road, she dropped the key down a drain hole. As she turned the bend, she saw the cat sitting on the opposite pavement, staring at her impassively.

Masha gazed back but didn't stop walking. "Are you coming too?" she asked. "I haven't got the basket. You'll have to walk." The cat bounded across the road and fell into step behind her.

When Joe came home that night, he was surprised not to find Masha there, but reassured by the note she'd left on the table. It was the kind of simple message any nervous but house-proud bride-to-be might leave. Joe felt a rush of pride as he read what she'd put. In curlier than usual handwriting, it read "Your Dinner Is In The Oven"

fish without a bicycle

Pagan Kennedy

I hurried down the staircase to our apartment, clamping two grocery bags to my stomach. One of the bags had split, and organic millet grains rained around my feet, bouncing down the stairs like tiny ping-pong balls. As I unlocked the door that day, that fateful day, I was thinking only about the war on the grain. A film played in my head—me in the near future, how I would kneel on the stairs with a Dustbuster to vacuum up the mess, how the situation would soon be under control.

I shoved my hip against the door to our apartment. It flew open. The doorknob slammed against the back wall. After two years, I knew how this should sound—a dull thud. But that night, the noise echoed through our apartment as loud as a gunshot, as if every room was empty. As if someone had taken all the furniture away.

They had. I glanced around the barren hallway, my stomach tightening. Where were the bookshelves that had lined the walls? Where was the rug? Under my feet, the scarred pine floors lay exposed. For a moment, I believed we had been robbed, until I noticed my boom box sitting demurely where shelves had once been, its cord behind it like a tail.

All of a sudden, I understood: he'd left me. I lost control of the grocery bags. They splatted on the floor. The rest of the millet exploded around my feet. A bottle of soy sauce ricocheted off the baseboard. Cantaloupes rolled down the hall like bowling balls. I stepped over the paper bags and edged my way into the living room to find out just how gone he was.

The videotapes stacked into teetering towers and the shooting scripts that papered the floor. All this had disappeared. He'd even yanked his posters off the walls. Now, one chair cast a long shadow on the pine floor. A roll of scotch tape sat on the windowsill. That was it. I had never known a room could be so empty.

My boyfriend—I prefer not to use his name—my boyfriend must have borrowed a van and thrown his stuff into the back. He would have worked so fast that half-moons of sweat darkened the underneath of his arms. Now he probably would camp out on someone's sofa until he found his own apartment. He would not come back. Once he reached a decision, he never second-guessed himself.

I crept around the kitchen and the bedroom, taking stock of what was gone. His thoroughness struck me as cruel: why had he bothered to take, for instance, the Econopak of Charmin toilet paper he'd bought yesterday? What he left behind was even worse: an old Valentine from me, sprinkled with glitter. A sweater I'd knitted for him.

Those first few hours I felt numb, rather than grief-stricken. Pain hadn't hit yet. It hovered in the near future, like a root canal scheduled for the next day at three o'clock. I jotted down a list of all the things I'd need now: toilet paper, rugs, shampoo, a Phillips-head screwdriver.

He called late that night, his voice so flat he sounded lobotomized. "I'm really, really sorry, Erica, but I had to."

That's when the pain hit. "What's wrong with you?" I began sobbing so hard I had to clutch my gut.

"OK, so maybe I didn't handle it in the best way, but I had to do something. You'll see that soon." He delivered this little speech in an ultra-calm tone of voice as if dealing with my accusations was just another chore, the final item on his breaking-up-with-me To Do list. "You're going to resent me for a while," he said. "But after that I hope we can be friends."

I slammed down the receiver. The phone rang again, rang and rang, until I unplugged it. I crawled into bed and curled around the one pillow he'd left behind. I tried to fall asleep, to go blank, but sleep had absconded with all the furniture just like my boyfriend. Ex-boyfriend. I had to get used to saying, "ex-boyfriend." I hunched around that pillow the whole night, sometimes trembling and sometimes lying stiff with my mind racing. The world had shifted around me to become a place I didn't recognize, settling with a bump like an elevator when it arrives at a new floor.

Just yesterday, I could have told you what I'd be doing for the next forty years. We would stay with his family in Michigan at Thanksgiving; we'd have a clutch out in our car; we'd maybe get married and maybe retire together on a ranch where he could make films. Actually, these had all been his plans, and he'd come up with them early on, back when he could spend an afternoon admiring one of my toes, cradling my foot to study the droll curve of my instep.

But the last year had been one long fight, interrupted by occasional backrubs, zucchini lasagna, and black-and-white French films on video. The fight: He would pace beside the bed, breathing noisily. "It's nothing you did," he'd burst out. "It's just . . ." and then he'd shake his head, dismayed when words skittered away from him. "I want . . ." he'd begin, and then cup his eyes, as if he were exhausted. The room would vibrate with all he could not say. I'd be curled up amidst a mess of blankets, sheets twisted around my legs like ropes, my cheeks itching with dried tears, waiting for him to say the final awful thing.

And now he had.

Thank God for Coffee

When the windows turned pale with sickly morning light, I sat up, hugging the pillow between my stomach and my knees. I was thinking about what would happen next, now that he'd taken away my life plan, just like he'd taken the rug. Months and years yawned ahead of me, endless white squares on a calendar.

Oh shit, I was single. Soon I would start dating. I vaguely remembered that it involved going to movies I wouldn't ordinarily see and having intense discussions in coffee houses with bearded men. But the details were hazy. Last time I had been single I had been twenty-nine; now I was thirty-three. That was a long sabbatical. Back in my pre-boyfriend era, no one had email addresses or used the word "dot com"; Princess Di still bopped around offering comfort to the dying, unaware that she would be the next to go.

Everything had changed in the last few years while I, Rip Van Winkle, had slept in the cocoon of a couple. Maybe dating practices had evolved into something I wouldn't understand; maybe people flirted using hand signals that would mystify. Were there any single men these days? I read somewhere that they had all moved to Silicon Valley.

I did not want to date. But worse than the dating was falling in love. It revolted me to imagine adoring some guy and then tumbling into bed with him and meeting his mother and moving in together and then ending up here again, hunched in sheets that still smelled of him. It seemed like this whole stream of events would happen over and over throughout my life, like some fever dream where you're running down a tilted hall, running and running but you never get to the end.

When the clock on the night table said 7 A.M., I pulled a blanket around my shoulders and padded into the kitchen, brewed some coffee and poured a bowl of cereal. I ate one bite of cornflakes, and couldn't touch the rest. But the coffee—bitter, black and silty—went down like medicine. A few minutes later, when the caffeine hit, I threw off the blanket and dressed in cowboy boots, a short skirt, lipstick, eyeliner, stuff I ordinarily wouldn't bother with.

I had plenty of time before work. So I locked the door to the apartment, *my* apartment, and went for a walk through the back streets of Northampton. My boots made crisp little clicks on the sidewalk, a sound I'd always associated with sexy and dangerous women. "Yes, yes, yes" my boots said to me.

The crisp air buzzed in my mouth like champagne. A car swept by, shadows sliding over its windshield glass. The man inside that car might be my next husband. Or, hell, I could give up men, move to Morocco and drug myself with the sun. Or join an ashram. Anything could happen. I had met my new lover, and she was myself, an unpredictable vixen who had swept me off my feet.

Until the coffee buzz wore off.

His Name

I'm aware that only a few pages ago, I vowed never to utter it again. But after three and half years of saying it every day that name is as hard to repress as a sneeze. Boyd, Boyd, Boyd.

The word used to act on me like a drop of whiskey, a flake of caffeine, a granule of methadrine. His name could conjure up the times when he'd love me the most, his Boyd-ness washing over me like a revelation: Boyd with the video camera over his eye, filming my left ankle; "Your tendons," he whispers, "Hollows." Or Boyd cross-legged in bed, a sheet gathered around him like a skirt, his hands swirling through the air as he explains that years ago he drove a Chevy van over the side of an embankment because he hadn't met me yet.

Later, I melted into the background of his consciousness as he fixated on other things: replacing the alternator in his car, applying for a grant, learning the secret ingredients of Pad Thai so we'd never have to pay for restaurant food again. Around him he created a whirl of machine parts, papers, receipts, videotapes; he squatted on the floor in the middle of it all. His long legs would be tucked under him, the sleeves of his jacket rolled up, his shaggy hair falling across his face. He had the lite, femme-y beauty of all those seventies glam rock stars, and his face, oh my god, bruised lips, high half-Cherokee cheekbones, sly eyes.

Say it to yourself: Boyd. Sounds like the past tense. "Tonight, we'll dance around in front of the mirror, get boyed up, and break some hearts." "He boyed me so hard I came in two minutes." Or think of it this way: it's the word that slams into the wall of a "d", ending with the finality of a car wreck. It could be the name of a dessert dripping with cream, a rifle, a bronco.

Boyd, Boyd, Boyd. When he first left, I'd chant it in my head, hoping to wear the word out, chew all the flavor out like a piece of bubble gum. But even now, a year later, it still carries a small charge, like the pop of static electricity. Boyd.

Saving the Connecticut River

The office, in the basement of a warehouse, reeked of fumes. The fluorescent lights flickered above steam pipes wrapped in asbestos foam. The coffee maker spit boiling water from its lid, but we used it anyway, risking third degree burns. My desk was buried under flyers for a meeting about toxic waste; thousands of pieces of paper that had to find the proper destination by next Wednesday. In other words, I worked at a non-profit.

For months, I'd been on the verge of quitting. It was a thankless task, protecting the Connecticut River from the inevitable demise, that polluted and lumbering old sweetheart.

But today, as I settled into my squeaky chair, I gave thanks for the piles of flyers on my desk. Even if Boyd didn't need me anymore, the Connecticut River still did. She always would. We called the river a "she" in this office. I had a distinct mental picture of her as a retired circus elephant still clinging to her trunk, chained up in a dirty cage, starved by her keepers. Now, as I turned on my computer, I felt tears stinging my eyes. Today, I could identify with the Connecticut River. I felt just as bad as she did. Poor old dear.

Janet, my co-worker, came in a half-hour late, with bagels for both for us. "I couldn't remember whether you liked sesame or not," she began. I silenced her by yanking her into my cubicle.

"Janet," I whispered, so the intern wouldn't hear. "He left me. No warning. Just gone."

She wedged herself in closer to my chair. "Who?"

"Boyd," I hissed impatiently. "He cleared out the entire apartment. Vacated."

Janet backed against the wall of my cubicle. "You're kidding."

In answer, I sniffed back a sob.

She petted my hair, smoothing it along my scalp. "No," she said after a few moments. "He can't really have left. He loves you, Erica. In a few weeks, he'll be back."

I don't mean this as an insult at all, because she's actually quite beautiful but Janet reminds me of Big Bird. She's off-balance—a whirring top, with blond hair piled on her head, tufts of it sticking out in every direction, and horn-rimmed glasses that slide down her beaky nose. She can remain an optimist under any circumstances: if you show her a report that proves that the groundwater in Western Massachusetts has been saturated with PCBs, she'll flip through it until she finds the one piece of positive news hidden in 1,000 pages.

"No, Janet, he won't be back," I said in a nasal, I'm-the-adult-here tone of voice, feeling a spark of pleasure at being able to smash her face into the shittiness of the world.

She crossed her arms over her purple sweater, assumed the S-shaped posture of women who have been told they're too tall. "This is so hard to take in. Last weekend, you guys are at Richard's, laughing like crazy, so relaxed. Of all the couples I know, you're the last ones I'd ever thought—"

"Were," I corrected. "Were the last ones you ever thought . . . would break up."

Then I slumped over on the desk, nestling my cheek on the computer keyboard. I closed my eyes.

"Erica?" she shook me. "Hello?"

"I haven't slept in thirty-six hours," I groaned.

"Listen, I know what to do." Janet popped up over the wall of my cubicle. "Ted," she called to the intern, "we have just learned there's been a toxic spill near Turner's Falls. We're going to have to investigate. Can you hold down the phones?"

"Sure," he said, looking scared. "Do you think any TV people will call?"

"If they do, keep it hush-hush."

Then Janet grabbed my coat and pulled me along behind her and out the door. "Don't be such a slowcoach," she called to me as we huffed along the sidewalk. After a few blocks, I realized we were heading towards her girlfriend's herb store. About six months ago, Cathy earned her degree in Chinese medicine and rented an upstairs room in a firetrap building where the floor tilted vertiginously. She had lined the walls with wooden drawers like the card catalogues that libraries used to have, as if she planned to file away herbs alphabetically. When you walked around the room, you'd hit pockets of air with different smells like cinnamon, rose, beeswax, wool, dog fur, dirt, grass. I liked to imagine that Cathy had constructed an invisible city inside that drab room, an architecture of smell that she had built. As you moved through the seemingly empty air, you explored boudoirs, bar rooms, root cellars, nurseries, and musty closets, identifying your surroundings only by scent.

I'd dragged Boyd in there once, but he'd immediately wanted to leave. "What a dump," he'd said on the stairs. I had been trying to convince him that we should detoxify ourselves, but he'd refused any part of it. I hadn't been to the herb store since.

Now Cathy greeted us at the door, wearing a white coat, a new acquisition. The outfit lent her an air of professionalism, which she badly needed, given her pink-streaked hair and her pierced eyebrow.

"Hey there, you," she said, and stood on tiptoe to peck Janet on the lips. Then she patted me on the arm, but stopped mid-pat. "Erica? What happened?"

I recited the story all over again, adding details that had just begun to strike me as important—for instance, how Boyd had left me with a two-bedroom apartment and no time to find a room-mate. How would I pay rent next month?

"You're better off without him," she said. As soon as I heard that phrase, I knew that dozens of people would repeat it to me over the next few months, and I would not believe any of them. "What a shock, though," she added.

She and Janet traded a glance. I remembered how Boyd and I used to do that, the telepathic reassurances we'd send each other over people's heads: "No, honey, we're not like them. We won't break up."

I decided to change the subject. "Do you have anything for insomnia?" Cathy sat me down, circled my wrist in her fingers, closed her eyes, as if she were listening for my pulse rather than feeling it. She breathed in time with me, and this smallest intimacy made my shoulders relax. Then she rooted around in some drawers, mixed up teas, and handed me a few vials of medicine as well. When I reached for my money, she shook her head. "It's on the house."

Back out on the sidewalk, I took the vial of St. John's Wort out of the bag, unscrewed the cap and drank a slug.

"You're only supposed to have six drops," Janet brayed, grabbing my arm. "Now why don't you go home and get some sleep?"

"You're so nice to me, Janet," I said and hugged her, spilling St. John's Wort all over her corduroy jacket. "Oh crap," I began brushing the beads of liquid that clung to the fabric.

"It's OK, Erica, geez. I found this coat in the dump. Here, stop that."

"I'm sorry," I blubbered, "for everything."

"Honestly, Erica, you need a nap." She jumped up the wall that ran along the sidewalk, as if to put a little distance between us, then tightrope-walked along beside me. As she windmilled her arms, the antenna of her hair bobbed up and down, like feelers.

I craned my neck to address her where she teetered on that wall. "Janet, I got so obsessed with that stupid relationship. It took every ounce of energy I had. My priorities got all screwed up. I didn't appreciate you enough. You and all my friends were there for me all along, looking out for me, and I never noticed."

Janet jumped down to the sidewalk all hunched over, then sprung up to her full height like some kind of toy.

"Like I said, you need a nap. Go home, honey. Take your drugs. Dream. Enter the land of nod."

"Thank you," I said, and patted her arm one last time.

As I walked back to my apartment, I made a mental list of all the friends I could count on: Janet, Cathy, Amy, Richard, Leo, Winnie, Mom, Allison. When I passed the Pink Teacup Cafe, I gave its warm brick wall a high-five—somewhere inside, my friend Richard was kneading dough, his hands in dainty gloves made out of flour. My friends. My friends. My friends.

Happy Valley—What's Wrong With That?

When I first met Boyd, he told me he planned to move back to Detroit. "Northampton's fake," he said. "A theme park. Detroit, you're scraping up against reality all the time."

"I don't want to scrape up against reality." I would say this in a wheedling, wounded voice; when he began criticizing our town,

I would be nearly in tears. I considered Northampton and its environs to be an extension of my own person. The Pink Teacup Cafe, with its loaves of fresh-baked bread puffing up in the old gas oven was my stomach; the shaggy ridges of the Holyoke range poking up at the end of our town, my feet; the scrub oaks growing wild and mossy in the woods were my hair. People call this part of Western Massachusetts "The Happy Valley" because in the nest formed by our diminutive mountains we breeze around on bikes, wearing hemp, waving at our neighbors who drive by in Volvos plastered with Ralph Nader stickers. Even the auto repair place at the edge of town flies a rainbow flag to celebrate gay pride.

Once he left me, I assumed he'd disappear into the soot of the industrial Midwest. But I was wrong. A week after he moved out, he left a message on my machine with his new address, a few blocks away. "Just so you'll know where to find me, if anything comes up," he said, in that nonchalant tone that he'd adopted with my answering machine. What, I wondered, did he expect to come up?

Still No Toilet Paper

For the next few evenings, when I trudged home from United to Save the Connecticut River, I'd remind myself that I needed toilet paper, because he'd taken the Charmin with him in his moving-out holocaust. I'd pass the plate glass windows of the CVS, but couldn't work up the courage to go in.

I may have claimed that Northampton belonged to me, that the town was an extension of my body. This is not quite true; my dominion did not extend to the fast-food restaurants or franchises. Those belonged to Boyd. If grapefruit was on sale at Price Chopper, he'd come home with fifty, fill the whole refrigerator with yellow globes. He could spend hours roaming the aisles of the CVS, searching for his own Holy Grail, a shampoo that was cheaper than Suave.

Now that we were broken up, I developed CVS-phobia. Walking past the store's entrance and hearing the hiss of the automatic doors could make my knees go quivery. I was terrified that Boyd would emerge from the store and appear in front of me on the sidewalk, a plastic CVS bag rattling in his hand, ebullient from having just bought shaving gel for only 99 cents. There was no way, no fucking way, I would ever go inside that fucking CVS again.

Yet, I had no toilet paper. This required a creative solution. I moved a package of coffee filters into the bathroom, using them as impromptu wiping devices. Only about twelve filters remained, which meant a horrible choice: caffeine or personal hygiene? To avoid that impasse, I instituted a new policy. I'd only use the filters in extreme circumstances. When I peed, I would "drip dry." Which meant sometimes I'd be stuck on the toilet for a while.

I brought the phone in with me. I called Amy, my longest-running friend in Northampton, who I know from college. We referred to each other as "old school chums."

"I'm urinating," I announced to her.

"I feel special. Thanks for sharing," she said. I heard the clack of her keyboard, and I knew she was fiddling with some Photoshop file as she talked to me, so really, it was only fair that I was peeing.

"How do you meet them?" I asked her. "I'm never going to be able to."

"It's easy. They're everywhere. But you will have to have your own apartment," she chirruped, in that perky way I found a tad annoying these days.

"Don't worry. It will all happen in good time," she added.

"Amy," I moaned. "I'm over thirty now. All the decent ones are taken. I'm going to be single for the rest of my life."

"Let me refresh your memory." The receiver thunked as she put it down on a table. I heard her footsteps as she crossed the room. She picked up the receiver again. "OK, where is it?" she said. I heard her flipping the pages of a book. "Listen to this," she said, " 'Despite media reports of a so-called man shortage, a simple check of the latest census population charts reveals there were about 1.9 million more bachelors than unwed women between the ages of twenty-five and thirty-four.' "

I clutched the receiver in my fist, and stared around me at the bathroom, the mold creeping up between the tiles in the shower, the windowsill where his bottle of Suave used to sit on top of jigsaw pieces of cracked paint. "I don't care what a simple check of the latest census shows," I groaned. "It's hopeless."

Sociology Section

Three and a half years ago, he was a stranger, lounging at a desk in the Northampton Public Library. I was browsing through Sociology. Just as I tried to squeeze past his desk, he jumped up, and sort of bowed before me.

"Come out on the steps and talk to me," he said. And then he added, "I want to ask you about the politics of Lena Wertmuller." Maybe that's when he hooked me. How many guys want your opinion about a Marxist female filmmaker?

"It's freezing out there," I protested, but I followed him to the granite stairs, where we slithered our boots around in the slush. He argued with me about art and gender, his breath issued from his mouth in puffs that climbed up into the sky and tangled in the snow-bobbing branches of the pines.

I was in the middle of answering one of his questions, cobbling together some opinion—when he cut me off.

"I know it's out of fashion, but I believe in love at first sight," he said. "And I have to tell you that I'm falling in love with you."

"You don't even know me. And I think that—"

"Will you marry me?" he interrupted. I had the impression that the proposal had flown from his mouth unbidden. It seemed to flutter around in the air between us, like a baby robin just pushed from the nest, all purring wings and startled eyes.

I wouldn't marry him. But I would go out for coffee.

That weekend, I had a paper due for a Biomass Energy Conference, and on top of that, I had promised to bring a cake to Amy's birthday party. Then, Friday night, he materialized at my door, as surprised to be there as if he'd been sucked into my house by a magnetic field. "I missed you," he said. It had been two days since the library. I yanked him inside, and we kissed for the first time, our mouths seeming to be a portal we passed through together, into a wet wonderland. We had sex all weekend. I forgot about the paper. I forgot about Amy, my friend for a decade. Forgot about everything but him, which unfortunately set the trend for the next few years.

Once Again, I Fail to Buy Toilet Paper

I was leaning against the stove, stirring my soup, listening to voices on NPR speculate about the situation in the former Soviet Union. And then, out of nowhere, an idea burst into my head: tonight I must go to CVS. After weeks of scampering down the street, ducking into doorways, all to avoid running into Boyd, *I would actually seek him out.* My heart started pounding. I became so nervous that I had to wipe my damp palms on a dishtowel.

"I need toilet paper," I told myself, even though this was not true. Two weeks ago, I had broken down in the aisle of the Food Co-op and bought a few rolls of Eco-Friend, the ridiculously expensive 100-percent-recycled brand with little flecks of black in the gray-colored paper. It had been my ambition, when Boyd and I were together, to be the kind of couple that stocked our bathroom with this speckled toilet paper, part of a larger fantasy in which we constructed a straw-bale house out in the woods and Boyd transformed from a moody filmmaker into a sweet-tempered goat farmer. But now that I had the toilet paper of my dreams, I saw how inadequate that really was. It scraped. I might as well wipe my bum with a nail file. More to the point, I suddenly grew nostalgic for the Charmin he used to buy, its bubblegum smell, its consistency of Wonder Bread. Boyd would buy it on sale, rolls and rolls

185

of it, then come home and dump it out into a pyramid on the bathroom floor. How rich we felt then, how padded and safe with all that toilet paper and no need to leave the apartment ever again.

I had to see him. I had to have Charmin. I pulled on my jacket, leaving the miso soup to cool on the stovetop. I couldn't eat anything now and slammed the door behind me. Soon, I was jogging toward the CVS sign, the white and orange glare that burned a hole in the black sky. I plunged through the door, into the aisles—Halloween masks grimacing from the shelves, boxes of condoms like candy, romance novels, reek of perfume. "Calm down, calm down," I chanted to myself. The inside of the store seemed to have warped, as if I were looking at it through a sheet of Mylar. I could hear myself panting. I whirled through the aisles, turning the corner into the Personal Care section, sure that I'd see him squatting on the linoleum, studying labels, waiting for me.

But he was not in Personal Care, was not anywhere in CVS. I halted near a display of Halloween buckets, plastic pumpkins grinning in rows. My heart began to slow. Why had I been absolutely sure that I would find Boyd in the Personal Care aisle of CVS? Why had I been absolutely sure that the final showdown between us would happen on this linoleum floor with a lite-rock song playing in the background blocking our emotions? What was the big deal anyway?

A haggard woman in a nurse uniform shoved past. A teenage kid in a smock rolled a cart full of boxes along the aisle. It was just an ordinary night at CVS, and I felt myself dissolving into an ordinary shopper.

I sauntered through the aisles, enormously proud of myself. I had descended into my own personal hell and survived. I had faced fear. CVS had no hold on me now. I celebrated with a six-pack of Charmin, a hot-pink toothbrush, and a tube of toothpaste flavored with fennel.

Arms loaded with booty, I stood in line at the register, gazing at the tabloid headlines about Hollywood divorces. Ahead of me a few shoppers shifted from foot to foot. The cashier intoned into the loudspeaker, "Price check on Kellogg's frozen waffles."

We were still waiting to hear about the frozen waffles when the automatic doors parted. Boyd emerged from the darkness. He wore the same army jacket as always, his gloveless hands red from the cold, dangling. His hair hung in coils, longer than I remembered. It hadn't occurred to me that his hair would keep growing after we broke up. His jacket whistled as he walked; his curls bounced with every step; he squinted his eyes as if he were trying to read fine print in the air around him. And that brought back so many of my memories of him—the way that his coat smelled in the snow and the taste of enchiladas cooked at midnight and the little "ha" of surprise he made in his sleep. All the anger I had managed to work up over the last few weeks—the great wall I'd erected—crumbled. I wanted him so much that my throat felt sore.

A woman stepped through the door and took her place at his side. She was my clone. I mean that she also kept her thick black hair in a ponytail, and she also stood just high enough to touch his shoulder with her nose, and she wore a thrift-store hound's-tooth coat.

I have no idea, to this day, what happened to the toothpaste, toilet paper, etc. gathered in my arms. Nor do I know whether he saw me. All I remember is diving through the back door of the CVS, and racing through the parking lot empty-handed. The world blurred—the cars like bubbles filled with ink, streetlamps flying by like comets, the thin mouth of a woman gawking as I ran past. When I reached the town green, I tripped over a tree root, and fell sprawling under an oak. My knees rammed into the dirt. I lay gasping for air, then rolled onto my back. Above, the leaves made lace in the sky. Footsteps approached, swishing-swishing in the grass and for an awful moment, I thought he'd followed me. But it turned out to be nothing but a hippie-dad-type man. "Nice night to look at the stars," he said without pausing, and walked on. Tears trickled down the side of my face. I sucked a long, wavering breath. I did not want to begin sobbing in the dead center of Northampton with dirt all over my pants.

Stupid idiot me. Why hadn't I guessed the reason he had vacated our apartment in twenty-four hours flat? Her.

Deconstructing the Personals

Sunday night, late, I should have been in bed. *The Valley Vanguard*, a smudgy alternative newspaper, lay in sections all over the kitchen table, scattered with cake crumbs. I had to find a roommate. But had I even made it to the Housing Section? No, I'd bogged down in the Personals, where I had begun a complicated statistical analysis. I wanted to prove to myself that there was a man shortage, just like Susan Faludi claimed.

Men Seeking Women: 245 ads. Women Seeking Men: 213 ads.

Oh damn, I thought, estimating an eight per cent surplus of women.

I tried to stop myself there before my mental processes became any more degraded and pathetic. Grabbing my copy of *Backlash*, I stared at the author photo. Susan met my eyes. She wore an endearingly out-of-fashion cowl neck sweater. You could almost hear her mind go click-click-click, the sound of knitting needles as they stitched together one thought and then the next and the next into a shawl of theory, just big enough to fit on a single bed, to keep a woman like me warm.

The book dropped on the floor with an explosion. My hands must have been shaking. I just couldn't be bothered to call into question the *New York Times, Newsweek* and the rest of the media conspiracy right now. It seemed of vital importance that I figure out whether any date-able men existed at all in Northampton.

I uncapped my red pen and ran it along the ads of the men who classed themselves "SWM"s. Not that I have a thing against white people. I am one myself. But I knew I could never love a man who tucked a "W" between his S and M. It implied all kinds of things, that "W". Wall-to-wall carpeting, premium cable channels. A job in computer sales that he'd explain over and over, but that I'd fail to understand. Multiplexes. Formative years spent in Connecticut. Photo albums full of his friends posing in human pyramids or shouting at the camera with beer cans. So with my red pen, I x-ed out every guy who referred to himself as "SWM". For good measure, I also crossed out all the men seeking "SWF"s. Slashing through the ads felt lovely, like exorcising all the prejudice in

Northampton in only a few minutes. But it left only about eight ads. "Caring, supportive musician, 40, into politics, Spanish literature, is seeking female, 22-32."

Not only did I x that one out, I marked it so hard that the newspaper tore, and the ad turned into a black hole. I could just picture this loser, lugging his guitar into a cafe to perform folk songs about Nicaragua (which he would showily pronounce in Spanish). He'd have a bad case of male-pattern baldness that he would try to make up for by growing his remaining hair long and draping it in a rattail down his back. After his set, he'd work the room, trying to sell his CDs, and even more determinedly trying to score with a flock of college girls giggling at the table in the back. He wants a twenty-two-year-old! Asshole.

I went through and slashed all the ads of men who refused to go out with women their own age.

That left one. "Chivalrous Christian gentleman, 35, never married, enjoys scuba diving and nature photography, seeks chaste and skinny Christian for a lifetime of love."

This Book is Brought to You By the Heft Family Foundation

You have no doubt heard of the Hefts of Newport, Rhode Island, who made their fortune in bird cages and pig feed—basically, anything an animal will eat, bat around the room or shit into has enriched the Heft family coffers. You probably also remember the scandal a decade ago, when Adolph Heft—an octogenarian who favored blue eye-glass frames—stated in an interview that AIDS was God's way of punishing homosexuals. The boycott nearly bankrupted the company. The younger Hefts had just announced a new foundation, throwing money at gay causes—also conservation, cancer and urban teens.

"We're the Heft wet dream," I told Janet. "We've got a gay indicator—you. And we do wildlife protection, which ties in with the pet thing. We're the perfect group to help them whitewash their corporate image."

For the first time in weeks, I worked intently, fingers flowing over the keyboard as I bullshitted my way through the first part of the proposal. That day last summer when we'd convinced three old ladies to help us pick up trash on the riverbank became a "rich program of community events designed to celebrate diversity." Our interns from Hampshire College, one of whom drove a Miata, turned into "at-risk youth." Though I didn't come right out and say it, I implied that through our "innovative outreach program" we'd discovered these kids selling their bodies for crack in the Springfield bus station and had rehabilitated them by imparting "the sense of hope that goes hand-in-hand with environmental empowerment."

I had discovered my own inner grant writer.

Suddenly It Was All So Obvious

Next morning, I dragged myself out of bed, made a cup of coffee on top of the rattling sheets of newspaper personals tattooed with red ink. Once the caffeine hit, I couldn't remember why I'd been in a depressive frenzy a few days before. Why had I been so worried about the stupid non-existent man shortage? I scooped up the newspaper pages into the hall, and stuffed them into the trash. Then I galloped down the hall of my building and emerged onto the street, where the trees magically grew out of the sidewalk, their leaves glowing scarlet and amber against the morning-glory-colored sky. Already, I could tell it would be one of those days when Northampton turned into a movie set, a cinematically perfect New England town. The air would taste as cold and crisp as a Jonah Gold apple plucked right off the tree.

As I ambled along, kicking the pink-and-red-polka-dotted leaves that decorated the sidewalk, I vowed to stop being so neurotic. Of course I would meet someone eventually. After all, lots of relationships last, why shouldn't my next? To reassure myself, I listed all the stable couples I knew. Let's see, Janet and Cathy adored each other. David and Jonathan just moved to Vermont together. Richard and Theodore. Alice and Mimi. Christopher and Anthony . . .

Suddenly the truth hit like a kick in the head. I stopped in the middle of the sidewalk and froze there. Now I saw the obvious pattern. Only gay people stayed together.

I hadn't noticed before, because the gay people explained so much. To listen to them talk, you'd think they'd had it just as bad as heterosexuals. "Cathy and I are trying to have as much sex as possible, before lesbian bed death kicks in," Janet would joke.

"Alice is such a little co-dependent nut," Mimi would tell me. "This must be why lesbians are always in therapy."

But she wasn't in therapy. None of them were in therapy. The gay people shared apartments crammed with hand-made pottery and mementos of their life together. They held potlucks to celebrate their anniversaries, the table overflowed with candles, glazed cranberries and red wine. They lounged on chairs covered with dog hair and sipped tea, relaxed in each other's loose-limbed embrace.

But the straight people, forget about it. In my immediate circle of friends, I could name one straight couple that had lasted. Mostly, the heterosexuals lived alone and gulped down Prozac. Even when they did manage to fall in love, the straight people invariably could not make a go of it without the help of professionals. Boyd and I had been to a couples' therapist. My parents had, too, only they called it "marriage counseling" back then. And they'd divorced anyway. Heterosexual desire seemed to be nothing but a bright and doomed comet that plummeted through the sky, scattering behind it a plume of therapy bills, condom wrappers and prescriptions, before it inevitably burned out.

I was so deep in thought that I'd begun pinching myself in between thumb and forefinger, which usually I avoid doing in public. Two women brushed past me, arguing about whether their car would get a ticket where it was parked. I thrust my hands in my pockets and began ambling down the sidewalk again, letting the swish-swish of leaves give a rhythm to my thoughts.

Ahead of me, a rainbow flag jumped and danced in the surreal blue of the sky, above a sign that read "Her-Story Books." I stopped in front of its brick facade, which was caked with flyers. I'd passed this wall every day and never bothered to read the haphazard messages until now. "Lesbian, Bisexual and Questioning. Support group for women coming out." "The Amazons. All-wimmin's metal band. At the Teacup on Sunday comehead-bang, rock out and play Scrabble." Layers and layers of flyers offered herbalist retreats, gender transition discussion groups, lectures about Mary Daly, motorcycle repair classes.

The posters fluttered in the wind, rained-on, raggedy, as if no one had bothered to clear them away for years. All except one, a crisp poster that had been stapled neatly on top of the others. "A Room of One's Own? How About a Whole House!" it offered. In a photo beside the headline, a woman about my age beamed with happiness: her buzz-cut hair and smudge black eyes gave her the look of a well-fed seal. She seemed familiar, though I couldn't say why. It took me a moment to realize that I'd seen her photo many times before. Her face was plastered all over town, this Sadie McGraw, licensed real-estate broker, winner of the Business Person of the Year Award, with testimonials available from hundreds of satisfied clients.

I leaned into the wall to squint at the photo. The corners of her nose and mouth didn't go crooked no matter how close you got. If only I were Sadie McGraw. My mom, for one, would be thrilled. Only a few days ago on the phone, Mom said to me, "It's a good thing you didn't marry him, Erica. I'm talking from a purely economic standpoint here. Did you know that when a woman is married, she loses two percent of her earning capacity *every year*. And then when you get divorced, you're truly fucked." My mom swears a lot. In fact, she's the only actual mother I've known who uses the term "motherfucker." She works as a cultural studies professor at NYU, where, I believe, they encourage you to cuss.

As I stared into the xeroxed eyes of Sadie McGraw, I realized that she was the kind of woman Mom had always wanted to be. Property owner. A woman who planned for her thirty years hence. An independent woman. Empowered. Invincible. A woman who did not let men destroy her earning power. A lesbian.

web diary of amp

Anne-Marie Payne

29 February 2000

Saw my friend Zoe outside the Le Tigre gig last night, looking pretty, her black eyeliner slick and thick and perfect. She asked how I'd got a ticket and I said "guest list" and mumbled it like I was ashamed, but really I was proud as hell. I felt like that Bukowski poem where he writes about his Gold Card and his BMW just to annoy his critics. I'm so sad, hubris floating round me like cheap perfume.

Inside was a tiny venue, red and dark, full of indie kids. All the old ugly blokes (like, 28), clustered at the back. The kids were down the front, excited, talking loud, showing off to each other. One waved a kiddie's light-up magic wand. Another—a boy—held a glow-in-the-dark green water pistol, which he pointed at the girl with the wand. Both boys and girls were fey, pointing knees, turning toes inward, tilting heads to the side, pouting and dimpling mouths and scrunching up their eyes.

I bumped into Little Neil who inquired about San Francisco (I'd spent January working there in my new incarnation as web yuppie writer-lady). He introduced me to his friend Nicky. "How do you know Neil, then?" I asked. "Oh, I just kept seeing him around, and finally I got up the courage to speak to him," she said. (How do they do that? All these people I meet now, these scenester kids, they do that. See each other at clubs and just start chatting and hanging out. I'd love to know how it works.)

Nicky introduced me to her friends Rhona and Charlie, warning me that Rhona was "scary." Rhona was a mammoth girl with lots of eyeblack and pink hair in bunches. She wore heavy chains round her neck and plastic beads, a Bikini Kill T-shirt, studded wristbands, and big, swishy jeans. Charlie wore wide jeans too, plus a T-shirt under a lurex '60s girl's dress, accessorized with plastic beads round neck and wrists, and lots of facial jewelry. He was confident and dismissive: 5 years and a million miles away from me.

The support band had a lovely name—Comet Gain—like comets having a race. I bought a drink and sat on a DJ record crate in the corner, tore a page from my notebook and started scribbling. I hoped no one could see me. I started to feel like I looked freaky, there on my own, all dressed up in red, scribbling notes on paper resting on my knees.

In the loo a pretty blond girl was fiddling with her hair in front of the mirror. "Gawd, your weather really messes up my hair," she drawled. "Doesn't it yours?"

"Mine's always curly," I grinned. Talking to American strangers was second nature now, after San Francisco. "Where are you from?"

She looked away. "New York," she said, dismissively, like I should have known.

"Wow . . ." I said, and looked at the wall. Perhaps people from New York weren't as friendly as people from San Francisco.

When Le Tigre were due to come on, I stood near the front. My bag was on my back. The blond girl from NY walked onstage. Oops. They joked around, set stuff up, then Kathleen came on to screams. She was pretty: hair in a ponytail high up on her head. We bounced along, and everyone knew all the songs. They made a cool trio: Kathleen in her yellow Le Tigre shirt; Johanna from the loos foxy in pink, Sadie Benning ugly-chic, all Sarah Lucas cool in a blue bodywarmer. She got cheers and yells of "foxy lady!" from the club V dykey contingent at the bar, five young ladies sporting matching '50s men's hairdos and Morrissey specs.

The gig was great. I bounced up and down till my toes

ached, sang along, even clapped after songs with my hands in the air, looking at the sleeves of my red and white frock glowing in the pink lights. But once it was over, what to do?

For a while I chatted to Mick, a guy with a girl's voice who runs a zine distro down in Wales. He writes beautifully. He was tiny, shy. He drove all the way up for the gig and had to drive off after to get to work the next day. I asked where he worked. A petrol station. I asked if he wanted to move to London. No, London was too unfriendly. It made him depressed. I felt bad because I knew my questions were making me look like a yuppie. I felt like a yuppie. I wanted to take him by his little gray shoulders and give him a shake till his pint slopped on the floor. "Don't work in a Welsh petrol station!" I wanted to say. "You write like an angel!"

I left Mick, pumping his arm like I'd learnt in America, then apologizing profusely for it. "Do you know who Jen the press officer is?" I asked as I made my excuses. "I've got to meet her." "Er, no," he said, and gave me a look. The get-away-from-me, you-careerist-yuppie look.

No press officer. She said she had a black fringe. I got a glass of water and sat at the bar. I could see myself in the mirror, all curvy-round in red, round curly-red hair, plump arms, red mouth. I felt conspicuous, like a lush or a roué or one of those other old-fashioned words I always think I'll end up being.

I wanted to leave so bad. It was just like the party I went to in SF: I wanted to sneak off, disappear, sneak out of the door, slip out of the world. I saw Little Neil handing out flyers for a disco he's having with Frances and Alex, and I smiled at him, but what was there to say? I stood up and leant against the wall. A boy in glasses stared at me quizzically. I got my things together and left.

I rode home listening to the drunks. A girl opposite detailed her straight A's at GCSE, masters and degree level. She was hurt at not getting some job. Loudly, drunkenly, her colleague commiserated. It was a loud drunk train and a loud drunk bus.

On the bus I wrote a hundred times "I can write short stories". Writing stories, I decided, was the perfect cover for my inadequacy as an indie kid. I couldn't talk to strangers and thought wands were affected. The new breed of indie boy, cute and confident yet wearing plastic children's jewelry, repelled me. The large girls scared me. The ubiquitous uniforms they all wore bored me. And I had a job: a proper job: writing, editing—responsible shit. No one else I knew had that, and they mocked my salary behind my back, I was told.

I would write stories about it all, I decided, and then my rudeness and shyness and meanness would all fall into place. I just knew it.

19 April 2000

After I got my hair cut at the Vidal Sassoon School, I was very depressed. It wasn't like the exciting depression my friend Lady Lucy had. She started drawing non-stop on napkins and cigarette packets and anything to hand, using felt-tip pens she had blagged off Crayola. Then she had a panic attack outside her horrible office job and had to quit and move to the country. Now she does performance art at disused cinemas and just got awarded lots of money to make prints. But me, my depression consisted of sitting in front of the telly, under the duvet, not wanting to go out.

That's as depressed as I get. I am a not-very-depressed person. Dan, the boyfriend, he gets depressed loads. So does Frances. And Anna's depressed nearly all the time. Everyone gets it. Some people even get a bit mad, and have to take Lithium and stuff. But me, I had a dodgy haircut and felt a bit sorry for myself and wanted to stay home. Whoo.

But, what it is, I had to go out. Even though I felt depressed, I just don't have any excuses not to go out anymore. Before I had loads: I lived in crappy South London and there was nowhere to go. Plus, I was an unemployed writer so I was horribly in debt and poor. But, for the moment anyway, I've actually got some work: beautiful freelance content producer work you can do from home, in bed, on a laptop, or in the office. Whatever you like. Last month, me and Dan ran away from South London, forever, I hope.

So, the situation here is, you've got The Lux Cinema if you want to see a film. You've got 2 cafes within a few hundred yards if you want coffee. You've got umpteen curry houses if you want a hot mouth and a full belly. You've got the Beigel Bake whenever you want it. And you've got lots of clubs that you can WALK BACK FROM. What you don't have, not anymore, is an excuse not to go out. Not even if your hair is horrible and you are intimidated by all the pretty skinny hipster girls and all the trendy blokes with "ironic" beards. Life's tough, eh?

So, eventually, I did go out. I didn't take my coat off all night, mind, because that was a bit like being under the duvet. I went to the cafe down the road where they were having this thing called Talkeoke, and it was ace. It was almost as good as staying in, but with the added bonus of being Out. And what's Talkeoke? Well, there's a round table with a hole in the middle. In the hole, there's a spinny chair. The host sits on that, while the guests sit round the table. The host has a mike and he keeps the conversation going. He spins round to different guests and fields interesting debates on various topics. The whole thing is filmed and projected onto a giant screen. And (of course, this being Multimedia Ditch) it's broadcast on the web. The host wore glasses and a Chinese print shirt. He had short dark hair and a smiley face.

Anyway Dan knew this guy Paul who was there, and Paul told Dan that the host was going out with the girl Sarah who was a guest at the table. And it was true, whenever the host looked at Sarah, his face sort of glowed, and he'd look at her for slightly too long, and smile even more than he already was. We vaguely used to know Sarah, via Paul, but she didn't recognize us. Dan whispered to me that Sarah used to go out with a mad crazy Estonian called Sergei, who ran an art gallery in a briefcase. The Attache Gallery had "shows" in the Tate, the Royal Festival Hall, the Whitechapel and the Lux, but then Sergei started playing all mind games with Sarah so they cancelled their visa-facilitating marriage, and now she's going out with the Talkeoke guy. All this gossip was fascinating to me. It's quite hard for me to figure out how to interact these days, so gossip is like a mini-tutorial in human relations.

The conversation, nimbly fielded by the host, swung

from art to relationships to blokes having orgasms without coming, and back again. I stood by the counter the whole night, drinking chocolate and watching the screen. I didn't feel my usual social confusion—didn't have to worry about whether or not I was being included in the conversation or whether I was absent-mindedly sucking my thumb (a habit I've never been able to shake) because no one was paying attention to anyone except the people round the round table. It was like being invisible. It was like watching telly, or being on the internet. Under a duvet (well, my coat), too! But I started to worry. What if that was the only way I could enjoy things these days? As an observer?

You see, everything people say about the internet (that it stops real-life interaction) is true. In the mornings I clean up some, and run to the shop that used to sell hats but now sells milk and washing powder as well, and then I watch Richard and Judy, then do bits for my website, or for other people's websites. Sometimes I'll go into town and work in the big internet cafe instead. And while I'm doing all this internet work I write emails to people who started writing to me because of my site. They're all really interesting and we write fun long emails. I guess it's the equivalent of gossiping with your work-mates because they seem to check their mail every 5 minutes and be online all the time like I am. It's all fine but. . . . I've never met them and they've never

met me and what this really means is that I'm alone
all day, with my cat Katrina, or the other people in
the internet cafe.

So now other people's lives have taken on the quality
of a series of short films. Even my friends' lives
seem like mini-docusoaps about confused young people
in the big city. Will Frances move to Berlin? Will her
band make it? Will Lady Lucy move back to London? Will
Andrea quit her job and become a gardener? Will Dee
get funding for his film? Will Lisa ever get out of
debt? And I feel like I'm just sitting there under a
duvet watching them the whole time. There's something
wrong. Is it me? Or is it nu meedja cultcha?

PS. As if to prove my point, Dan just came in and told
me all the streets are blocked because it's Charlie
Kray's funeral. Apparently there are big burly secu-
rity people in dark glasses, and loads of policemen,
and hearses and Rolls Royces and floral tributes saying
"Charlie" in one hearse and "Gentleman" in the other,
and loads of East End people saying "Ahh, the Krays,
they were all right really," all getting off on the
glamour and history of it all. You see what happens
when you go out, instead of staying in bed all morning
with your laptop and your chapstick and your diary and
the cat? You get to go to famous gangsters' brother's
funerals. Right, that's it. I'm getting a life. Really.
I've just got to update my website first.

27 May 2000

It's 3 am and I'm online to Sovac77. I can tell he's pissed off by the way he's typing. Characters hit the screen, rapidly piling up: typostrewn. He's even using abbreviations, which he never does: wtf for "what the fuck," ppl instead of "people." He doesn't smiley. I've been on the computer for five hours straight, and I'm gagging for bed.

> Sovac77 says:
>> what did you think about what elfie said
>
> Sovac77 says:
>> she is so arrogant, the waty jonno
>
> Sovac77 says:
>> way*
>
> Sovac77 says:
>> sticks his head up her arse whatever she says
>
> Sovac77 says:
>> writing about her holiday
>
> Sovac77 says:
>> wtf is th a t about
>
> Sovac77 says:
>> why should we care about that?
>
> Sovac77 says:
>> Ion, are u there

His words have been streaming up the screen but I've not been looking. I've been perusing "the forum," the place where Sovac77 and elfie and jonno and I and at least fifty others encounter each other daily. It is an electronic bulletin board where users leave messages for each other. They are listed in date order: most recent first, earlier today, yesterday, last week, last month. They are mostly boring; at first they seemed to me to consist of little more than people posting "is anyone on? I'm here! Speak to me!"

"Get into the forums," my editor had said. "Liven things up a bit."

Tick, elfie, faeriechick, emerald, Incholate Jest, Lowlito, Hippygirl. Names, not people. But slowly their stories formed, jigsawlike. Faerie, lover of ketamine and her husband. Tick, obsessed with WWII. Lowlito, with a criminal record as long as his tattooed arms, but never as big as the love for his 2 y/o daughter. Their stories developed and unfolded before me: soon I was logging in—undercover, of course, I never said where I worked—to catch all the latest gossip. Never mind my real friends, my boyfriend: never mind Frances moving to Berlin or Lady sobering up: I wanted to know whether Tick and elfie really did meet up and shag in real life; whether Incholate Jest was really cybering emerald AND faerie, as his hints in the forum suggested; whether Lowlito would manage to teach his kestrel

to fly off the leash; whether LAN would find more
programming work.

London, are you there?

I raise my right hand and press my fingers hard against
my screen-dazzled eyes. It's boring waiting for people
to answer you, and I feel bad for Sovac. Quick typing
is a bonus in the online world: you can express yourself sharper, quicker: you have recourse to adjectives
that two-finger typists daren't even commence; as a
result, your "online persona"—the you that you project
into cyberspace—is fuller, bolder, more dramatic, more
interesting, more "real" than it might otherwise be.
Sovac is real to me—at this moment realler than my own
boyfriend, who is asleep in the bedroom—and I don't
even know what he looks like; never heard his voice.

"Amp, what are you doing?"

I freeze; red rushes to my face as I hurriedly mini-
mize windows.

"It's 4 o'clock. What are you bloody doing?"

"Nothing!" I turn round in my chair and smile
brightly. Dan is standing in the doorway, hair ruffled, eyes half-closed: his T-shirt ending at the top
of his thighs.

"Nothing. Just finishing some writing."

He grunts, mutters a curse, and shuffles off to bed
like an old man. I turn back to the screen only when
I hear him shut the door. Sovac's text flutters up the
screen, drifting like a black snowbank. My eyes hurt
as I scroll through, slowly locate the "C" and "Y" and
"A" keys with my left index finger.

15 April 2001

Four A.M. And I'm awake again. Ho hum. One of my feet
is tucked under me and the acrylic leopard fur of my
slipper rubs against my right thigh. The sleeves of
my dressing gown—nylon, I think it is, and covered
with a hothotHOT pink and yellow and orange flower-
print, like a Versace dress gone to hell—are slipping
down my arms towards my elbows. And my eye, it hurts
like I've been poked in it. I suppose it's because
I've been crying. Sniff.

I haven't been crying very much, OK? I'm not a girl.
Well, I mean I am, but . . . I've been crying in a
very surreptitious, steely way. With the covers over
my head and my thumb in my mouth. Or, alternatively,
lying on the rug (It's a tiger print rug, but there's
not a theme going on here—leopard skin slippers or no
leopard skin slippers) with my head resting on it, one
eye pressed closed against the wool, the other staring

straight at a knot of fluff which might as well bear a small sign saying "you need to hoover, you lazy, unsuccessful excuse for a competent human being." So either some fluff got in my eye or my eye got too squashed or my eye has still got some unexpressed tears in it. But they'll never get out now, these recalcitrant tears, because I've rubbed the eye so many times that the tears are probably squashed against the back of my eye. I can just picture 'em, cartoon legs waving, teardrop bodies no longer curved and plump but smashed squashed flat against the circle of my eyeball. Tough shit, tears. You can suffer too.

At 5 P.M. British time the American woman called up and said "I've got bad news" and I sat in the chair and the boyfriend looked up at me, and I gave him the thumbs down sign, whilst trying to keep my voice very calm and mature and rational. The American told me my job, my lovely dreamy job, was coming to an end.

Ever since then, I've had Elaine Paige and Barbara Dixon in my head, singing "Nothing is so good it lasts eternity . . . Perfect situations must go wrong," in quivering operatic falsettos. Do you remember the song? It was number one for ages in the early '80s. My mum loved it. If I could see Paige and Dixon right now I'd bang their heads together for writing a crap-pyass song that years later was to form the smug mental soundtrack to a night of job loss angst.

A poke in the eye and early '80s opera songs stuck in my head.
Whatever next? Oh, I know.
Now I've got to write a new CV.

Fuck!

Friday 18 May 2001
Underwear Over The Internet

A voice came into my head and told me I should sell my underwear over the internet. I had always considered making money from sex to be a perfectly fine thing. This is not to say that I did it. But it had always seemed a fair swap. And I had read many feminist books that saw it that way, too.

I sat down on my chair and tried to make sense of it. I could sell my underwear over the internet and that way I would still be making money from the internet. But, of course, would anyone want to buy the underwear of an out-of-work content producer in her late twenties?

Item One: Black, sheer "lace"-effect panties, polyamide/viscose/cotton/elastene mix, made especially for H&M. These are the knickers worn on the day she discovered the website had lost its funding. At the end of the day they were found tangled up with her big baggy skater-style jeans at the side of her bed. Jeans/knickers/belt were still looped around her left foot when she passed out from tequila consumption. A black Converse One-Star sneaker was also tangled up with the jeans, caught inside the right leg.

Item Two: White sheer panties, pink trim, small pink ribbon rose decoration. Polyamide/elastene/cotton mix. These are the knickers worn on the day she was on the internet for ten hours, posting meaningless messages to strangers on a Bulletin Board, pausing only to make tea, pick up a telephone bill from the mat by the door, and visit the bathroom. In the bathroom she spoke to her reflection in the mirror, defending herself against its silent accusation of atrophy. Please note that repeated washings have robbed these knickers of their initial enthusiastic dazzly-whiteness.

Item Three: Black, sheer, '50s-style "Big Pants," with black roses in raised embroidery, small ruffle round legs, tiny black ribbon on waistband. Worn the night she met said strangers from Bulletin Board in an unfashionable bar in Central London. She stood on the bar's second level, looked down on hundreds of drunken heads, and felt the fabric work its way between her buttocks as she bent down to fetch a cigarette from her handbag. It was a non-smoking area but she and two

213

other girls smoked anyway, with the intimate complicity of new acquaintances. As she stayed out all night these knickers command a higher price than the others: also, they are her personal favorites.

It would never do, would it. Would it? Though I had originally dismissed the idea, it began to take on a new luster. Knickers have an awful lot of power for such little things. Perhaps the underwear of out-of-work content producers in their late twenties is an untapped market? Perhaps it is a niche, like the vacuum-wrapped knickers of Japanese schoolgirls sold in vending machines in Tokyo. The voice continued nagging. "You have to make some money somehow. This is not a school holiday: this is your life."

I picked at a hole in the chair; the stuffing was beginning to come out. There was a small speckling of yellow stuffing on the floor under the chair. Evidently I had done this before, without even realizing. Everything in my flat was broken or distressed in some way. Once I had found this charming, carefree, artistic, but now, when people came over, I began to imagine their eyes running over the battered chair legs and then turning to my legs and imagining my legs were battered and ruined too.

I firmly believed that you are what you eat: I had eaten only candy for three months when I was seventeen

to make myself taste sweet, and whenever I had a slice
of greasy pizza I would begin to imagine myself
oleaginous as the peppers and mushrooms that slid
around on the top of the slice. But perhaps I had got
it all wrong; you were in fact what you sat on, and
all my insides were on display, scattered all over the
floor, gathering dust.

23 July 2001

LET'S GET METAPHYSICAL

Bejeezus, this is gettin' ridiculous. I have not
worked for two and a half months. Hey, make that
three. Let's be honest now. Three months. Twelve
weeks. Ninety-ish days. Yes, I could work it out of
course. I could be exact. But that would entail maths,
wouldn't it. It would entail getting my diary,
pointing at things, counting things up. Not fucking
likely. No, my brain, and my ass, have decided that
they are ON STRIKE.

ASSUMPTION MAKES AN ASS OUT OF U AND. . . .

My ass, however, has an excuse. (Unpatriotic as it is,
I prefer the American pronunciation of the word. The
British equivalent, arse, with the "r" stretched long
and flowing fruity from the throat, is far too redo-
lent of the genuine, wobbling, split-cheeked, shit-
ting actuality of the thing. The Americanism is, I
reckon, more like the idea of an arse: a plump, clean,

cuppable, sexy thing that never, ever poos.) My ass
has an excuse because my ass is dragged down to the
gym every day or so and trounced around to wickedly
bad house music. Hence my ass is more up-in-the-air,
higher and prettier, than it has been since, ooh,
April, when I last had a job and survived on coffee,
ice-cream and giant Kit-kats. Nonetheless, my ass is
still on strike.

FLIRTATION HOPES DASHED BY PRESENCE OF MORE ATTRAC-
TIVE FRIEND
The furthest my ass, and I, have been in the last
week, is to the cafe on the corner, about 50 yards
away from my house. (Again, yes, I could count that
distance. I could be precise. But then I'd have to
measure it. Which means I'd have to get up. YuHUH.
That's gonna happen.) The cafe has green tiles outside and big lattes inside, and it has ALL the latest
magazines including obscure ones like **Pure** and obscene
ones like **Wallpaper.** It has sofas and one cute boy who
works there on Mondays even though he never, like
never, ever, ever, ever flirts with me. Though he does
with Francesca. Or did. Once. Bastard. Fuck him and
damn him to hell.

WOMAN SITS IN COFFEE SHOP DEBATING WHETHER OR NOT SHE
IS "COOL"
Last Monday I went there with Claudia. Claudia does
dresses. Claudia was wearing an outfit she had made.

The skirt came down to the ground and trailed behind her, catching cigarette butts and ring-pulls in its wake. She wore a black top with a high neck and these sweet little arm things, as though the bottom part of the sleeves had got bored of being attached and had decided to make a run for it. Claudia wore purple sunglasses indoors the whole time. "Gosh," I thought to myself. "I'm sitting in a cafe with someone who wears sunglasses inside. I think that means we are cool. Well, at least, she is, although I am not wearing any make-up, and my shoes are covered in nightclub juice."

FRIEND'S DESCRIPTION OF DEPRESSION IGNORED IN FAVOR OF THOUGHTS OF DRAGONS
On Wednesday I went there with Scott. Scott is a boy. He's thirty, but he's a boy. It's as if his skin grew too big for him, and he stayed small inside. He's got the eyes of a boy, and the smooth, pale skin of a boy. But the skin bags down now, loops stomachly over his jeans, ripples beneath his long-lashed eyes. Scott wears caps like a boy; draws cartoons for a living, like a boy, speaks in puns and wordplay, like a boy. We talked dot.bomb and the perils of unemployment. "I hope it's not like the last time I was unemployed," Scott said. "I never opened the curtains. I lay in bed all day. I didn't speak to anyone. At least this time, I've got the people on the internet message board I go to."

Guilty of similar pajama-clad internet crimes, I kept

my gob shut. Metaphorically, at least. In actuality,
I parted my lips just enough to exhale a plume of cigarette smoke. It would be pretty impressive, I thought
to myself, if I could blow smoke out of my mouth whenever I wanted, like a dragon. When I was angry, or
wanted to convey disdain, say. Like every time the
counter boy didn't flirt with me. Puff. Angry smoke,
like a naughty witch. Apparently, dragons sleep on
mounds of gold. It would be great if I had a mound of
gold. A heap of gold. A pile of gold. A mountain of
gold. A mountain of gold as high as the ceiling. I
smiled at Scott.

PORTUGUESE CAKE COMPARED TO MAN'S NAVEL BY WOULD-BE
WRITER
On Thursday Jill wore all red, working the Marilyn thing
with her platinum ringlets and her red lipstick which
pressed red caterpillars onto the white paper coffee
cups. She insisted on buying cakes for me. Cakes and
sandwiches were half price after 4 pm. The donut was
plump and full and tempting, like an unpopped orb of
bubblewrap. And the natea, the Portuguese custard tart,
well, it dipped low and perfect within its pastry moor-
ings. I wanted to push my tongue into it the way I sometimes longed to shove my tongue into the delicate
sand-dusted navel of a strange man on a beach.

PETTY CRUELTIES "ENRICH LIFE," GIRL ARGUES
On Friday I went to a different cafe, not the green-tiled

one on the corner. I lied. Sorry. The truth can eat my
ass. I got on my little black bicycle and actually rode
to a cafe on Curtain Road, up near Old Street. As I was
unlocking my bike from the garage I could hear my cat
meowing. She'd been locked in the garden. I started
calling her name. Her cries doubled. I went over to a
gap in the fence. I peered through. I called and blew
kisses at her. Her big green eyes gazed up at me through
the gap, and her little pink-and-white mouth opened to
meow. I kicked the stand of my bike away and rode that
bad boy into the sunset. In the cafe with Jason I ate
chocolate brownies. I wiped the crumbs from my mouth with
a tissue imprinted with the words "I LOVE BOYS." It
started to rain and I thought about the cat. I'd like to
say that in addition to my brain and my ass, my morals
have also gone on strike, but it's simply not true. I
sacked them ages ago.

This week I shall be mainly looking for a job.

07 November 2001
From: Amp
To: Diane@open-uk.com
Subject: Headset Jockey

!This message has not been sent!
Well, I don't see anything in your excessively exhaus-
tive rules about not writing, ma'am. No email, fine.

No internet, natch. No reading of magazines, books, or newspapers; no colored nail varnish; no strong perfume; no bracelets; no personal calls; sure! No problemo! But, ma'am, on your list I see nothing regarding opening a fat heavy white Paperchase notebook with a Fawn Gehweiler drawing stuck to the front cover and a WINK (Hoxton fashion boutique) sticker glued to the back. I see nothing forbidding the grabbing of a purple Pilot G-Tec C4. I see no ruling pertaining to the scribbling down of details of my friends' sex lives. Though I am sure this is just an oversight on your part, ma'am. For you are truly an efficient and proactive Head of Reception and Office Manager, ma'am, and I would indeed like to commend you on your skills.

You are harsh, ma'am, but fair. You run a tight ship: but the boat does not rock too much, indeed. Ma'am, I would like to commend you. The headset you provide us with does not snuggle inside the ear canal, leading to early deafness and a hideous infusion of a stranger's earwax: it is a padded, folded black fabric—leather? PVC? Pleather? a quick sniff cannot verify—that rests lightly on the ear and does not cause excessive sweating. Your interactive intranet-based internal phone list is far and away the best designed and most efficient I have ever used: the caller places a request; the first few letters of the name are typed in, and, bing! The screen displays the staff member's full name, photograph, extension number, job title, line manager and co-workers in clickable user-friendly glory. This, I like.

Ma'am, you must note that it is extremely rare for a state of liking to be reached by myself when I am doing this kind of work. When my left ear is all flattened and hot; when a slender steel microphone sits an inch from my lips; when my cheeks and tongue ache from the plum they have been arching around all afternoon (b/f says that the blow jobs I perform on days when I have been doing this kind of work are sublime, for the requisite bits are already flexed and limber): in this state, ma'am, I am unhappy: generally, I like nothing.

Best Wishes
Amp
Temporary Receptionist
Open Interactive, Clerkenwell

It is in this state that I have spent the past week. I buy Alpen, expensive and sugar-dusted, to tempt me from my bed. My skin, unaccustomed to make-up before 9 am (nay, before 9 pm), rebels. I ride the shiny black German bike, but, unusually, I do not pretend I am Dutch as I do so. I don't imagine canals. I don't sing songs at the top of my lungs. I eschew earmuffs. I compress my mouth into a line, and every day I cycle the wrong way down St John Street. Crossroads are so confusing.

Why am I here? Accursed gender-specificity; headset jockeying is as female as endometrial shedding. "Receptionists," quotes the American Bureau of Labor (sic) Statistics website, "are charged with a responsibility that may have a lasting impact on the success of an organization—making a good first impression." Your list informs me to smile, ma'am: and smile I do. In the bathroom I rub Vaseline on my teeth: at the desk, my lips slide slickly into the requisite grimace. Were I male, I would be—what—working in a post room? A courier?

I am too sullen to be boycrazy, though it might provide respite. The couriers' hirsute faces trap asphalt, speeding cars, oily puddles, gyratory systems, radio crackle, breezes. They fill the reception area with the scent of freedom. Their feet clack briskly across the wood floors: they thrust objects at me: pens, delivery notes, packages. Then they are gone. I shift in my chair; my buttocks are numb. The pressure of my thighs makes me contemplate depilation. I make a Z shape: rest on my toes; my useless high heels are daggers pointing to heaven, threatening the vengeful god that traps me here. I drop my pen and reach for it: am jerked to heel by the headset.

"Receptionists tend to be less subject to layoffs during recessions than other clerical workers, because establishments need someone to perform their duties even during economic downturns."

Oh goody.

30 November 2001

Tuesday: Stumbled into an old enemy. Stringy hair streaming from bobble hat. Wizened face winking. Lips rubbering round flat northern gargle. "Illl-lYYYYAAAAAHHHHH!!!!!!" Shit. We stood by the homeless person sitting outside the Star Garage on Shoreditch High Street, just opposite the Rainbow Sports Bar—the scuzziest place within a three-minute walk of my house—and talked about "meeeooooowwwwsic." He opened his bag to show me the records he had bought at Small-fish, and a fly flew out! Ewwwwwwww!!!!! I can't believe I used to fancy him. Damn my eyes!!!!!!

Wednesday: Club Surplus, Public Life, Spitalfields. Piled new make-up on top of old and got there for mid-night, just missing the avant-jazz Japanese experimental band, thank fuck. Public Life used to be a toilet, allowing some web designer I got talking to to announce "I remember when this were all toilet round here," and thinking he was talking about Shoreditch, I replied "Think you'll find it still is." Twat. Me, I mean.

The place was lousy with German boys. My favorite German boy was the one with the massive head. Not all the German boys have the dorky black glasses, but most of them do, and my favorite one does, so I spent a while talking to him about shoe-shopping and dog-eating in Shanghai whilst drinking cheap beer and trying desperately to keep my eyes off his Marlboro Reds. Prob'ly I was only using him to get closer to the cute cylinders. No jawache, no fluids dribbling across your face, and if you do it right you don't even disturb your lipstick. S'no choice really, is it.

Thursday: Wander Shoreditch like a Chinese-silk-jacketed vagrant, searching desperately for a free drink or at least a guest list with my name on it, hawking misery into gutters, rooting round in my pockets and discovering only 7 of your English pence, 3 Dutch guilders and a lump of hash too small to be of use to anybody—about the size of my ex-boyfriend's cock, in fact—sobbing in empty garages as I lock up my shiny black German bike, the last, and soon-to-be-pawned, modicum of my respectability. I've not even had any reception work for a week, and all my money's gone. Luckily I'm on the list for the Kitty-Yo night @ 93 Feet East, where Maximilian Hecker is cute and Couch are boring and Frances' girlfriend Morag flirts with me because of my green chiffon trans-parent top, leading my boyfriend to add lesbian-fear to his lexicon of insecurities. Bless!

Friday: My pits stink, my ears ring, and my tummy rumbles. Must get some breakfast. Must apply for 20 jobs, but write nonsense instead. Want to write my nonsense in a speedy-hot streak of brilliance. Instead I go plod, plod, plod. Oh, later, Cafe Kick Shoreditch High St table football with ex-models turned pop-video directors with allegedly huge third legs, but I didn't get to see leg so what do I care. Not inconsiderable breasts—not mine, I might add—pulled from tops and not inconsiderable nipples sucked—by said nipples' owner—in full view of bar. Kingsland Road Thai noodles blown off in favor of physical and emotional collapse and fight with b/f in which he accuses me of being upset at not having had chance to experience the third legs of various male models in the years I have been with him. I laugh a hollow laugh.

Saturday: Boring. Sunday: Boring. Weekends are for moribund office-bound wankers, and I am wild and free, though open to offers.

Monday: Stockpot, then Ghost World at Wardour St Odeon, then Coach and Horses on Greek Street where stared at by menz on stools, despite being with b/f. Is it the top again? I realize I should have washed top rather than just spraying it with Anna Sui eau de toilette, as combo of semi-visible undies plus intoxicating me pheromones clearly too much for the poor menz.

Tuesday: Editorial meeting at Planetmedia offices on Strand. If I pitch some decent ideas, I might land some freelance work. Explain theories on Jamie Oliver's over-large tongue—think cunnilingus, lay-deez—and its respective effects on male and female psyche. Greeted with "are-you-crazy" stares from the writerly menz who then go on to discuss ideas for "If Sperm Was A Drink." I nearly retch at thought of Yop spunk, juice-box spunk, spunk delivered daily in milk-bottles. I declare that menz should at least taste sperm before making heartless jokes about it. I feel it is deeply insensitive for bunch of straight males to make jokes from the misfortunes of others. Gargle then giggle, y'getme?

My ideas are rejected.

After meeting started drinking at 5 pm, then cocktails in Freuds—I fuckin' love Freuds—with writerly menz and Al and beautiful record company press officers Jodi and Janine. By eleven we have slimmed to hardcore of Al, myself and lone writerly menz Pimpdaddy. Off to Soho and Bar Solona, snorting Pimpdaddy's coke off the table in booth, dancing to Ricky Martin, meeting kerayzzee dude and chick Rina and Dean who were stripper and "Director, Enterprise Online Channel, e-Enablement Team" for Cable and Wireless respectively, getting offered pole dancing lessons and copywriting job, well sorta: "No! You can't do a line of coke offa my clit!

Gimme a JOB!" Our heads are a lousy mess of booze and drugs and we are kicked out at 3 am and we are taken by mad homeless man called Jimmy to late-nite drinking dive in Soho which costs five quid to get into and four quid for a beer, which we suckle like mother's milk.

I get talking to scaryman who teaches me exactly what to do should I get caught by police with a gram of coke and 2 e's stuffed down my bra, not that that would ever happen, right; but then scaryman wants to be my boyfriend for the rest of the night so I get Pimpdaddy to be my boyfriend instead, only without like tongues or sex or nuffin, so Pimpdaddy tells me to tidy up, has a jealous fit, designs a few leaflets for the Open University, then yells at me to get off the internet and go to sleep. More crazy Australians buy me and Al and Pimpdaddy more beer. These are officially The Best Australians In The World Ever after Rina and Dean. Then it is 6:30 and we go to the 24-hour Chinese restaurant that plays house music despite Pimpdaddy's protestations that it does not exist. More beer is drunk, more coke is inhaled but it all stops working KA-BOOM! Just like that. Tube it at 9 am with Al (she goes off to school still drunk) amongst wide-eyed Central Liners, stinking, sleeping, suddenly self-loathing. Shiver on sofa under blanket. My real boyfriend points at me and laughs. I groan. And if you think that is the last time I am going out in the world ever, you'd be right.

29 January 2002

"I suppose you want to know what happens next, all the
Edward Gorey details and all, not that it's any of
your business. Well I'm going to tell you anyway, as
punishment"
Bruce Labruce, "Not That It's Any Of Your Business"

Christ, It's been too long. I've forgotten what you all
look like: your eager li'l faces, eyes shining and
squinched up with enthusiasm, wanting WORDS, and FACTS,
and STORIES. To be honest, I didn't want to give you
the stories. I felt like having some SECRETS for once.
These ruby-red lips were SEALED, a subtle smile playing
across them, eyelashes modestly lowered, my diary
snapped locked shut, hidden under a pillow, wrapped in
newspaper. I wanted to keep my life to myself: to hug
my bons mots to me like a horsehair blanket; forfeiting
glamour for mystery and volume for silence. Don't worry
though, dudes, cuz dat shit is, like, totally over.

Prepare yourself for a bumpersized funpack of blather.
Best pull up a chair, light a fag, demand a massage
from the Thai houseboy. This is some long sheeyat, k?

Let's talk about work.

I'm either incredibly lucky or incredibly naive or
incredibly lazy or, incredibly, all three. Not for
these ginga ringlets or the dusting of schweet

freckles across my nose, or my breasts which are still, incredibly, incredible. Though I blush, shyly, at the mention of it. Can't you see. Look, blushing. No, It's because for the past three years I've completely avoided having a "proper" job. I've skived round on the dole whilst running a tiny free pink zine, which I even managed to get the man at the dole office to distribute for me, god blessim. I've worked for a teen girlz website and earned fuck-loadsa cash and been flown to Silicon Valley to work. I've written for an irreverent TV spinoff site, getting paid to indulge my obsessions with Craig David and Jamie Oliver and penis size and lesbian sex. I've even earned thirty smackers an hour simply to blather about pensions. You could say I rode the last economic boom like a sweaty trucker rides a parking-lot ho, and, hey, you'd be right.

But I've always been freelance. I've been the stranger, the perpetual nu girl, the wacky kid in the corner, paid to have ideas and make people laff an laff till their noses run, or to tidy wayward sentences and knock slack paragraphs into shape. I'm the one whose name nobody knows. I'm the one who doesn't have her own phone line. The one who realizes after a few days that it doesn't matter whether or not she wears make-up, cuz ain't no one lookin in her direction, not even her nominal boss. Freelance is da business, boyee.

Freelance was way cool, and hey, at last, so was I.
I worked for Excite and the big evil megacorp whose
products fill your house. I worked for a TV company
on a cool-ass web spinoff from an oh-so-zeitgeisty
dot.com drama. I drank coffees from paper cups whilst
walking down the street and talking into a tiny phone
through red-lipsticked lips. I ran a website. I had a
business card. I was nu meedja. And the whole time,
who was my inspiration and role-model: the thorn in
my side, the pointy boot in my ass?

It was Ella G.

Who?

Ella G. was perhaps the original self-styled web
celeb. I was Content Producer at Excite while she was
Senior Content Editor in a different department. I
stuffed a load of AMPs in an envelope and I delivered
them via internal mail with an effusive hand-written
note which declared that I was here working on the
teen site and I had been a big fan of hers for years
and would she do an interview with me? And she never
wrote back, the slag, the bitch, the black-haired ho.
No wonder I never bother to do interviews any more.
Jes' blather on about myself instead. Teach myself to
pee standing up and use bizarro menstrual devices to
give myself something to write about. Fuck interviewing web celebs, I thought: I'll become one myself.

Some time towards the end of my tenure in SF, I stood behind Ella G. in the queue (not the pee queue, though peeing onto her back surreptitiously whilst standing might have been just reward for her silence)—nono, the queue for the in-house coffee 'n' bagel bar. This was Silicon Valley in early 2000, after all, and a flashy web company wasn't a flashy web company 'nless it had its own bar selling lattes/mochacinos/frappes/fruit shakes/whatever, staffed by underpaid Mexicans who would endure the rudeness and material stink of the San Francisco dot.commers.

I finished my stint in San Francisco without speaking to Miz G., though I would regularly visit her site and look at the pages wherein she would brag of her fame and her desire to become even more hugely renowned. I'd cut my eyes at the heavily photoshopped pictures of her, whispering, "you're not as pretty in the flesh, biatch." I'm a supportive femuhneest sista like dat, y'see.

But things have changed. Now even the celebiest of web celebs are Out-Of-Work Content Producers jus' like l'il ole me! Maura dot com? Laid off. Tom of Plasticbag.org? Laid off. And it was with no small amount of glee that myself and Jo Insomnia noted that even Ella G. was affected by the recent dot.com slump, um, just like we were. Is it possible to laugh at someone for sitting in the same gutter as you? I'm not sure,

but we gave it a shot. Schadenfreude, jealousy, ambition—ugly things, suffusing your skin and hair like a
golden shower, leaving you feeling just as stinky when
you wake up the next morning.

But no more. Are you ready for this, cuz I wasn't,
despite six months of preparation and longing—I got
a job!

The guy at the recruitment agency was quite fit, which
probably helped. Not that these things matter, of
course, whaddaya think I am, shallow? But when you've
been inhabiting a world of headset jockeying and
temping agencies, and all you know is:

- climbing stairs
- handing your CV to the receptionist
- drinking the minging coffee
- ticking the little boxes
- taking a pointless typing test
- dealing with the knockbacks like a goodgirl

—then one tends to grab one's joy where one can,
and if one's joy lies in sitting on—I mean, near—
the face of a pleasantly-planed blond twentysome-
thing, then so be it.

I was hella surprised. Never in my frickin' life have

I got a job from an interview. Let alone a real job: copywriting, editing, project managing. Y'know. Responsible shit. I thought they could smell it on me: freelance, unconventional, headstrong: weirdo. Normally people just read my stuff and say "you'll do" and hire me, not see me first. My writing is a better ambassador for me than I am, baybee. But all they smelt was the Anna Sui perfume and the Poppy King lip gloss and the Aveda Shampoo and the niceness. All they saw was a page tracked birdfoot with proofing marks, and a piece of prose whipped into shape with personaltrainer fingers, and nuggets of knowledge: solid, genuine, flickering mica facts of website minutiae.

I am not going to say where exactly I work because the thought of my boss with the shiny hair discovering this site and all my blather makes shivery cold run through me like ice cream. Basically, I work for a charidee fashion campaign (darling), writing and editing, scanning and doctoring photos of Jodi Kidd and Liberty Ross and the like, hassling reluctant strangers for copy, composing email newsletters, updating the website with scientific info and stories of fundraising campaigns.

My my, things have changed. The fridge is not full of free "sodas" and five different types of mineral water and we don't get free ice creams on Fridays like we did at Excite. There are no fizzy wine and dips parties on payday every month, no champagne-stuffed fridge, no expenses, no free biscuits, no fine selection of Earl Grey and Assam teas like there was at Planetmedia. It's Typhoo and Nescafe and a payslip that I have to squint at to make out the miniscule sum that flows as a tiny stream into the giant lake of my overdraft.

I can no longer afford new trainers and paper-cup, lipstick-printed coffee—and let us all heave a collective sigh of sorrow for the poor li'l web girl, for what is a web girl without her coffee? Nonetheless, the biggest surprise I've ever experienced, except when I grew tits, is this:

I like my job.

After work last week, I found my favorite prostitute card ever in a phone box on Tottenham Court Road. It features the above phrase scrawled in magic marker: no photo, no list of skills; just a sentence describing sheer unadulterated pleasure in getting regularly screwed for very little money.

I have pinned it to the noticeboard above my computer, and every full-time, properly-contracted day, I look at it, and I smile.

the happening

Laura Hird

I wake with the cold, tight-headed, empty sense of an impending family day. Annual leave is precious and it galls me to waste any of it with cousins' brats, my foul auntie and my mother's inevitable tears after a few glasses of Asti Spumante.

There's an unpleasant and unfamiliar odor in the bed beside me. Rolling onto my back, I feel too warm. The side of my thigh suddenly touches flesh, the slight contact eliciting a grunt from someone at my side. Gently retrieving my leg, I lie rigid, trying to recall something, anything. It's not until I hear the burr of light snoring that I can bear to look. Extremely hazy recollections of the latter part of the office party make this almost unbearable.

Who the hell is that? There's a teenage boy in my bed. A smelly angel with a dirty face. I haven't been in bed with a teenage boy since the neighbor's son used to babysit when I was nine. What the fuck is going on? Afraid to move or breathe, I wonder if this is what being scared-stiff feels like. It's not just the fact that my bed-mate could be anyone—a sleepy burglar, a sensitive rapist. It's trying to remember what happened and none of it explaining this.

There was the thing at work. God knows how much wine I had with the lunch before moving onto serious G&T's. Socializing with colleagues always puts me terribly on edge. Outwith our work-roles it's as if we're complete strangers. Did I ask Bob about promotion? Oh Jesus. I've just had this vision of Marion, Bob and I in the Bistro. How did we get there? Didn't Bob buy champagne and keep trying to snog me? I definitely remember cold, wet lips bearing down. Beyond that there's just this bad, scary feeling.

Quietly extricating myself from the bed I stare at the boy. Is he naked? Not really wanting to know I nonetheless lift the duvet a little and stare underneath. He is naked—slim, pale, beautiful, dirty and naked. He'll think I'm a pervert if he suddenly wakes up, but despite this, I can't seem to stop looking. Have I already had him?

Reluctantly curtailing my voyeurism, I trace a path of clothes to the living room. My bra and screwed-up dress entwined, muddy Dr. Martens, superman tights (sunny-side up), dirty jeans encasing suspect yellow-stained white y-fronts. Checking he's still asleep I rifle the pockets of his inordinately heavy jeans for some clue to his identity. A mobile number scribbled on a betting slip looks vaguely familiar. Who do I know with a mobile? I'm sure Evelyn's 0374. The front pockets are so crammed with coins they can't even muster a rattle as I search. I find a packet of Rizlas and a lump of hash wrapped in a rag of tinfoil in the little pocket at the front. Then I think I hear a noise from the bedroom and haphazardly stuff everything back.

"Hello," I endeavor, shakily. No response. When I go through to the bedroom he's still snoring. Closing the door quietly behind me I accost the phone. It's no good, I'll have to pick Marion's brains. I'll be cagey, though, as I hate confessing to black-outs. People fill your memory gaps with things they can use against you. Never get drunk with work-mates. I'm always telling myself that. I dial the number.

It's worse than I thought. Marion tries to say I dragged Bob, my boss, shy-Helen-the-Finance-Officer and her to the Bistro. They supposedly had other things arranged but I became persuasively aggressive. I knew she'd make up bullshit like that. Bob and I were allegedly all over each other. Helen left because he tried to neck her on the way back from the Ladies.

"He actually offered us a lift. After what, about a liter of Grouse and that bloody champagne. Unbelievable. And remember him grabbing that girl's breast at the bar. Why didn't they chuck us out?"

"Pretty excruciating," I agree, clueless.

"Sorry, Cath. You know I was going to come for the meal but after all his shite with the waitress, God, why do people like that drink?"

"The three of us went to a restaurant?"

"You what?"

"I mean just you, me and Bob?"

"Don't you remember? I left before we got a table. Did you stay for the meal? God, Cath, how could you? Did he keep trying it on?"

Jesus, this isn't making any sense. Mystery boy will wake up at this rate. "No Marion, see, It's just like ... well ... I met someone. Was anyone else with us when you left?"

She laughs. "What, a man?"

"Yes."

"Is he there now? Sure it's not Bob? I thought I was going to have to throw a bucket of water over the pair of you."

"Oh please, I feel sick enough as it is."

"So what happened? Did you shag this bloke?"

This is hopeless.

"Look, Cath, I better go, I have to get into mother-mode. Merry bloody Christmas."

"Not as merry as yours by the sounds of it."

Putting the phone down, I go back through to the bedroom. Rummaging in the bedside table for my Prozac, I'm aware of the duvet at my side moving.

"Morning, gorgeous!"

Grabbing my wrist, he pulls me gently towards him and gives me a grubby kiss. I recoil at the smell of me on his breath. He flutters his long eyelashes, sleepily.

"Thanks for letting me stay."

I'm aghast. A man is actually thanking me for sleeping with him and I've no idea who he is.

Ruffling his spiky hair he asks if he can have a wash. His request makes him blush. Pointing out the shower, I get a couple of bath towels from the airing cupboard. Once I hear the water going on I start picking up his things, folding clothes over the arm of the settee, then moving them to the upright chair when I realize how filthy they are. I take the cannabis out of his pocket again. By now the tin-foil has effectively disintegrated. I loved getting stoned when I was younger, but all my friends are straight these days, sobered-up by childbirth. Impulsively I bite a bit off, smoothing the teeth-marks with my finger and hide it amidst the Christmas cards.

Anticipating a silence when he gets out, I switch on the

television—cartoons, a sickly American children's film, a throng of singing Christians, or the fuzz of Channel 5. Switching it off, I go to make some coffee.

Did we meet him in the restaurant? Surely they wouldn't let someone that dirty into a place where people eat? I remember Bob standing with his raincoat on. Did he leave when the urchin appeared? Where the fuck did he come from?

A vision in steam, naked to the waist comes out the bathroom. Beneath the grime he is even more beautiful. I invite him through to the kitchen for coffee. He has a lovely smile.

Sitting opposite each other, I watch him spoon four sugars into his mug. Taking a cigarette from a packet on the table, he offers me one. Where did they come from? Were we through here last night? Why can't I remember?

"Or do you fancy a Christmas spliff?"

Oh no, the blow.

"I don't mind."

Retrieving his jeans, he comes back, fumbling through them. What if he notices they've been interfered with? He'll see teethmarks on his dope, I know he will. "I should have a wee bit left," he says, taking it from his pocket. Oh God, he's noticed. "Aye fine, plenty," he reassures, proceeding to roll a joint.

Let him do the talking. He has an unfair advantage—he knows what happened and I don't. He looks up as he crumbles hash.

"Have you recovered then?"

"From what?" I ask tentatively. He raises his eyebrows and grins.

"Last night."

"I was pretty drunk," I explain, but it is really a question.

"I think we all were."

"All?"

He shuts his eyes and looks like he's imagining something extremely amusing then hands me the joint. Lighting up, I inhale deeply. Maybe this'll help me work up the nerve to ask him. Oh, but I can't admit not remembering whether we had sex. I'd be devastated if someone said that to me.

"No offense or anything, but I didn't think much of your mate."

"What mate?" Was Marion lying to me? Was she here?

"Bob, wasn't it?"

"Bob, my boss?"

"Boss?" he chuckles in seeming disbelief.

"What about him? What was wrong with him?"

He looks at me as if I'm mad.

"Strangely enough, the recovery position for someone having an epileptic fit isn't throwing them out in the snow. Thanks for letting me back in, I felt terrible. Someone stole my medication when I was sleeping."

I return the joint to him, even more confused now.

"Where? Here? Someone pinched your medicine when you were here?"

"No, outside the shop, where you met me."

"What do you mean?"

"Argos, my room-with-a-view, you know? Phenobarbitones too. They'll end up having a fit themselves. Divine retribution, I suppose."

"Sorry, I still don't understand."

"That's where I sleep. It's compact but it's home, you know."

My jaw does a Gordon Brown. There's a homeless person sitting opposite me, a fucking down-and-out, drinking my Gold Blend. I picked up a dosser outside Argos in front of my fucking boss? This is ludicrous. "When did Bob leave?"

He's obviously amused that I can't remember.

"You threw him out after he tried to throw me out. You were great, my hero."

He crosses his heart with his hands.

That's maybe not so bad. Bob was so pissed he was probably completely obnoxious. How could I forget someone having an epileptic fit on my carpet, though? Please make Bob have left before anything happened between me and the Artful Dodger. I don't even know his name and can't conceivably ask now.

Downing my coffee I take the mug over to the sink, light-headed from the drugs.

He offers me another puff and I decline. "No, no thanks. I'm going to have to get my act together. I'm going to my mother's. How about yourself?"

He shrugs, finishes his coffee and goes to get dressed. When he returns, I can't stand it anymore, I have to know.

"So where did we meet you? I don't mean to be rude but my memory's gone."

Blushing again, he pulls on his filthy combat jacket.

"I asked you for money. Your pal invited me for a meal with the pair of you. He said if he gave me money I'd spend it on drugs.

I've not had a proper meal in weeks, so thanks. It was my Christmas dinner, I suppose."

What a patronizing bastard Bob is. What must they have thought in the restaurant? Two extremely drunk business people and a tramp. To my relief he walks towards the door. I'd feel such a heel having to ask him to leave if he's just going to be sitting in a shop doorway for the day. God, I've shagged a homeless person.

He kisses me as I unlock the door. Soap disguises the sex smell from earlier.

"Thanks for everything, pet. I don't suppose you'll want to see me again, but I want you to know, you're a really kind person."

Could it be that innocent? Have I actually done something extremely charitable? Bought a homeless man a meal, saved him from having a fit in the snow, let him stay at my house on Christmas Eve and given him what was probably his first fuck in years.

"I'll know where to find you if I do," I say, making a mental note never to walk up the South Bridge after dark again. As I wish him Merry Christmas and begin closing the door, he suddenly looks extremely perplexed. Don't let him ask if he can stay, please.

"One thing. I have to say it. I'm sorry."

Dread renders me incapable of responding.

"It's just . . . I would have preferred if it had just been you and me, you know, not the three of us. I only joined in because you asked me to. I don't usually go with guys. You won't think any less of me, will you?"

men like palm oil

Kadija Sesay

She soiled her clothes deliberately with palm oil whenever she went home, just so she could hang them outside and watch them as the sun magically made the golden stain disappear.

In England, she would have spent five pounds on stain remover; hand washed her palms raw; churned her clothes at least twice in the machine and yet the palm oil would still have left a faint but unmistakable outline, embedded in the fabric. A permanent sign of her messy eating ways.

So she sat in the sun, baking; watching her T-shirt baking and becoming so hot that it stung the spot where she had had her rubella injection as a child, where there was still a small dent on her left upper arm that resembled a miniature round window ventilator.

But soon, the extended length of time in the sun made her head hurt, ridged her forehead and made her squint. But the stain hadn't gone yet though, and she was adamant—this time—that she would see this natural disappearing act. She had even tried to stop blinking, in case she missed the moment, because if she smeared palm oil on her clothes every day, her cousins would consider her careless—or crazy. She could hear how the reports would flow back to her mother. "You know, Auntie K, we see now why Zainab can't get a man—let alone keep one." "Ee too light 'ed," and Auntie K would shake her head, desperate at the thought that, although her thirty-two-year-old daughter was beautiful and intelligent, she was also crazy—no grandchildren for her, and Auntie K was already fifty-eight herself.

Yet Zainab had come to learn, through her many failed liaisons, that compatibility had nothing or little to do with culture, religion or astrological signs. It didn't matter if his Jupiter was rising or if he made her Venus eclipse, or if they met on the day that the moon was a crescent.

What mattered, she knew, were the odd, nondescript things that no one but absolutely no one else had—the things that really made someone "individual"—and this had nothing to do with how deep your spirit was. For her, it was if the man she met liked round, yellow, happy faces as much as she did, or if his dog-eared paperbacks were ironed more lovingly than his underwear or if he only ate the green Smarties, willing to get his fingers stuck in the long round tube in public, to ensure he got the last, stubborn one. Or if he licked the chocolate off her fingers as she nibbled squirrel-like, to get the hazelnut out of Cadbury's Whole Nut chocolate bar. And it had to be Cadbury's. One man she had flown to New York to be with substituted Cadbury's with Hershey's. That's when she knew the relationship was over.

She would know the right man when she met him; she would

look in his eyes and tell him to herself that "in a past life, we were from the same tribe."

"Zainab! ZAINAB!"

Her head jolted forward. Was that her name her aunt was calling? In England, she would have responded straightaway, by shouting back or speedily getting up to move towards the screeching voice—usually her mother's—without delay. But here in Sierra Leone, where so many women had her name, it was like being called Jane, so she continued to sit, letting the voice wash over her head. Besides, her aunt rarely bawled for her like that.

"I SAID, ZAINAB, WHERE ARE YOU!"

That shout was definitely for her.

She felt conscious about shouting back "Yes, Ma," so she shouted as she would have done at home in London. A weak "Coming."

"Well, cam. Na whetin yu de wait for?"

Something was wrong. What had she not done (apart from be married) or done? Her aunt rarely, in fact she couldn't remember ever hearing her, sound so agitated with her—and she never spoke to her in Krio, although Zainab constantly asked her to.

"Zainab. Your uncle has some very important business guests who have turned up unexpectedly. You must help."

With what, she said to herself, but stayed silent as her aunt continued.

"Both the girls are out, so you have to serve them instead."

Serve them?

"I've already offered them beer, so it's only to get the food ready. But I have to go out too. Can I leave it up to you?"

She was still dozy from the sun and this was all registering very slowly.

"Yes auntie, of course."

Well, she could never say "no" at any rate—say yes first, think about it after—because whatever it was, she had to do it anyway.

"Good girl. I know Auntie K has raised you properly."

Zainab looked down at what she was wearing, a *lapa* and long T-shirt, emblazoned with a provoking statement, "Danger, Educated Black Woman"—enough to incense many Black men in England who would just get het up and accuse her of demoralizing the Black man. But here, African men? They would just laugh derisively and dismiss her like a child from their sight. She decided to change.

"What are you staring at? You are fine, just wear your *enkincha* properly, you look like a clown."

Zainab raised her hands and took off the piece of cloth she had tied sloppily on her head, so as not to get sunstroke, then slowly started to re-tie it properly. Her aunt snatched it from her hands and did it for her.

"Quick now, do you think they have all day to wait for you? These men are hungry. They want to eat."

Zainab stood patiently, feeling like a ten-year-old having her shoelaces tied, whilst her aunt fiddled around with her head wrap.

"Ah-hah! It makes all the difference. Well, I'll leave you to it. If you need any help, call for Saidu. He'll lay the table whilst you sort out the food."

"Auntie, how many of them?"

"Oh, just four, plus your uncle, five."

Yuk! A full house. If it had only been one or two, she could have been in and out in minutes; at the beck and call of five men, she knew she would be in the kitchen for some time. And it was so hot! How did the women here do it?

As it was, it wasn't so bad. Within half an hour she was relieved, but it was a half hour that was to change her life.

She took down her aunt's best china, that she had bought no doubt from Petticoat Lane Market on one of her visits to London when she purchased stocks of shoes and matching accessories. She rinsed them through with boiling water to keep the food warm. Thank goodness the rice had been cooked before she was called—she always burned it, her mother despaired.

"How can any man want you if you burn the rice all the time? Do you want to give him heartburn?"

"My husband will be a better cook than me, Mother," she had stated.

Her mother stared at her as if she had said something sacrilegious.

"So, you will not cook for your husband?"

"I'll be too busy—being successful."

"Fine, so you will let another woman come and cook for him, fine. Just see how long that marriage will last!"

Zainab smiled. One day her mother would realize. She would wake up and realize that her daughter had no intention of getting married. Men, like palm oil, she thought bitterly, were hot when they met you—intent on making their presence felt, bit into you, like *pepe*—with a deep need to make an indelible mark on your life. But when the taste for you became familiar, they faded, very quickly and all you could hope for was that they left no more than a faint stain that would eventually wash out of its own accord.

She leant over the fire, scooping the rice into the fake Ming serving dishes with an intricately carved locally made wooden spoon. Then she took another large ornate serving dish and ladled the palm oil stew into it, before placing it in the microwave. Bits of dried fish nestled amongst the small green leaves of chopped up *crain-crain* in the rich reddy-brown palm oil. She liked the smell of this one: the processed palm oil in jars in England, that her mother bought when they were growing up, was bright yellow and stank the whole house all day. She remembered spitting it out, when she was a child, as soon as she put it in her mouth, then when her mother wasn't looking, wrapping it up in tissue—the extra strong man-size type—and stuffing it down her knickers to throw away.

Quite often, though, her mother was too close by and she would have to sneak into the toilet and flush it. She would usually get caught a couple of hours later, as the telltale oil rose to the surface in tiny spots. But it was either that or get a huge stain on the front of her dress, that would look as though she had pissed palm oil on herself.

Yet this deep amber solid oil had a cultivating sensuous smell that blended in with the natural incense of the climate; sweet cloying of over-ripe mangoes; home brewed *omole* and body sweat. It was more obvious to her now, why palm oil was good for the skin—but she couldn't work out its part in the making of bombs. In her mind, she conjured up a bomb made out of palm oil, exploding, sprinkling the earth with spots of its provocative perfume; its odor rising, stimulated by the sun. Everyone who smelt it would forget what they were doing and make love. Spots of palm oil licked from limbs, ears and tips of noses. Strangers would wrap themselves like tissue around each other to ingest more palm oil. Fingers massaged its thick smooth yellow lotion on elbows and behind knees, fingers massaged yellow sweat behind ears.

She smiled at the idea as the "ding" of the microwave made her jump.

"Have you set the table, Saidu?"

"Yes, Ma."

She looked at him slightly annoyed. She wasn't a "Ma" yet; well probably to his little eight-year-old self she was, over thirty and unmarried, so she turned her frown upside down.

"Hold the door open for me, would you, Saidu."

She carried the heavy rice dish from the kitchen into the dining room. Where were they?

She put the dish on the table and then went to get the stew. When she went back in, she heard their bellowing from the verandah. She moved towards the voices and waited patiently until her uncle noticed her standing there. It gave her time to look at the pot-bellied men, well, all but one, the slimmest and youngest, and quite good-looking in fact—who would probably age into a belly too.

Her uncle interrupted her thoughts.

"Bring water and hand towels," he snapped.

How could she have forgotten? She felt more than stupid, she felt uncouth, but she went to fetch them quickly—where was Saidu?—to the dining room where they were now moving to.

And the beer? Her uncle looked at her, annoyed. She went hot as he looked her up and down swiftly, settling his eyes on the T-shirt that she wished she had changed, his annoyance turning to amusement. He placed his hand firmly on her wrist and pulled her closer to the table.

"This is my niece, Zainab, from London," he said with a grin. "Very intelligent gel, you know. Her mother sent her here for us to find her a husband. You can see why, can't you?"

He pointed to her T-shirt that made his guests laugh. Except for one pot belly; he was too busy appreciating the stew. She watched him as he licked palm oil from his thick-set finger and caught it deftly with the tip of his tongue as some of it ran down the edge of his hand. Her eyes and mouth watered as if she were eating chocolate. If she spread palm oil all over her body, would he slowly skim it off with his tongue, lick palm oil off her breasts, catch it with the tip of his tongue as it slid down and he caught it before it dripped off the end of her nipples? He made his eyes small, as he caught her watching him. He wagged his sucked palm-oiled finger at her.

"You know, you and I, in a past life, we were from the same tribe."

She prayed silently for herself to him that the sun would not bleach the palm oil from his finger.

love story

Caren Gussoff

April 15, 2001

Dear Michael,

I was referred to you by Katherine Merrill, an associate of your sister Deedee's from her ashtanga yoga class at the YMCA. I am interested in applying for the open position as your girlfriend, and have enclosed my resume.

For the past several months, I have been attending disastrous art openings showcasing pretentious under-thirty photographers all emulating the mid-'80s Cindy Sherman; gulping down syrupy drinks masquerading as martinis in rubber-upholstered bars catering to dot-com success stories, media outfit marketing managers, and *Sex and the City* female extra look-alikes; and sitting next to young men close to my age on city buses without starting conversations, but smiling at their mouths. I have also been trying to quit smoking, watching *Comedy Central*, browsing clearance racks at Macy's, and looking up airline prices to places I know I will never go.

Katherine briefly explained the requirements of the position, and while I am not a natural blonde, I am an air sign, childless, and my breasts are real. I enjoy barbecue and shooting pool, and also have a phobia of street performers. I have not yet dated a systems administrator, but I do understand the attraction to Open Source Linux, like Dr. Pepper, have read *The Sandman*, and am familiar with popular role-playing games, past and present. Upon reviewing my other qualifications, I believe you will find I am flexible, a quick learner, and am detail-oriented.

I would be available for an interview over dinner at your earliest convenience, and references are, of course, available upon request. I look forward to hearing from you.

Sincerely,
Hannah L. Meinecke

Hannah Laurel Meinecke

Objective

I am seeking a long-term relationship with a man, older than eighteen and younger than forty, having both long-term and short-term memory intact; a diet beyond brick cheese, tinned meats, malt liquor, and day-old bagels; and a childhood free of squirrel, cat, or sparrow killing (slugs OK, grasshoppers on a case-by-case basis), who will never tell me he is a lesbian trapped in a man's body, and with whom I have a few interests in common, can have some fun, and spend time under blankets with.

Skills

- Enjoy the following: *Highlander, Hogan's Heroes,* the *World Wrestling Federation,* Mr. Bungle, demolition, things flavored with nacho cheese and/or hot sauce
- Can cry in the night without sound, without shaking, even when it seems the grief will pull my throat into my mouth
- Can create a meal using three ingredients, all leftover and stock even in a bare pantry, then throw it up until my nose bleeds
- Can view a computer's internet history, recognize porn site URLs, and keep silent

- Am generally unthreatening to mothers, sisters, and ex-girlfriends
- Can displace and/or sublimate my anger and fear onto traffic, baristas, lines at the ATM
- Can shave/wax so it seems I am hairless or that my body hair grows naturally in a stripe
- Know how to fix a two stroke engine, am trainable on four stroke
- Understand Valentine's Day is not important/meaningful/significant in and of itself
- Can find hidden places to drip dry my bras

Experience

1978 / Eddie Capone
Eddie had bowlegs and a walleye, but I loved him. One time, I gave him toenail clippers that had a small knife for cleaning under nails. Not too long after that, I asked him the hilarious gag-joke, "Are you a Homo sapien?" and he dug out a scrap of my knuckle with it. I still have that scar.

1982 / Jonathan Steinberg
I was the only girl invited to Jonathan's ninth birthday party, so our mothers decided we were in love. They seemed to like that idea, maybe because we were the only two Jewish kids in town, and maybe because we were both kind of fat. Other than the one time he pulled down his pants, which at the time seemed upsetting, he was pretty nice, and as I remember, he played the drums. I don't remember if I went to that party.

1985 / David Heller

David Heller only wore hockey jerseys, and his best friend was an actual albino, pink eyes, transparent skin and all. After school, all the latchkey kids went to the Grendale County Public Library because we could read *National Geographic*, Judy Blume's *Forever*, and D.H. Lawrence. One Monday, Clarissa Kahn went into my backpack and showed David Heller my blue canvas binder where I'd written Hannah+David Heller over and over in pencil until the lead was shiny. He looked at it, and then never again looked at me, even when we were Biology lab partners three years later.

1986 / Alex Parris

Alex taught me to smoke and about Motorhead and Iron Maiden. He had blackheads all over his nose that I liked to look at. He'd also let me hold his skateboard. We got along great until he developed a glue habit bad enough to hold up his mother at knifepoint. He got sent to live in Lawrence, Kansas with his real father, and the letters stopped maybe a month later.

1987–1991, on and off / Tyler Gonzalez-Warren

I noticed Tyler immediately, even though he ate lunch with the learning disabled class. He was gorgeous, plus the only boy in town with lavender hair. I'd recently started listening to the Smiths and wearing ripped black tights. We were intense, and watched *Sid and Nancy* too many times. The first time I ever got drunk, I broke his nose with the butt end of a Jim Beam bottle. We would have stayed together probably, except he developed this annoying habit of fooling around with every other girl in the world but me.

1990 / Lowell Cole
Lowell. Well, Lowell, he dated everybody.

1991 / Andy
I was depressed, fat, and eighteen. The day we met, he wore a shirt silk-screened with the Batman symbol with large droopy tits, labeled "Batgirl" underneath the graphic. This was when I lived in rural Vermont; there were sheep. The pickings were, as they say, slim. My parents moved to Miami, and I was alone in the world. I was eighteen, and he was interested. Afterwards, I was ashamed.

1992 / Ian Lipscar
Ian's father was the Australian ambassador, and he rode to class every day in an outsized black Cadillac. He took me on a date to see *Heavy Metal* at the theatre on campus, and while I was in the restroom, dripped three hits of liquid acid into my soda. That was the last time we went out.

1993 / Kirsten "Yuki" Nakazawa
It was college, and I had to try. Jell-O shots were involved.

1993–1996 / Tracer Connery
Tracer began a short-lived trend of living with motorcycle-riding, cello-playing, Taoist chemical engineers from Texas. I eventually

dumped him for Jack (see directly below). Tracer had great capacity for kindness, which most often lay dormant. I learned a lot from him, in spite of his mystical physics-spirituality Dancing Wu Li Masters bullshit, like how attempting consummate rationality in both behavior and emotion can take one far, far over the cliff of irrationality. Basically, most of the time, he didn't pay attention to me at all. He has nice parents I still send Christmas cards to.

1996–1998 / Jack Pappadis
Jack was my last motorcycle-riding, cello-playing, Taoist chemical engineer from Texas. He had surprisingly long eyelashes, and after being together for two years, convinced me to move cross-country to San Francisco with him. He left first, to find us an apartment, with only a backpack and his motorcycle, leaving me with his Quattro packed with our belongings, in a sublet apartment I had to vacate within one week. He then disappeared. When he resurfaced, he told me he went to Mexico to blow his head off. He couldn't do it, so he went to a Zen monastery in Las Cruces to get his head together. He then disappeared for another two weeks, and when he called then he said he cheated on me several times with one girl (who incidentally later becomes my best friend) but that he was still in love with me. I moved to Portland instead, throwing his clothes out the window as I drove, and later pushing his car into the Willamette River.

1998 / Ray from the deli
Ray was very small and very Italian and very pretty. He'd give me

free refills on my sodas and discounts on my cigarettes, and so, I let him take me out. I discovered we had nothing in common, except that he grew up two towns from me, where the mall was. Our two-week relationship was based solely on that fact, reminiscing specifically about one store on the second level, called "For Lovers Only," the kind of place that sold jelly beans in medicine bottles labeled "horny pills," and fake shit and vomit.

1998 / Matt B.

Matt was a day trader who had been sleeping on an air mattress in his ex-stepmother's living room for eight months when I met him. We were not serious, maybe together for two months. He never called when he said he was going to, and explained that with weird excuses like "I didn't feel so good last night. I've had diarrhea. But I was thinking about you." He later overcame this by developing this habit of calling my friends at 4 A.M. to cry about our break-up.

1999 / Matt H.

This Matt once pulled a lint ball out of his ass and showed it to me while we were at the supermarket checkout line. He'd smoke old cigarette butts out of other people's ashtrays. When we went out, he would never enter a club, concert, or bar with me. He would enter first, get his hand stamped, and come back and get me. I later found out he'd been charged with printing mediocre quality counterfeit IDs on an iMac, escaped from prison, and created himself a new identity. He would, however, use his real ID to get into the club. Apparently, even he found his own work shoddy.

1999 / Ethán H. Rose

Ethan was not my type, down to being uncircumcised. He would listen to only one western swing tape in his car stereo, over and over. I quickly learned the words to "Take Me Back To Tulsa." His eyebrows were placed beautifully on his face, but otherwise, he looked suspiciously like Jim Nabors. He was an artist, and painted elaborate pictures of animals with wheels. I realized Ethan was a variation on Andy (see above), except that now I was depressed, skinny, and twenty-six, and that while Ethan was interested in me, it was only in how I looked sitting in the passenger's seat of his car with him, listening to "Take Me Back To Tulsa."

1999-2000 / Shane Riordan

I met Shane in a chat room, and while we saw one another twice, our love translated only via fiber optics. We wrote earnest emails, and had extensive fetish-based phone sex. I was pleased because for once, I was dating the all-American tough-guy black-belt quarterback, one whose nose had been broken so many times it was straight again. Because he almost never had to look at me, my actual face, into my eyes, I learned his secrets, that he loved Laurie Anderson and *Jesus Christ Superstar*, kept his dead pet lizards in the basement deep freeze, had dreams about wearing medieval ball gowns, and therefore, because I knew all this, we could never move beyond being apart, never actually be together.

April 20, 2001
RE: Girlfriend application

Dear Hannah:
Your application and resume for the position of girlfriend has been received. You seem really cool, and Katherine really thinks I will think you're cute, so I have selected you to enter into the second round of interviews. To expedite this process, I have included some pre-screening questions, and request forms for letters of reference. If you could, please complete the questions and return them at your earliest convenience. The letters of reference may be completed by any persons you deem appropriate, and should be returned to me by the recommender in the addressed, stamped envelopes I have also enclosed.

If you are determined to be a good fit, you will be contacted for an in-person interview, most likely over lunch.

1. How do you handle conflict?
2. If you were a ride in an amusement park, which ride would you be?
3. Where do you see yourself in five years?

And lastly, what can you add to what I have already asked you that should make me want to date you?

Thank you for your time. I look forward to completing your file.

Best wishes,
Michael Duffy

April 22, 2001

Dear Michael,
Thanks for the prompt and positive response. Letters of reference are on their way, and answers to the questions follow this note.

I hope to hear from you soon.

Sincerely,
Hannah M.

1. How do you handle conflict?

It would depend on the conflict. I am known to my friends and acquaintances as a tough bitch, but in romantic relationships, especially when the conflict concerns how I hang my towel on a rack, forgetting you only drink whole milk, or that your car's upholstery smells like my perfume, I become quiet and weepy, meekly submissive, or oddly defensive. This is all geared to manipulate you into feeling bad. This behavior is a classic example of Skinnerian operant conditioning in which my romantic behavior is controlled by response patterns, originating in childhood. My mother was afflicted with a rare form of late-occurring adolescent idiopathic scoliosis, which left her unable to figure skate in the 1968 Grenoble Winter Olympics. My father had to drop out of law school to support her, and his brand new son, and later, his baby daughter. My brother, from an early age, was an underachieving stoner, so my parents focused their explosive unfulfillment and dissatisfaction on me, in the form of consummate perfectionism. I am to recompense for three malnourished lives, when in reality, I am not sure they ever prepared me to live my own.

2. If you were a ride in an amusement park, which ride would you be?

I think I could be one of three, at different times: the Guess-My-Weight game, a Tilt-A-Whirl, or an emotional roller coaster.

3. Where do you see yourself in five years?

I'm not sure. In exactly five years from when I read this, I'd like to be in Las Vegas, sipping martinis by the poolside, which while it doesn't seem possible right now, as gin makes me queasy and you couldn't pay me enough to be that undressed in an uncontrolled environment, stranger things have, as they say, happened. If you told me where I'd be now five years ago, I'd never had believed you. I thought I'd be happier, richer, not living in a shitty apartment filled with build-it-yourself Formica shelving, with two bum knees, working temp jobs to buy family-sized bottles of SAM-e and keep up payments on a 1986 Suzuki Samurai.

And lastly, what can you add to what I have already asked you that should make me want to date you?

I make great fruit pies, and have been told that I suck cock like a porn star.

To the recommender:
Please complete the information requested on this form. If you need additional space, you may attach your pages to this form.

Your comments will be held confidential, so your candid and timely completion is appreciated.

Please return the completed form directly to me, in the addressed envelope provided.

NAME: *Tracer Connery*

1. Please state your relationship to the applicant. Include how long and in what capacity you have known her.

Hannah and I are distant close friends, the kind where you only speak once or twice every few months, but when you do, it is an absolute pleasure to catch up on their news. I have known Hannah for eight years, beginning initially as my girlfriend. She later dumped me for some sorry punk-ass turkey that broke her heart and ran off with all her money. That satisfaction, combined with me moving away and cultivating a new group of friends that only know Hannah through my carefully chosen stories, has allowed us to maintain the type of friendship we have.

2. If you dated the applicant, please list the dates, intensity, and by which scale you are evaluating these factors. All evaluators should summarize the course of their relationship to the applicant, and if possible, comment on the applicant's communicative abilities.

I began seeing Hannah in late 1993. I was looking to get out of a dying relationship with my high-school sweetheart that was going nowhere except obsessive, on her part. Hannah was standing outside the dormitory in combat boots and a 1950s sundress, smoking clove cigarettes. She was radiant, hair falling down her back in ringlets like curled ribbon, smudged black eyeliner. To me, she was a law of nature, as sure as I believe that General Relativity is the exact true theory of gravity. I'd say we became extremely intense very quickly, intense in that my only other relationship was with my high-school sweetheart, who as I mentioned was obsessing over the fact that I was now in college and she was not and that I was most likely looking for a reason to break it off with her, which was as true as momentum equals mass times velocity, even though she was no longer actually interested in me either. With Hannah, I could cultivate my newfound sophistication and freedom, drinking faux absinthe and espressos, seeing art films accompanied by live organists, claiming to read Thomas Pynchon, protesting plutonium production, and discussing Democratic Socialism.

Hannah is a great communicator. She's a great debater. In her way, she ruined me for other women. This was counter-intuitive for me to learn, as counter-intuitive as that hot water can in fact freeze faster than cold water in a wide range of experimental conditions. I loved Hannah's strong opinions, and this led to me dating a string of insipid, agreeable girls in post-dump retaliation.

3. Please compare the applicant's potential to that of her peers, and to that of other women you know who are pursuing long-term relationships.

Never have I had the pleasure of examining such a prime example of a gracile female cranium, with a rounded chin, small mastoid process, under-developed occipital protuberances, and a perfectly vertical forehead.

4. Please indicate your overall endorsement of the applicant.

Let me know if this doesn't work out with you two, OK? I have been thinking of upping my contact with her, lately, on long nights when I can't sleep, the TV turns to infomercials, and I wonder where I went wrong. After all, we have a history together, and everyone knows as the number of bonds between two atoms increases, the bond grows shorter and stronger.

To the recommender:
Please complete the information requested on this form. If you need additional space, you may attach your pages to this form. Your comments will be held confidential, so your candid and timely completion is appreciated.

Please return the completed form directly to me, in the addressed envelope provided.

NAME: *Casey Meinecke*

1. Please state your relationship to the applicant. Include how long and in what capacity you have known her.

Hannah is my little sister by three and a half years. I've known her all her life. I helped diaper her. How does that stupid song go, from that movie? From crayons to perfume and shit? I just saw that movie on TV the other day. Yeah, I've known Hannah since diapers. Wait. Stop thinking about her ass, little man.

2. If you dated the applicant, please list the dates, intensity, and by which scale you are evaluating these factors. All evaluators should summarize the course of their relationship to the applicant, and if possible, comment on the applicant's communicative abilities.

Hannah's my sister. You want me to summarize her whole life? That I need two or three beers for, and man, I'm writing this too early in the morning.

She can communicate just fine. It was no problem for her to tell on me when I gave her noogies or rope burns or I vomited behind the sink or the time I had my 11th grade girlfriend Josie sleep over. She also screams when you tickle her. And now she nags me with ease about going back to school, getting a job, eating better, wearing my seatbelt, and not spending all my money on pot.

3. Please compare the applicant's potential to that of her peers, and to that of other women you know who are pursuing long-term relationships.

Dude, that's gross. She's my sister. I can't think of my sister like that, compare her to girls I'd date. She'd better not act like that.

I dunno. I guess she's pretty good-looking, compared to most girls. And she is fucking smart. She always got A's, and was reading some shit.

My friends all always liked her too, because she was really cute, and while she was smart and all, she liked sports too and I taught her a little bit about cars.

4. Please indicate your overall endorsement of the applicant.

My sister kicks ass. You break her heart and I will find you and bite off your ear.

To the recommender:
Please complete the information requested on this form. If you need additional space, you may attach your pages to this form. Your comments will be held confidential, so your candid and timely completion is appreciated.

Please return the completed form directly to me, in the addressed envelope provided.

NAME: *Savannah-Marie Creed*

1. Please state your relationship to the applicant. Include how long and in what capacity you have known her.

Hannah's my best friend. We met a few years back when her boyfriend at the time was cheating on her with me. In my defense, Jack told me she was just his roommate. When we found out about it, we decided we liked each other better than we liked him anyways. We call him Mr. Wonderful. He had one eyebrow, and was less than, say, gifted in his male endowments. He had taste though. That's for sure.

2. If you dated the applicant, please list the dates, intensity, and by which scale you are evaluating these factors. All evaluators should summarize the course of their relationship to the

applicant, and if possible, comment on the applicant's communicative abilities.

We've never dated, although we totally would if we went that way, you know? We have sat on her living room floor, drunk, on numerous Saturday nights, wishing we could be attracted to each other because we would be the happiest couple in the world. Besides, how great would it be to call our exboyfriend and tell him WE'D fallen in love? Plus, we could do the whole talk-show circuit.

Anyways, Hannah and I just clicked immediately. Mr. Wonderful had picked two similar women's heads to fuck around with, which probably made it very easy on him. Our names even rhyme a little. We like almost all the same things, except Hannah will eat Ranch dressing on just about anything and I think that is disgusting. She also has this thing for Ministry and other 1980s dirt/art dance music that I just do not get.

She's like my sister. I can tell her anything, and I do. Except when she tries to act like my mother, she always has very intelligent advice and would do just about anything she could to help someone she loves. Hannah doesn't care about much, but when she does, she gives herself totally to it.

Her communicative abilities are high. You can always count on Hannah telling you what she thinks, even if sometimes she talks in circles to get there.

3. Please compare the applicant's potential to that of her peers, and to that of other women you know who are pursuing long-term relationships.

I guess I'd be a peer, in this case. Hannah ranks as high as I do in my mind and I rank myself pretty high. We are both smart and beautiful and funny, and consider ourselves low-maintenance. Hannah has just one problem that I don't. Since our Mr. Wonderful-sharing days, I tend now to flock to sensitive, indie, lactose-intolerant guys, while she tends to chase around cyborg assholes.

4. Please indicate your overall endorsement of the applicant.

I give her 5 stars, thumbs up, a must see, the tops, can't miss. After all, you are the company you keep, right? We come as a set. You may want to start thinking about some nice Emo-indie rock boy you know for me.

May 5, 2001

Dear Hannah,

After interviewing all finalists, I am pleased to offer you the position as my girlfriend. The full job description and potential compensation is below.

If you would like to accept this position, please sign the end of this letter, and return it to me no later than seven (7) days of receipt. We could meet at that tapas place you mentioned at your interview.

I look forward to getting your acceptance.

Mike

TITLE: Michael Patrick Duffy's Girlfriend
ANTICIPATED START DATE: May 15, 2001
JOB DESCRIPTION:
First, we'll sleep together too soon, not really knowing enough about each other. It'll be pretty exciting, so we'll start going out a lot and talking on the phone each night and sending cute emails from work and having frequent sex. After a few months, you'll tell me you love me, and I'll say it back to you, because I almost mean it, I think it's what you want to hear, and I don't really mind. You'll meet my friends, and you all will get along, because they will think you're hot, and you think they are sort of cute, in helpless, funny, burping/farting ways. You'll be sure and tell me you landed the best of the lot. We'll continue going out and doing fun stuff—like activities, like dates—ice skating and nice dinners and film festivals and car shows, but as a few more months go by, we'll mostly be going to my apartment because I have a Play station 2, a DVD player, ordering pizza, seeing each other every day but not really doing anything at all. By this point, I've taken a piss in front of you, you've left a box of tampons under my sink, you've met my parents and I've spoken to yours on the phone a few times. We may have already had our first fight, one about not going out quite as often, or me not making a huge deal about our six-month anniversary.

Things are pretty serious between us.

After eight or nine months, I'll be getting less interested in having sex with you. Not that I'm not interested in sex. In fact, you may catch me beating off to porn once, nothing too serious.

When you notice how infrequently we fuck, you will work really hard to get my attention, buying fancy and embarrassing string outfits from Victoria's Secret or someplace. You will think I'm not attracted to you anymore, and while that isn't the truth, I won't be able to vocalize what is, and instead I will tell you maybe I need some space.

You will be insecure because I won't touch you, and this will make things worse. You will act a little needy, or maybe pushy, and I will feel bad because I really do care about you. We will have many long, long talks, where you will cry, I will break something, and we will end by having the sex we were arguing about in the first place.

We will then spend several more months suffering through this. I won't want to be the one breaking up, even though I don't know what happened, but that nothing is easy anymore, so I will be an asshole, or maybe I will cheat on you, so eventually you will break up with me. You'll cry, and leave some desperate messages on my voice mail, but eventually we'll promise to be friends. Some time will pass, and one of us will ask the other to go do something fun, or something where we need a date, like to an acquaintance's wedding. We will then get drunk, romantic, and misty-eyed, winding up back in bed, and it will be amazing, mind blowing. I will then wonder why we broke up in the first place. I'll want to get back together, and you'll agree, because you never quite got over me, we were maybe really in love the first time, we're meant to be together, and deep down, you think you know me better than anyone, that I really am a good guy on the inside.

FIVE YEAR GROWTH POTENTIAL:

After approximately one year, we will move in together.

The exact same sequence of events as above will then repeat as if none of it had happened in the first place. I may try and systematically trash your self-worth with snippy comments and the power of my supposed rational intellect, my cold objectivity, and detached demeanor until I drive you finally to think that I am most likely insane and you wish you never met me in the first place.

The exact same sequence of events as above will then repeat as if none of it had happened in the first place. I may try and systematically trash your self-worth with snippy comments and the power of my supposed rational intellect, my cold objectivity, and detached demeanor until I drive you to marry me, and buy a condo in an area that quickly becomes gentrified.